GREAT LIVES
Human Rights

Human Rights
GREAT LIVES

William Jay Jacobs

Charles Scribner's Sons • New York

Injustice anywhere is a threat to justice everywhere.

—MARTIN LUTHER KING, JR.
"Letter from Birmingham City Jail"

Charles Scribner's Sons Books for Young Readers
Macmillan Publishing Company, 866 Third Avenue, New York, NY 10022
Collier Macmillan Canada, Inc.

First Edition   10 9 8 7 6 5 4 3 2 1

Printed in the United States of America
Cover illustration copyright © 1990 by Stephen Marchesi. All rights reserved.

Library of Congress Cataloging-in-Publication Data
Jacobs, William Jay.
  Great lives: human rights/William Jay Jacobs.
  —1st ed. p.   cm.   Includes bibliographical references.
  Summary: Biographical portraits of twenty-nine individuals who fought for human rights, from Roger Williams and Thomas Paine to Eleanor Roosevelt and Martin Luther King.
  1. United States—Biography—Juvenile literature.
  2. Human rights—United States—Juvenile literature.
  3. Reformers—United States—Biography—Juvenile literature.
  [1. Reformers. 2. Human rights.]   I. Title.
  CT215.J33 1990 920.073—dc20 [920]
  89–37211 CIP AC   ISBN 0-684-19036-2

Contents

Foreword

From the very day of America's birth, July 4, 1776, this nation has celebrated the idea of human rights. Thomas Jefferson stated in the Declaration of Independence as "self-evident" truths the beliefs of Americans, then fighting for freedom from British rule, that:

> . . . all men are created equal, that they are endowed by their
> Creator with certain unalienable Rights, that among these are
> Life, Liberty, and the Pursuit of Happiness.

It was to secure those basic rights, said Jefferson, that people first created governments. If ever a government failed to protect the people's liberties, he continued, "it is their right, it is their duty, to throw off such government, and to provide new guards for their future security."

More than two centuries have passed since the signers of the Declaration mutually pledged "our Lives, our Fortunes, and our Sacred Honor" to the cause of human liberty. So delicate, so fragile a flower is freedom that many times since 1776 it has seemed unlikely that the dream of the Founding Fathers could survive.

"Four score and seven years" after Jefferson penned his immortal words, President Abraham Lincoln was called upon to deliver a memorial address to honor those who had died on the bloody Civil War battlefield of Gettysburg,

Pennsylvania. On that field of conflict the president rededicated the nation to the revolutionary cause of human freedom. A great war was being fought, said Lincoln, testing whether "any nation so conceived could long endure." Looking over the military cemetery where he spoke, Lincoln declared that:

> . . . We here highly resolve that these dead shall not have died in vain—that this nation, under God, shall have a new birth of freedom—and that government of the people, by the people, for the people, shall not perish from the earth.

During the Great Depression of the 1930s, with fully one-third of the nation "out of work, out of luck, out of hope," President Franklin Delano Roosevelt still refused to give up on American freedom. While many of the world's "great minds" spoke with awe of Hitler's Germany and Mussolini's Italy as "the wave of the future," Roosevelt never once despaired of democracy. He demonstrated that a democratic government could deal with crises—political and economic—without depriving people of their freedoms.

That faith has not faded. Based as it is on a belief in the capacities of individual human beings, it has echoed through the corridors of our national experience. It is the central theme of what has come to be known as "the American dream." "Americans," said President Woodrow Wilson, "are idealists working in matter." From the beginning we have searched for material security—prosperity—without sacrificing the rights of individual citizens to make choices about their own lives.

It is not always easy to strike a proper balance between order and liberty, between the needs of the society and the needs of the individual. Nor, having once achieved that balance, is it easy to keep it. Governments, even our own government, tend to take on more power, not to give it up.

Who, then, is left to stand for the rights of individuals? How, in a democracy, can we prevent those with the majority of votes from tyrannizing over the minority? Always there have been a few courageous personalities, including the remarkable men and women portrayed in this book, who have persisted. Together they make up that class of heroic leaders who, often in the face of great odds, continue to struggle to free the human spirit from ignorance and prejudice.

In the pages that follow you will find stories of familiar heroes in America's human rights movement—people such as Benjamin Franklin, Eleanor Roosevelt, Martin Luther King, Jr. Probably you already know them as shapers of America's past. But you will also find stories of people seldom discussed in books for young readers—people like Cesar Chavez, the leader of poor farm workers; Dorothy Day, the founder of the Catholic Worker Movement, who shared a life of poverty with Americans left outside of our society's general prosperity; Clarence Darrow, a lawyer who defended the rights of unpopular clients, especially the "underdogs" in society.

For the personalities discussed in this book the struggle for human rights did not end with independence from Great Britain, or the death of slavery, or the passing of the Great Depression. They understood that always there are new battles to be fought. Always there are new foes—self-seeking leaders eager to limit human freedom and to make the decisions in other people's lives.

They understood, too, that the task of defending freedom cannot be left to a tiny band of individuals like themselves. Everyone must share in it. Martin Niemöller, head of the largest church in Germany in Hitler's time, summed up our shared responsibility for protecting human rights with this story:

> I was living in Germany and I did not like Hitler but I did not do much about it. Hitler came for the Jews and I said, "I am not a Jew," and I didn't do anything to help them. Then Hitler came for the Communists and I said, "I am not a Communist," and I did nothing to help them. Then Hitler came for the labor leaders and I said, "I am not a labor leader," and I turned my back. Then they came for the intellectuals and the artists. I said, "I am not an intellectual nor an artist," and I turned my back again. Then one night I heard the sirens wail; I heard the truck turn into my street; I heard the storm troopers pounding up the stairs; I heard them bang on my door. I started to scream, "Help me," but I knew, through my own fault, there was nobody left to hear me.

Like Pastor Niemöller, Martin Luther King reminded us that we are all part of one great human community. In his famous "Letter from Birmingham City Jail" he wrote that "Injustice anywhere is a threat to justice everywhere. We are caught in an inescapable network of mutuality, tied in a single garment of destiny."

Thus, although the personalities included in this book emerge from different social backgrounds, deal with different social problems, they are still united, for all of them share a common vision that America can somehow be a better place to live. They all believe that one day it may live up to those promises that, beginning some five hundred years ago, first lured pioneers and immigrants to this strange, unexplored New World.

We can come to know these champions of human rights. We can better appreciate their struggle to expand our right of free choice. By knowing them we can make them our companions, perhaps even our models. If we do, our lives will be richer for it.

WJJ

PART I

Human Rights in a New World Setting

Anne Hutchinson

1591–1643   Champion of religious liberty and the rights of women
in colonial America

Anne Hutchinson's life seemed settled. In 1633, at the age of forty-two, she was living quietly and comfortably in the English countryside. The wife of a wealthy landowner, she was the mother of fourteen children.

Ten years later, in a wilderness cabin in North America, Anne Hutchinson lay dead in a pool of blood. Around her sprawled the butchered bodies of all but one of her children.

What brought her to such an end? Why had she come to America?

The story of Anne Hutchinson is one of great courage. A person of strong beliefs, she stuck to her ideas, finally at the cost of her life. As a result those who live after her in America have greater freedom to think as they wish, for she helped bring to America the idea of freedom of religion.

Anne Hutchinson and her husband, William, came to Boston in 1634. It was then a town of about a thousand persons in Massachusetts Bay Colony. Most of its citizens had left England hoping to find religious freedom in North America.

The Hutchinsons came for the sake of John Cotton, the minister whose church they attended in England. When Cotton decided to come to America, the Hutchinsons gave up their comfortable life to be with him. Anne was herself the daughter of a minister. Even as a child she was interested in religious discussions.

William Hutchinson soon became a leader in Boston. Anne, intelligent and kindly, became one of the most popular women of the community. She was also a skilled midwife, a person who

A nineteenth-century engraving of Anne Hutchinson. *Brown Brothers.*

helped women have their babies. That was important because in Boston it was not thought proper for a male doctor to be present at a childbirth.

Before long the women of Boston looked on Mistress Anne, as they called her, with respect and love. Some said that when she delivered a baby she seemed almost a partner of God, helping Him to bring a soul into the world.

But Anne Hutchinson was not happy just taking care of children and doing laundry. She had a fine mind. She stud-

ied the Bible and took part in the religious life of Boston. That was not unusual, since everyone in Massachusetts Bay was interested in religion. They all were concerned with what might happen to their souls after death.

Soon after arriving in America, Mrs. Hutchinson began holding meetings of women in her home. She would discuss with them the sermon preached in church the Sunday before. Church members sometimes did this, and certainly there was no law against discussion in Boston—even though there were laws against many other things people liked to do.

But Mistress Anne did not stop at just discussing the ministers' sermons. She talked about her own religious ideas.

According to Mrs. Hutchinson, the most important thing about religion was God's love. A person, she said, should speak directly to God. Just obeying the laws of the church and government was not enough to get into heaven. Good deeds were not enough. God was a mystery, said Anne Hutchinson. A minister might help people. But sooner or later each man or woman would have to talk to God in his or her own way in order to find a place in heaven. People could not get in by building up good credit for obeying the church. Instead they had to love God and believe in Him. That was not something just to think about; it was something a person had to feel.

These ideas at once stirred up a storm. All of Massachusetts Bay was excited. If Mrs. Hutchinson were right, said her enemies, nobody would have to obey the laws. Each person would make up his or her own mind about what was right and wrong. And if everyone spoke directly to God, what need would there be for ministers? Ministers would lose their jobs. For that matter, what need would there be for the church?

John Winthrop, the governor of Massachusetts Bay, and John Wilson, a leading minister, were furious. They both said that Mistress Anne was putting all of Massachusetts Bay Colony in danger. Savage Indians were all around, they said, and if people did not obey the laws of the church and the government, the colony would fail. Men could refuse to serve in the army, could refuse to pay their taxes. The people would all believe different things. They would be divided against each other. They would stop respecting government officers and the ministers. Moreover, if the church were endangered, then everyone's chances for getting to heaven would be endangered, too.

At first many people lined up on the side of Mrs. Hutchinson. The women of Boston sided with her. So did Sir Henry Vane, who was elected governor of Massachusetts in 1636. Her brother-in-law, the Reverend John Wheelwright, gave sermons using her ideas.

Anne Hutchinson's strongest friend was the Reverend John Cotton, whom Anne and her husband had followed to America. Mrs. Hutchinson thought he was the only minister in Massachusetts who spoke the truth about God.

All went well for a while, but then things changed. When Henry Vane lost the next election for governor to John Winthrop, Vane sailed for England. Next John Wilson called a meeting of all the churchmen in Massachusetts. Those churchmen were angry and afraid, so they declared that Anne's ideas were wrong and dangerous. The General Court, which made the laws for Massachusetts, banished the Reverend John Wheelwright for defending Mrs. Hutchinson.

That left only one powerful friend—John Cotton.

Perhaps Cotton feared that the people of Massachusetts would take sides, some for Anne Hutchinson, some against her. If that happened, the colony would not be united against its enemies, the Indians. Perhaps he just did not have as much courage as Mistress Anne. Whatever the reason, John Cotton changed his mind.

He said that Anne Hutchinson was a good woman, a just woman, but that

A nineteenth-century engraving of the trial of Anne Hutchinson. *The Bettmann Archive*.

her ideas were not right. He told Anne to admit she was wrong, even if she did not believe it. She refused.

The General Court put Anne Hutchinson on trial. It was not a fair trial. Nobody tried to find out whether she was right. Instead she would have been found guilty just for saying that people did not always have to obey the ministers, and she had already said that before the trial began.

"Mrs. Hutchinson," said Governor John Winthrop, "you have broken the Fifth Commandment, 'Honor thy father and mother.'"

"You are not my parents," said Anne Hutchinson, sensibly enough.

"Father and mother means all those who make the rules," Winthrop replied. "And when there are rules, they have to be obeyed."

"Not when those rules are against the word of God," said Anne Hutchinson.

"Enough!" cried John Wilson. "She has thrown dirt in the judges' faces!"

Winthrop agreed. "Say no more," he commanded Mrs. Hutchinson. "The court is satisfied. You are no longer fit to live in this community. You must leave."

It was the dead of winter, snow covered the ground, and Mistress Anne was expecting still another child. Not even the stern judges of Massachusetts could send a woman to wander in the forests of New England at that time. She was allowed to remain in Boston until spring.

Once again John Cotton begged her to say that she had been wrong, that she would obey the ministers. All would be forgiven, and she would be allowed to remain in Boston for the rest of her days.

But when Anne Hutchinson came again before the church elders she would not lie about her beliefs. The Reverend Wilson read the final sentence declaring Anne Hutchinson to be in the hands of the devil. She was banished from Massachusetts forever.

Anne Hutchinson rose and left the church, never again to return.

In the spring of 1638 she and her family packed their belongings and moved to Rhode Island. Roger Williams, who had been made to leave Massachusetts for trying to keep the church separate from the colony's government, was already there.

John Wheelwright, William Coddington, and others who believed in Mrs. Hutchinson's ideas joined her in Rhode Island. She helped Coddington start the town of Portsmouth. When her husband, William, died in 1642, she moved to Long Island. The next year she moved to Pelham Bay, close to what is now New York City.

There, in the wilderness, a band of Narragansett Indians attacked and burned her home. They killed Anne Hutchinson and all of her children but one, a daughter who later was bought back from them by Dutch settlers.

So, unhappily, ended the life of Anne Hutchinson. It is hard to say whether she was right or wrong in her ideas—each person must judge that for himself—but there is no doubt that she was a woman of great courage. She believed in freedom of religion and was willing to stand by her beliefs.

Nor is she forgotten in Massachusetts. On Beacon Hill in Boston, where all can see it, stands a statue of Anne Hutchinson. She was among the first of many strong women who helped build a tradition of human freedom in the New World.

Roger Williams

c. 1603–1683   Colonial American clergyman; advocate of religious freedom

Young people always have asked the question, "What will become of me in life?" Through much of human history, though, there were fewer possibilities than today. If a boy's father was a farmer, the chances were that he would be a farmer, too. And girls had even fewer choices.

Young Roger Williams, growing up in England nearly four hundred years ago, had something else to think about in planning for the future: religion. Religion was the burning issue of the day— the question that was tearing Western Europe apart. In the religious wars of the time, nations fought long and bloody battles over it. Neighbors came to hate and kill each other over matters of faith.

It was in 1517, less than a hundred years before Roger Williams was born, that an obscure scholar-priest named Martin Luther nailed his Ninety-five Theses to the door of a church in the German city of Wittenberg. The Ninety-five Theses were a challenge to debate Luther's angry charge that the Roman Catholic Church had become too powerful and was using that power badly.

Since Luther and his followers protested strongly against the evils they claimed to see around them, they became known as Protestants. The Protestants called for major changes and reforms in the church, or, as the movement itself came to be called, a Reformation.

Luther urged people to make up their own minds about religious questions by reading the Bible for themselves. As a result Protestants demanded sermons based on Bible reading, preached by teachers called "ministers" instead of by priests. They also demanded simpler, more understandable church services and less costly, less formal church buildings.

Protestants argued that their reforms would return Christianity to the original ideas of Jesus Christ himself as explained in the New Testament. Loyal Catholics were furious. They warned against changing the ways of the Roman Catholic Church.

What was at stake in this complicated argument among Christians? Why were people so upset by it that they were willing to fight—even to kill—to be sure that their way of looking at things won out? One answer is that in the late Middle Ages and early modern times Christians in Western Europe, including England, believed that life was short, something just to be gotten through. The *real* life would come *after* death. That "afterlife," they argued, would not be short; it would last forever. And it would be lived either in heaven, alongside God and the angels, or in hell—with the devil.

Both Protestants and Catholics agreed that the church played an important part, maybe even the *most* important part, in helping people to escape an afterlife of horrible punishment in hell and to gain the greatest reward of all, salvation—an eternal life after death in heaven. But which church? And how should it be set up?

Such ideas were argued bitterly by the most able, intelligent, and powerful men of the day. Thus it was only natural that young Roger Williams, a bright and ambitious lad growing up in London, England, would be fascinated by them. Even before reaching his teens he had decided to study the Bible and become a Protestant minister, working in the service of God.

Williams probably was born in 1603, although his exact date of birth is uncertain. His father owned a tailor shop on Cow Lane, displaying his wares, as most London merchants did, from street-level windows. The family room and kitchen extended back to the rear of the store, with bedrooms ranged above on the second floor.

Along with studying the Bible, young Roger Williams learned the newly developed art of shorthand. Sometimes he took down in shorthand the sermons of ministers at Saint Sepulchre's Church. It was there that he attracted the attention of Sir Edward Coke, a well-known and respected London lawyer.

Coke, impressed with Williams's intelligence, hired him as a secretary. Then, in 1621, he provided a scholarship for him at the Charterhouse School to prepare him for college. Often he spoke of Williams as a "son."

Williams liked to sit in Parliament, taking down in shorthand Coke's stirring speeches on the rights of the individual in society. It was Coke who, in 1628, drafted the famous Petition of Right and led Parliament in its successful struggle to force King Charles I to accept it. Many items in the Petition of Right later became part of America's own Bill of Rights, such as the idea that no person should be put in prison unless convicted of a specific charge.

Young Williams listened in awe as Coke championed the rights of the people. Later the great lawyer's beliefs would play a crucial part in his own life.

In 1627 Roger Williams graduated with honors from Cambridge University, again on scholarship. Two years later he was ordained at Cambridge as a Protestant minister.

At Cambridge Williams was known as a serious, disciplined scholar. Students there were expected to be present for morning church services at five o'clock and for breakfast at six. Latin was the language required for all classes and examinations. Excellence in debate was stressed. It was a thorough, rigorous form of education, intended to produce leaders in law, government, and the church.

In 1628 Roger Williams became per-

sonal chaplain to Sir William Masham, a country gentleman. He settled down to a pleasant life at his employer's country estate in Essex. Before long he met and fell in love with the niece of a wealthy and powerful woman on a nearby estate. She agreed to marry him, and Williams asked the aunt's permission to proceed with the marriage.

Until then everything in life had flowed easily for Roger Williams. True, he was not a rich man. Still he clearly was a youth of promise—energetic, an eloquent speaker, physically strong, intelligent, charming. In his family he had been loved. He had been treated with favor by the great Sir Edward Coke. In school and college he had known nothing but success. Unaccustomed to disappointment, he was used to being liked and accepted. In fact he expected it.

To Williams's great surprise, the young lady's aunt refused to allow the marriage. She considered Roger Williams an unsuitable husband.

At first Williams pleaded. Then, angry, he threatened the aunt about her chances of entering heaven, a matter, he said, that should concern her since, because she was aged, her "candle was twinkling and glass near run." That only made things worse, much worse.

Nothing helped. Williams brooded. He turned gloomy. Then, a few months later—his lovesickness healed—he married Mary Barnard, who worked in Sir William Masham's household.

For much of his life Williams would behave in a similar way. He would take an extreme position and then, defeated, recover quickly.

Love was not the only matter claiming Williams's attention. At about the time of his marriage he learned that Archbishop Laud, a powerful defender of the Church of England, had learned about him and considered his religious ideas dangerous. Always outspoken, abrasive, Williams had publicly declared that the Church of England, although Protestant, was still too much like the Catholic Church. It should be made simpler, "purer," more like Christianity in the time of Jesus. People who held such beliefs were coming to be known in England as "Puritans."

Many Puritans already had left England, settling in the Massachusetts Bay Colony in America. There they hoped to set up what they called "a Zion in the wilderness"—a place to worship God in their own way: "a new Heaven in a new Earth."

In December 1630 Roger Williams and his wife, Mary, set sail aboard the ship *Lyon*. After a rough crossing in high seas and intense cold, they arrived near Boston on February 5, 1631. The Massachusetts General Court (the colony's assembly), pleased with the arrival of a new shipload of settlers, declared a day of Thanksgiving.

Almost from his first day in Massachusetts Bay Roger Williams found himself in trouble with the colony's leaders. Those men, familiar with his knowledge and his skill as a preacher, offered him a position as minister to the Boston congregation, the most important congregation in the colony. To their surprise, he refused.

The Boston church, he explained, did things too much like the Church of England. It also mixed religious matters too closely with matters of government. Church and state, declared Williams firmly, should always be kept separate. People who believed that were known at the time as "Separatists."

As a result of his dispute with the colony's leaders Williams spent his first two years in the New World not at Boston, but at nearby Plymouth Colony. That settlement was made up of the Society of Pilgrims, led by Governor William Bradford.

Yet even at Plymouth, a colony that welcomed free ideas, Williams was considered too advanced in his thinking. Bradford wrote of him as "unsettled in judgment . . . He is to be pitied and prayed for. . . ."

Next Williams became minister in the town of Salem, a part of Massachusetts Bay. Again and again he clashed with the colony's leaders, especially the shrewd and scholarly Puritan minister John Cotton. In his sermons Williams charged that it was wrong to think that only Puritans knew the truth about God. Scores of great cities and nations had flourished in history, said Williams, without holding to Puritan beliefs. In his view there were many ways to understand the mysteries of God. Therefore all religions, not just one, should be tolerated. And *none* should be persecuted.

Another of Williams's positions offended John Cotton and the elders of the Bay Colony even more—his stand on the treatment of the Indians. Williams reminded the leaders of Boston that before sailing to New England they had promised to convert "the savages" to Christianity. They had raised money for that purpose. Instead they had taken the Indians' land and otherwise mistreated them. It was possible, charged Williams, that Massachusetts Bay did not even have proper legal title to the land on which the colony had been built.

Finally Williams continued to point out the danger in failing to separate church and state. People and governments, he said, were already "corrupt." If the church became corrupted, too, by contact with government, then there would be no way for people to be "saved"—no way for them to get to heaven. And after all, reasoned Williams, providing the machinery for getting to heaven was the principal reason for a church in the first place.

At last John Cotton and the Massachusetts General Court lost all patience with Williams. Finding him a nuisance to have around, they charged him with "divers opinions" that, said the assembly, were "erroneous and very dangerous." Infuriated, Williams refused to be silent. He defied the General Court, preaching stronger and stronger sermons, writing angry letters to the church leaders. They demanded that he stop. But he refused.

On October 9, 1635, the General Court found him guilty of preaching "new and dangerous opinions" and ordered him to leave Massachusetts within six weeks. But because he was ill and his wife was expecting a second child he was permitted to remain until spring, on the condition that he would not meanwhile spread his beliefs among others.

Returning to Salem, Williams soon began preaching again. The General Court sent soldiers to seize him and place him on a ship that was about to sail for England.

Secretly, however, Governor John Winthrop, who, like Sir Edward Coke, treated Roger Williams like a son,

A nineteenth-century oil painting by Peter Frederick Rothermel depicts the banishment of Roger Williams. *Copyright © 1989, The Rhode Island Historical Society.*

warned him of the coming arrest. Just before the arrival of the soldiers in Salem, Williams and a few followers fled on foot into the wilderness, into the midwinter snows of New England.

Roger Williams survived the winter of 1636 only because of his friendship with the Indians. At Plymouth and Salem he had traded with the Wampanoags and the Narragansetts. He had slept in their wigwams, eaten the smoked bear meat dipped in maple syrup that they prized so highly. He had given them gifts. He had learned their languages. The Indians had saved his life when, as he later recalled, "I was sorely tossed for fourteen weeks in a bitter winter season not knowing what bread or bed did mean."

In the spring of 1636 he crossed the Seekonk River and at a great spring of fresh water pitched camp. It was on that spot that he established his colony, naming it Providence. The land was a gift of Canonicus, chief of the Narragansett Indians.

In the summer Williams's wife, Mary, joined him at Providence, along with their second daughter, whom they named "Freeborn" in defiant pride over their independence from the rule of Massachusetts.

Soon other settlers followed Williams to live among the Narragansetts. Among them was Anne Hutchinson, who also had been banished from Massachusetts for daring to say that salvation did not depend on obeying the laws of the church and the government.

With the help of Williams, Mrs. Hutchinson and a band of her followers gained title to the islands of Prudence and Aquidneck (both part of Rhode Island). Williams purchased the islands for forty fathoms of white beads, ten coats, and twenty hoes. But those items were only token gifts to the Indian chiefs. As Williams explained, "[A] thousand fathom would not have bought either [island] . . . and not a penny was demanded. . . . Rhode Island was a gift of love." It was the love that the Indian chiefs Canonicus and Miantinomi had for Roger Williams.

By 1643 Rhode Island had grown to include four communities: Providence, Portsmouth, Newport, and Warwick. The tiny colony quickly became a haven for those who had suffered persecution for their beliefs. Often, as in the case of the Quakers, Williams disagreed with the ideas of the new settlers. Yet he always welcomed them to Rhode Island and firmly defended their right to practice their religion. At that time no other place in the English-speaking world offered such complete freedom of conscience.

Williams himself was changing, too. In 1639 he declared himself a "Seeker," saying that there was no one true religion. Never again was he a member or an official preacher of any church. Instead, for the rest of his life he gave himself over to seeking the truth about God, allowing others to make up their own minds.

Not only did Williams offer religious freedom to people, he also made Rhode Island a place for political freedom. All heads of household had a voice in government. The "town meeting" gave anyone who wanted to speak a chance to be heard. From the beginning there was strict separation of church and state. Persons of every class and occupation had a chance to rise to positions of leadership. Few societies ever have been so lacking in class consciousness.

Before long Rhode Island became a place of refuge for the poor, as well as those in other colonies eager for religious liberty. Since anyone in good character in need of a place of safety was admitted, the elders of Massachusetts sneered at Williams's colony. They referred to it as "Rogues Island" or "The Sewer of New England." And because Roger Williams believed in equality they called him a "Leveller."

Under attack, Williams stuck to his beliefs. In his book *The Bloody Tenet of Persecution*, he argued that it was wrong to force people into one supposedly "true" belief. That, he said, was

against the teaching of Jesus Christ. Christ, said Williams, was a prince of peace, not of persecution. Hence, in Rhode Island Catholics, Jews, and even nonbelievers were given full citizenship.

Beginning in 1647 an assembly of the colony's towns began meeting. That assembly passed a code of laws based on Roger Williams's statement that "the Soveraigne, originall, and foundation of civill power lies in the people . . ." and that "a People may erect and establish what forme of Government seems to them most meete. . . ." More than 125 years would pass before similar words found their way into the Declaration of Independence. In politics, as in religion, Williams was ahead of his time.

In 1654 Williams was elected president of Rhode Island, a position he held for three terms. For the rest of his life he held some public office, always refusing to accept pay for his work. Twice he traveled to England to defend the colony's legal rights. He served as peacemaker between bickering groups within Rhode Island, usually on matters of land ownership.

Frequently he was called on, too, as the only person acceptable to both the Indians and the English to prevent war between the two sides. But when war came, like the brutal King Philip's War

(1675–1676), he sided with the English, helping to plan the fortifications of Providence.

Even in old age Williams continued farming, trading, taking part in public affairs. Then sometime early in 1683, at about the age of eighty, he died. At the simple burial ceremony beside his house, guns were sounded in a military salute.

All his life Roger Williams had believed in every person's right to think freely about religion and to share in the common good through a free government. Such ideas, drawn from the finest, bravest minds in England, were not original with him—but in Rhode Island he put them into actual practice and made them live.

Grudgingly, even Cotton Mather, the crusty old Puritan minister, agreed.

In more than forty years of exile, wrote Mather, Williams "acquitted himself so laudably that many juditious persons judge him to have the root of the matter in him. . . ."

Since the time of Mather, other generations of Americans have come to believe that Roger Williams "had the root of the matter in him." Stubborn and argumentative, he nevertheless trusted his fellows, whether Indians or Englishmen. And they returned his trust, even those like Governor John Winthrop who, in expelling him from Massachusetts into the harsh wilderness, had made him "the most outcast soul in America."

They respected him for his honesty, his generosity, his open-mindedness, but most of all for his desire to live a life in the cause of all humanity.

John Peter Zenger

1697–1746   Printer whose trial for libel helped establish the principle of a free press in America

The story has it that an American tourist in the Soviet Union once began boasting of the many freedoms that American citizens enjoy. "In my country," he said, "I could stand on a busy street corner and openly criticize the President of the United States, and nothing would happen to me."

"That's nothing," said the Russian. "Here in my country I, too, could stand on a busy street corner and criticize the President of the United States, and nothing would happen to me either."

Although the story is told in fun, it illustrates a basic principle of free societies—the right to speak without fear against those in power. Today Americans expect to have that right. Some say that we take it for granted. But even in America the rights of free speech and a free press were not always enjoyed by all citizens. Nor did winning those freedoms come easily.

One of the first incidents testing the right of Americans to criticize their government took place in New York, when it was still a British colony. At the center of the controversy in that colony was a humble printer, John Peter Zenger.

Zenger was born in 1697 in the Palatinate, an area of Germany devastated by the religious wars between Catholics and Protestants. When he was thirteen, Zenger's family left Europe, hoping for a better life in America. During the difficult ocean crossing his father died, leaving two other children besides John Peter. To ease his mother's heavy financial burden Zenger served for eight years as apprentice to a printer.

By the end of his apprenticeship Zenger had become skilled at his trade. He set up his own printing shop in New York City. Before the triumph of British armed forces in 1664 New York had been a Dutch colony. Therefore many of Zenger's customers still brought him materials to be printed in the Dutch language. He also printed the first arithmetic textbook to be published in the colony.

In the year 1732, when our story begins, New York City had a population of about 10,000, including approximately 1,700 Negro slaves. There were only about 1,500 houses in the city. And near what today is traffic-snarled lower Broadway, hunters experienced little difficulty in bagging a fine dinner of wild birds.

It was in that year that William Cosby arrived from England to take up his duties as governor of the British colonies of New York and New Jersey.

New Yorkers already had heard rumors about Cosby. Visitors whispered that as governor of another British colony he had been greedy for money, arrogant to the people he ruled, foul tempered, and willing to use force to get his way.

Soon the rumors proved all too true. On arriving in New York he immediately demanded the right to keep for himself a large part of the money he collected in taxes. Then he set up a new treasury court to be sure that he actually received the money. When Lewis Morris and Rip Van Dam, two of the colony's leading officials, tried to stop him, Cosby dismissed Morris and tried to fire Van Dam.

Governor Cosby gave the colonists other causes for complaint. He destroyed a deed assuring the Mohawk Indians their right to keep certain lands. He demanded that if New York settlers went to live on newly opened farmlands they give him the personal use of one-third of the land. Then when Quakers in Westchester County refused for religious reasons to swear the usual oath before voting in an election, Cosby would not let them vote. He did so even though they were landowners and always before had been allowed to vote by "affirming" instead of "swearing."

Before long two political groups formed in New York. One group, or political party, sided with Governor Cosby, saying that he had the right to rule as he pleased. The other party opposed Cosby. It included the majority of the people, not only the lower and middle classes but some of the wealthiest and most respected men of the colony, among them James Alexander, Cadwallader Colden, and Philip Livingston of Livingston Manor.

Cosby, however, controlled the colony's only newspaper, the *New York Gazette*. When he refused to allow his opponents to make any statements against him in that paper, they decided to start their own newspaper, calling it the *New York Weekly Journal*. To publish the paper for them they hired John Peter Zenger.

Not well educated, with only a fair command of the English language, Zenger probably took on the task for financial, not political, reasons. James Alexander and Cadwallader Colden almost certainly wrote most of the articles in the *Journal*. But since the writers' names did not appear in print it was Zenger, as publisher, who was legally responsible for the paper's contents.

Soon the *Journal's* sharply worded attacks on Governor Cosby were causing great excitement in the little colony. The paper's circulation soared. Cosby, never able to control his temper, became livid with rage. His wife declared publicly that the people responsible for the newspaper's mischief deserved to be hanged.

On November 5, 1734, Governor Cosby had the colony's council order that numbers 7, 47, 48, and 49 of the *Journal* be burned in public by the common hangman, or "whipper." Those particular issues, it was charged, contained verses and songs that tended to hold the government in contempt and "to disturb the peace." Town officials refused to permit the whipper to burn the papers, but the sheriff had one of his slaves carry out the order.

On November 17, by order of Governor Cosby, John Peter Zenger was arrested. He was not allowed to speak to anyone or allowed pen, ink, or paper. Judges fixed the bail for his release at far more than he could possibly pay. And when he admitted that he could not raise the money he was thrown into jail. By putting Zenger behind bars, reasoned the governor, perhaps he could at last silence the paper.

Cosby did not stop there. He also signed an order disbarring Zenger's two lawyers, James Alexander and William Smith—taking away their right to practice law in the courts of New York. Without them, the outstanding attorneys in the colony, Zenger's chances in court appeared slim.

To Cosby's astonishment, however, the *Journal* continued to appear every Monday. Zenger later reported that he gave his wife and servants necessary instructions "through the Hole of the Door of the Prison." Meanwhile, largely by the efforts of James Alexander, a new lawyer agreed to represent Zenger at his coming trial. That attorney, Andrew Hamilton of Philadephia, was at the time probably the finest lawyer in America.

The trial of John Peter Zenger. *The Bettmann Archive.*

The trial would prove memorable—a high point in the history of Britain's North American colonies, with lessons that apply even today.

On the day that Zenger's trial began, August 4, 1735, the courtroom was packed to capacity. Rich and poor alike turned out, most of them supporters of the almost penniless printer who already had suffered through nine months of imprisonment. Everyone present knew that if Zenger lost his case they, too, would be helpless before the power of Governor Cosby.

Cosby himself had chosen the judge to preside over the case. He had tried to choose the jury, too, but failed. As the proceedings opened the prosecutor read a long list of charges against Zenger. He had published, it was charged, "false News and seditious Libels" intended "wickedly and maliciously" to "scandalize and vilify His Excellency, the Governor . . . ," thus stirring the people to revolt against the government.

Andrew Hamilton, nearly eighty years old and suffering from a painful case of gout, rose to defend Zenger. To the surprise of Governor Cosby and the judge he admitted at once that Zenger had published the issues of the *Jour-*

nal in question. But, argued Hamilton, merely publishing something hardly made it libelous. It was up to the government, he said, to prove that what Zenger had printed was *false.* If the material was *true,* then the jury should find the defendant "not guilty."

"Nonsense!" replied the prosecutor. All that the jury had to decide was whether Zenger had, indeed, printed the statements. After that it was up to the judge to decide whether they were true.

Not surprisingly, the judge ruled against Hamilton. He could not take the risk of allowing the brilliant Andrew Hamilton to prove that what Zenger had printed in the *Journal* really was true. Nothing would be more embarrassing to Governor Cosby.

Hamilton now had no choice. Turning from the judge's bench, he addressed the members of the jury directly. "It is to you we must appeal," he said, "for witness to the Truth of the Facts we have offered, and are denied the Liberty to prove. . . . The suppression of Evidence ought always to be taken for the strongest Evidence." Leaving it to *judges* to decide whether a defendant's words are false or not, declared Hamilton, makes having a *jury* useless.

If a person in government, continued Hamilton, can simply charge someone with lying and not have to prove it was a lie, any coward can "cut down and destroy the innocent." Must people be silent in the face of a wicked ruler?

Then Hamilton reached the heart of his argument. The right of a person to complain against government is a "Natural Right," he said. It is a right that all people have. It is the law of "Nature's God," as well as the law of this country!

Less than forty years later, in composing the Declaration of Independence, Thomas Jefferson would echo the words of Andrew Hamilton. "The Laws of Nature and of Nature's God," said Jefferson, entitled the American people to independence from unjust laws and unjust rule.

As Hamilton faced the jury that pondered Zenger's fate, he began to summarize his case. If, he reasoned, all that must be proved is that a thing was said, is any person safe from the government? Is anyone secure in expressing one's thoughts? Under such circumstances, who would dare speak out against a government that injured and oppressed its people?

Hamilton paused. Then he concluded. "The Question before the Court and you, Gentlemen of the Jury, is not of small nor private Concern. It is not the Cause of a poor Printer, nor of New York alone, which you are now trying: No! . . . It is the best Cause. It is the

Cause of Liberty . . . The Liberty . . . both of exposing and opposing arbitrary Power . . . by speaking and writing Truth."

The jury, amid cheers from the crowded courtroom, found John Peter Zenger not guilty. The next day he was freed.

As Andrew Hamilton departed by ship from New York Harbor the guns of vessels anchored there fired salutes in his honor.

With the aid of James Alexander, who had taken careful notes, Zenger soon afterward published a complete record of the trial. He continued to print the *Journal* on a regular basis until his death in 1746. After that his wife and one of his sons carried on the business.

Governor Cosby died within a year of the trial and was replaced by a more generous and popular administrator. Meanwhile much had changed. The people of New York and of the other colonies had come to realize that they could stand together against an unjust, unfair ruler—and win.

It is no accident, then, that a leader in the cause of the American Revolution would one day look back on the trial of the poor printer John Peter Zenger and call it "the morningstar of liberty" in America.

Thomas Paine

1737–1809   Political theorist and pamphleteer whose *Common Sense* hastened the writing of the American Declaration of Independence

He was known as "the filthy Tom Paine" to President John Adams and "that dirty little atheist" to a later president, Theodore Roosevelt. During his lifetime his books were banned and publicly burned by the hangman. Fashionable gentlemen in English clubs liked to wear his initials, *TP*, in nails on their bootheels as if to grind down his ideas with their every step. Even in death he was not safe. His bones were dug up, taken to England, and eventually bought by a used-furniture dealer, after which they were lost to history.

On the other hand, many people, then and now, rank Thomas Paine among the greatest fighters of all time for the cause of human rights. "The equal of George Washington in making American liberty possible," said Thomas Edison.

Emerging from a youth and early adulthood of almost total obscurity, Paine became the companion of Washington, Jefferson, Franklin, and Napoleon. Clearly one of the leading figures of his time, he was also one of the most controversial.

Who was this strange man? What did he do to make himself so dearly loved by his friends and so bitterly hated by his enemies?

For the first thirty-seven years of his life Paine gave scarcely a hint of the glory—and the tragedy—that one day would be his. Born the son of a corset maker in Thetford, England, he withdrew from formal schooling at the age of thirteen to become an apprentice in his father's corset shop. For three years he put up with cutting strips of cloth, sewing, and being polite to customers.

Then he ran away, hoping to join the crew of a British warship. His father caught up with him and returned him to the shop. For two more dreary years he made corsets. At age nineteen he left Thetford for good, with few regrets.

At once he went to sea. But that life did not suit him either. He settled in London, forced to find work at the only job he knew but continued to detest: making corsets. After setting up his own shop in the city of Dover, he married. Less than a year later his wife died.

Next Paine became an exciseman— a tax collector. His job was to visit stores and taverns to decide what taxes each merchant should pay. Four years later he was fired, accused of filling out tax forms concerning goods he had never even examined. Desperate for a job, he confessed his crime and pleaded for a second chance, using the word *humbly* six times in his letter of apology to the Board of Excise. Although never a "humble" man, he knew it was either that or a return to the world of corset making.

He got his job back, but not for long. Soon he was fired as a troublemaker. He had tried to organize other tax collectors into a workers' union, in those days a serious offense.

For a time he taught school. Then he worked in a tobacco shop. Although Paine was deeply in debt, he married again, this time at the age of thirty-four. His wife was ten years his junior. Three years later, for reasons Paine always refused to discuss, the marriage broke up.

At that point in his life Paine considered himself a failure. Unknown, he had few friends, no money, and few marketable skills except, perhaps, for a way with words, a talent he used occasionally to earn a few shillings by writing newspaper advertisements.

It was then, in 1774, as he stood at the brink of middle age, that Thomas Paine's fortunes miraculously turned. Somehow he arranged to have a personal interview with Benjamin Franklin, who was serving in England as an agent for the American colonies. To Franklin, Paine appeared "an ingenious, worthy young man," a person of good sense with a clear mind. The two shared a burning interest in science and scientific experiments.

Armed only with a letter of introduction to a relative of the distinguished Dr. Franklin in Philadelphia, Paine booked passage on a small ship bound for the New World. Before leaving he sold or gave away what few possessions he owned.

During the week that he sailed, in the autumn of 1774, an assembly of angry delegates from all the American colonies was gathering in Philadelphia to consider the grievances of the colonies

This portrait of Thomas Paine was painted in 1857 by Bass Otis. *Independence National Historical Park Collection.*

against the King of England. The assembly was the First Continental Congress. A storm of trouble was gathering between the colonists and the "mother country." Paine fully understood the risks he might face. But like millions of other immigrants to America's shores, the possibility of a change in his life, a chance to improve his situation, made him willing to gamble.

Within three months after landing in America Paine had won a job writing for the *Pennsylvania Magazine*. One reason for his failure in England was a passionate interest in reading, attending lectures, learning—doing the things he liked to do instead of the things he was paid to do. Now his literary interests began to bear fruit.

He wrote strongly against the evils of slavery and the slave trade. In America those practices flourished even in Philadelphia, "the city of brotherly love," a city dominated by the Quakers. He also spoke out against titles of nobility, something he thought would not survive in a wilderness continent so far removed from the royal families of Europe. For pleasure he wrote humorous pieces and articles about scientific experiments.

Gradually more and more of his columns protested Great Britain's treatment of the American colonies. Was it fair, he asked, that colonial goods could not be sold to another country without first being sent to England to pay a tax? Was it fair that colonial raw materials, such as iron and wool, had to be sent to England for manufacture into finished goods in British factories, providing jobs for British workers? And worst of all, was it fair, asked Paine, that the colonists should be taxed by the British Parliament but have no representatives in that Parliament?

Even before Paine's arrival in America serious clashes had taken place. The British had tried to raise money to pay the cost of the French and Indian War by passing the Stamp Act. That act placed taxes on colonial newspapers, pamphlets, and legal documents. But the colonists had resisted and Britain had backed down. Parliament had also backed down after colonial resistance to another attempt at taxation, the Townshend Acts.

Then came the Tea Act, a small, seemingly harmless tax on imported tea. Colonists in Boston reacted to the new taxation by heaving chest after chest of English tea into Boston Harbor. Losing patience at last, the British government took severe action by passing what the colonists called the Intolerable Acts. In those laws Britain closed the port of Boston and dispatched red-coated regular army troops to maintain order in New England.

The result was war. American min-utemen fought pitched battles with British troops at Lexington and Con-cord.

Tom Paine, who had been in America only a few months when the fighting began, watched the unfolding events with intense interest. From the opening of hostilities at Concord Bridge—"the shot heard round the world"—Paine cried out for American independence from England. Why, he asked, should Americans fight merely for their "rights as Englishmen"? It was only "common sense," he said, to fight for freedom from England.

Feverishly Paine scribbled down his ideas, working night and day to produce a brief, clear, highly readable little book. Finally finished, he entitled it, in keeping with his argument, *Common Sense*. When it was published in January 1776, he sent the first copy to Benjamin Franklin, who had made his coming to America possible.

Common Sense burst on the American scene like a skyrocket. In it, Tom Paine dared to question the right of kings to rule free people. He denied the value of America's continued connection with Britain for trading purposes. Moreover, he said, just because America had flourished as an English colony was no reason to say it always should: "We may as well assert that because a child has thrived upon milk, that it is never to have meat." Looking at the vast American wilderness to the west waiting to be explored and settled, Paine wondered, "Is it right for an island to own a continent?" Already, said Paine, American troops had been in battle. Was their sacrifice to be in vain?

Everything that is right or natural pleads for separation. The blood of the slain, the weeping voice of nature cries, 'TIS TIME TO PART.

Paine's book soon was being read throughout the colonies—even being read aloud to crowds of people who were illiterate. Still, he received little profit from the book's sale. Not copy-righted, it was printed or hand copied freely. Paine continued to live in a cheap boardinghouse in Philadelphia.

But now there was a difference. His name was becoming known every-where. His ideas lifted the flagging spir-its of Americans at a time when news from the battlefronts was almost all bad. "*Common Sense*," declared George Washington, "is making a powerful change in the minds of many men."

Before long Paine became a friend of Thomas Jefferson. Despite Jefferson's enormous wealth and Thomas Paine's poverty, the two saw eye to eye. They especially agreed on one basic princi-ple: that "all men are created equal."

COMMON SENSE;

ADDRESSED TO THE

INHABITANTS

OF

A M E R I C A,

On the following interesting

S U B J E C T S.

I. Of the Origin and Design of Government in general, with concise Remarks on the English Constitution.

II. Of Monarchy and Hereditary Succession.

III. Thoughts on the present State of American Affairs.

IV. Of the present Ability of America, with some miscellaneous Reflections.

A NEW EDITION, with several Additions in the Body of the Work. To which is added an APPENDIX; together with an Address to the People called QUAKERS.

N. B. The New Addition here given increases the Work upwards of one Third.

Man knows no Master save creating HEAVEN,
Or those whom Choice and common Good ordain.
THOMSON.

PHILADELPHIA PRINTED.
And SOLD by W. and T. BRADFORD. [1776]

Wrote by one Thomas Payne
in the year — 1776.

The title page of *Common Sense*, 1776. *The New-York Historical Society.*

It has never been proved, although some scholars insist it is true, that Thomas Paine helped write the Declaration of Independence. What *Common Sense* did, though, was to create a mood that made Americans willing to fight the war for an altogether new purpose—to set up a free country in which they could rule themselves.

Brought up as a Quaker, Paine hated war. But he believed that sometimes it was necessary. Soon after the publication of his book he enlisted in a Pennsylvania army division. After a short period of service General Nathaniel Greene chose Paine as his personal secretary.

The war dragged on. Defeat followed defeat for the ragged American troops. There was little money for weapons and supplies. To some colonial leaders the situation appeared hopeless. One night, using the top of a drum as a desk, Thomas Paine penned the opening words of *The Crisis,* the work for which he will always be remembered:

These are the times that try men's souls. The summer soldier and the sunshine patriot will, in this crisis, shrink from the service of their country; but he that stands it *now* deserves the love and thanks of man and woman.

Surely, continued Paine, victory would not be easy:

Tyranny, like hell, is not easily conquered; yet we have this consolation with us, that the harder the conflict, the more glorious the triumph. . . .

Freedom, declared Paine, has a price:

What we obtain too cheap, we esteem too lightly: it is dearness only that gives every thing its value. Heaven knows how to put a price upon its goods; and it would be strange indeed if so celestial an article as Freedom should not be highly rated. . . .

Just before the Christmas of 1776, General George Washington gathered his forces alongside the Delaware River, preparing for a daring raid into British-held territory. His crossing of the Delaware would become one of the great events of the Revolution. Before he launched the attack Washington divided his men into groups. To each group he had officers read aloud the words of a short pamphlet that had just arrived from Philadelphia. It began: "These are the times that try men's souls. . . ."

As Tom Paine predicted, triumph did not come easily. But it came. In 1781, at Yorktown, Virginia, to the tune of fifes playing "The World Turned Upside Down," Lord Cornwallis surrendered his sword to General Washington. Then he marched his troops to waiting ships and sailed for England.

During the war years Paine had sworn a new oath, one that he himself had written, to become a citizen of the

United States of America. He had been named secretary of the Committee on Foreign Affairs. He had written new installments to his *Crisis* papers, sixteen in all by the end of the war. And, finally, he had been made a member of the American delegation that, with Benjamin Franklin in the lead, convinced King Louis XVI of France to send men, materials, and money to help defeat the British.

At the end of the war George Washington invited Paine to dine with him. They drank wine from silver cups. Washington arranged the payment of a fee from Pennsylvania for the work Paine had done—"services more useful than the sword." The state of New York granted him an estate of 227 acres of land and a gracious mansion at New Rochelle, beside Long Island Sound. The University of Pennsylvania awarded him an honorary master of arts degree.

For a time it appeared that Tom Paine, so recently a shabby, hungry adventurer lodged in a filthy rooming house, would settle down to live the life of a country gentleman, a life of ease and contentment.

But it was not to be. Perhaps the best—and also the worst—was yet to come for Paine.

In April 1787 he sailed for Europe with two purposes in mind: to visit his aged parents in Thetford and, on the way, to present his original design for an iron bridge (bridges in those days usually were made of wood or stone) to the French Academy in Paris. It was to be a short tour for the now internationally honored Thomas Paine. Yet he was not destined to return to his adopted country for fifteen years—and then, in disgrace.

At first all went well. The Academy of Science praised the model he had brought of his bridge. At Thetford, however, he found that his father had died and that his mother was a helpless invalid. Still, he was well received in London as the author of *Common Sense.* Joseph Priestley, the scientist, befriended him and persuaded him to build an actual full-scale iron bridge, not just a model. He did. Constructed on Paddington Green, it became one of the wonders of London. He also invented an improved form of crane. Finally Paine experimented with oxygen in the air even before Lavoisier became famous for his findings on what he called "phlogiston."

But politics was still Paine's great concern, especially the plight of the oppressed and the needy. Upon hearing that exciting changes were taking place in France he traveled there, hoping to play a part in the fast-moving events.

By the time he arrived, the Bastille,

a notorious prison, had been seized by the common people and its prisoners freed. Paine, known by the French as a friend of revolution—one who hated kings and monarchies—was given the old key to the prison. Happily he sent it on to George Washington, father of America's revolution against King George III of England.

In France a new revolution was beginning. As Paine put it, his "heart leaped with joy." When the French middle class set up a National Assembly, Paine was sure that the monarchy was finished. He looked forward to the establishment soon of a new government, a republic, like that of the United States.

Not everyone agreed with Paine's view of what was happening. The English leader Edmund Burke expressed shock at the course of events. Burke, who had been a strong friend of the American cause, feared disorder in France. Paine could not understand Burke's uneasiness about change. Partly in reply to Burke, Paine angrily rushed into print a brief but important book, *The Rights of Man*. In it he argued that people everywhere have the right to choose their own form of government and, when necessary, to change both the government and their rulers.

That idea—of limited government, serving the people—had been at the heart of America's Declaration of Independence. But in the Europe of 1789 it still was considered shocking. Defenders of the English and French kings shook their fists in anger at Paine's daring, perhaps even dangerous, language. Was he not, they charged, urging people to take arms against their governments? To rebel?

Overnight *The Rights of Man* sold 100,000 copies. Paine gave all the royalties he made from the book to a British organization that demanded an end to the monarchy and the founding of a democratic government. In a second edition he called for new laws in all countries to help people in need—the poor, the old, the sick, the unemployed. He called for freedom of religion and a free press. Overjoyed, the French National Assembly conferred on him the honorary title of "Citizen." He was now Citizen Thomas Paine.

In England, meanwhile, the government had acted to ban the printing and sale of *The Rights of Man*. Paine was charged with being "a wicked, seditious, and Evil disposed person" who had offended "our Lord the King." Police were ordered to arrest anyone found with a copy of the book. Paine himself, faced with arrest and almost certain death, fled the country at the very last minute, barely escaping his pursuers. He took refuge in France.

In Paris he was a hero. Wherever he was seen, people cheered him. Parades were held in his honor. Banners on housetops carried his name. He was elected a member of the French National Assembly. He was appointed to a committee to draft a new French constitution.

The France that Thomas Paine dreamed of was based on the motto of that nation's Revolution: "Liberty, Equality, Fraternity." He hoped to end the tyranny of rich over poor. And he hoped that people would act decently toward each other out of reason and good sense.

It was not to be. When King Louis XVI tried to flee, he was captured and sentenced to death. Thomas Paine was one of those in the National Assembly who voted to spare the king's life. King Louis was beheaded. And from that moment the Revolution turned violent. Instead of reason came the Reign of Terror. One execution followed another. Finally the Revolution turned against Paine. He was expelled from the National Assembly for being too moderate. Then one night, while he slept, police officers knocked at his door. They had come to arrest him. Like so many others who had helped to make the French Revolution, he became its victim.

Yet Paine did not lose his head to the blade of the guillotine. Month after month he languished in his cell at the once-luxurious Luxembourg Palace, which had been converted into a jail for French nobles and political prisoners. Ill with fever, sometimes delirious, he was given little food or medicine. Meanwhile hundreds were taken from the palace, thrown into carts, and driven to the guillotine, where they died before crowds of cheering Frenchmen.

At last the official order for Paine's death was readied. Authorities wrote a final confession in his name, admitting past lies and crimes, and distributed the confession to the press. But just then Robespierre, the evil genius of the Reign of Terror, himself felt the chill blade of the guillotine. Almost at once the Terror ended.

James Monroe, newly appointed American minister to France and an old friend of Paine's, claimed him as an American citizen and demanded his release. Within two days Thomas Paine was again a free man. He had spent ten months behind bars, nearly every moment of it at the very brink of execution.

Old, sick, penniless, his hair turned white during his imprisonment, Paine went to live in the Paris residence of James Monroe. There he slowly recovered his health, meanwhile completing work on his new book, *The Age of Reason.*

In the opening passages of that book he declared:

I believe in one God, and no more. . . . I do not believe in the creed professed by the Jewish church, by the Roman church, by the Greek church, . . . nor by any church that I know of. My own mind is my own church.

Jesus Christ, said Paine, was "a virtuous and an amiable man. The morality he preached and practiced was of the most benevolent kind." But it was difficult, according to Paine, to believe the story of his "being the Son of God."

To many people living in so religious an age, such ideas seemed dangerous. "The atheist's Bible" is how they described Paine's *Age of Reason.* He was called "the drunken atheist," "the arch-beast and liar," and other names. Some Frenchmen urged their new government to kill him for his part in starting the Revolution, which had sent hundreds of priests and ministers to the guillotine. From England and America torrents of abuse descended on Paine.

In October 1802 Thomas Paine returned to America. He had been away for fifteen years. Though he had been a popular hero when he had left, not a single person was waiting at the dock to greet him on his return. Old friends had turned against him, calling him an "unbeliever." Women he passed on the street turned their eyes to avoid him. He was abused and snubbed by "polite society." Still, Thomas Jefferson, by then President of the United States, received him warmly at the Executive Mansion in the new capital city of the nation, Washington, D.C.

Sadness and loneliness marked the last years of Paine's life. At New Rochelle he found that his fine mansion had burned to the ground. Then, while living in a cottage on the estate, one of his own workmen fired a musket at him, missing by inches. Later he suffered a stroke, which partially paralyzed him. Always careless about his appearance, he became even more untidy.

What little money he had, aside from his estate, he gave to needy friends. Finally he moved to a boardinghouse in what today is Bleecker Street in Manhattan's Greenwich Village. It was there, on June 8, 1809, that he died at the age of seventy-two.

For many years afterward it appeared that Paine's enemies had won. His name remained cloaked in scandal and lies. In time, however, people began to read his works again. "I never tire of reading Thomas Paine," said President Abraham Lincoln.

Today few Americans are more

greatly honored for standing up for a belief in freedom, regardless of the personal cost. Blacks and women, whose plight he championed, consider him a hero. Seldom has the cause of human rights had a more steadfast defender.

Benjamin Franklin

1706–1790 Statesman, printer, scientist, and writer

On January 17, 1706, Benjamin Franklin was born in a little house on Milk Street in Boston. He was the tenth son in his family. The Franklins were very poor.

When he was born the neighbors may have said, "Oh, well, another child at the Franklins'. Not much chance that he'll ever amount to much in life."

Eighty-four years later, when Benjamin Franklin died, people all over the world mourned his passing. Franklin was better known in his time than King Frederick the Great of Prussia, or the famous French philosopher Voltaire, or the English scientist Sir Isaac Newton.

Poor Ben Franklin of Milk Street, who went to school only two years in his entire life, grew up to know kings. He was given degrees by Harvard and Yale colleges in America and by the finest universities of Europe. He matched wits with outstanding lawyers in Great Britain. His scientific discoveries and inventions were famous everywhere. His writings were translated into many languages. He was a hero of the American Revolution. Some historians think he was the greatest of all Americans.

Franklin's father taught him to read at an early age, hoping that he would become a minister. But there were too many children to feed. Ben was taken out of school when he was ten and put to work in his father's business—making soap and candles.

Ben tried that but soon decided to become a printer. It seemed a good choice. He liked to use words. Besides, one of his older brothers had a printing shop. So Ben went to work for him.

Together they published a newspaper, the *New England Courant*.

Soon Ben Franklin was an expert printer. Once, when his brother was in jail, he put out the paper all by himself. Still, the two brothers did not get along well. In October 1723, at the age of seventeen, Franklin left Boston. Several days later he arrived in Philadelphia. Alone in a strange city, with only a Dutch dollar and some copper shillings in his pocket, Franklin started his new life. He stopped at a baker's to buy some bread. Since his pockets were full of extra socks and shirts, he tucked one long loaf of bread under each arm and munched a third loaf as he walked confidently down the street.

So what if he didn't have any money? He had a skill that people needed. And he believed in himself.

Before long young Benjamin Franklin was doing well. He took a job in a printing shop. He made friends. He learned to be an even better printer. People liked his work.

At the age of twenty-four he started his own printing business and his own newspaper, the *Pennsylvania Gazette*. He wrote most of the newspaper himself. Many of the things he said were very funny, so people bought the paper to laugh at the jokes.

Franklin worked hard and saved his money. And he took special care that others knew it. He never let people see him wasting his time hunting or fishing. He wore simple clothing. When he bought paper for his printing press, he himself wheeled it through the streets of Philadelphia in a wheelbarrow.

"Aha!" people said. "We can trust this young Ben Franklin. He works hard and is careful about his business. That is the kind of printer we need!"

The Pennsylvania Assembly chose Franklin as its printer. Ben printed copies of the laws and all the lawmakers' speeches.

Franklin was becoming an important person. His name was well known in Pennsylvania. Meanwhile he had married the daughter of his first landlady in Philadelphia, although she could neither read nor write. He and his wife raised a family of four children.

What finally made Franklin famous throughout the colonies was *Poor Richard's Almanack*. Almanacs once were very popular. They told people interesting things about farming, about the moon and stars, about great men and women of history. Franklin wrote an almanac that had all of those things. In addition it had old sayings that he put into language that even people who had not been to school could understand. Jokingly he said that the almanac had been written by a simple farmer called Richard Saunders.

"Poor Richard" said things like:

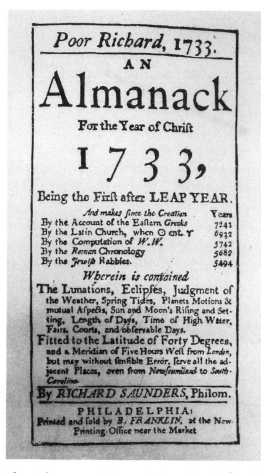

Poor Richard, 1733.

AN

Almanack

For the Year of Christ

1733,

Being the First after LEAP YEAR.

And makes since the Creation   Years
By the Account of the Eastern Greeks   7241
By the Latin Church, when ☉ ent. ♈   6932
By the Computation of W. W.   5742
By the Roman Chronology   5682
By the Jewish Rabbies.   5494

Wherein is contained

The Lunations, Eclipses, Judgment of the Weather, Spring Tides, Planets Motions & mutual Aspects, Sun and Moon's Rising and Setting, Length of Days, Time of High Water, Fairs, Courts, and observable Days.
Fitted to the Latitude of Forty Degrees, and a Meridian of Five Hours West from *London*, but may without sensible Error, serve all the adjacent Places, even from *Newfoundland* to *South-Carolina.*

By *RICHARD SAUNDERS*, Philom.

PHILADELPHIA:
Printed and sold by *B. FRANKLIN*, at the New Printing-Office near the Market.

The title page of *Poor Richard's Almanack for the Year of Christ 1733*. The almanac brought Franklin fame throughout the colonies. *Brown Brothers.*

"Early to bed, early to rise makes a man healthy, wealthy, and wise"; "A penny saved is a penny earned"; "The early bird catches the worm"; "The sleeping fox catches no poultry."

People throughout the colonies began talking about Ben Franklin of Philadelphia. Parts of the almanac

were reprinted in England and France. Ministers used it in their sermons. Lines from it were written on walls of buildings. Clearly Ben had become famous.

He honestly believed the things he said in *Poor Richard's Almanack*. He believed in being thrifty and working hard. He believed that people were good and could become better. They could improve themselves.

In his own life Ben Franklin always was busy trying to improve himself. He taught himself to read French, Spanish, Italian, and Latin. He taught himself history and mathematics. But his special love was science.

In every spare moment he studied science. He invented the "Pennsylvania Fireplace," a stove that gave more heat in a room at less cost. It became known as the Franklin stove and was used throughout the colonies. He invented a special clock that had only a few moving parts. He invented bifocal eyeglasses. He found out new things about storms on the Atlantic coast and about how to drain swamps.

In June 1752 Franklin made his most important scientific discovery. He had been doing experiments with electricity. It was fun for him. He even had made his own electric battery.

One stormy day he and his son William prepared a kite with a metal tip on it. They attached a key and a piece of silk to the kite string. Then they flew the kite. Lightning flashed. Franklin touched the silk and nothing happened. Then he touched the key and got a shock. It was an electric shock.

What Franklin proved was that lightning is a kind of electricity. Immediately he put his discovery to good use. He told people to put metal rods on their houses. The rods would attract the lightning and pass the electricity down through a wire to the earth. Then the houses themselves would not be hit and burned by lightning. Many lives and homes were saved because of Franklin's discovery.

His work with electricity is a good example of how Franklin put ideas to practical use. He was curious about many things, but what interested him most was solving problems. When he saw a puzzle he worked at it. And if one way did not succeed, he tried another and another until he found the right answer. By solving problems, Franklin was making a better life for himself and those around him.

Franklin spent much of his time in Philadelphia doing things to improve the city. He got people interested in paving the dirt streets with cobblestones and keeping streets clean and well lighted. He helped start a free public library and a hospital. He started a high school that later became the University of Pennsylvania. He organized

both the police force and fire department in Philadelphia. And when he saw how long it took to get mail delivered in the American colonies, he set up a postal service. It delivered the mail faster and helped to bring citizens of the colonies closer together.

In the same way that he improved the world around him he tried to improve his own personality. His goal was extraordinarily high: to rid himself of faults and become as "perfect" a person as possible. He even made a list of the ways he could be a better person and then worked at those things one at a time.

It seemed to him that God would reward those who lived good lives. But he thought of God in a different way than the Puritans had, or the men of Columbus's time. Franklin believed in God and said that people should give thanks to Him. But he said less about God's power to punish and much more about God's love. God was wise and good, said Franklin. Otherwise, why would He have created the world and put such wonderful creatures as human beings here?

In Ben Franklin's mind, what God wanted most was for people to be happy and do good to each other. To Franklin, happiness should come in a person's lifetime as well as in heaven.

By the time he was forty-two years old, in 1748, Franklin had made enough

In this mezzotint by Edward Fisher after a painting by M. Chamberlin, Benjamin Franklin is portrayed with a lightning rod in the background. *Metropolitan Museum of Art, New York City. Bequest of Michael Friedsam.*

money to retire. That gave him the time he wanted. He could have made more money and become richer. Instead he decided to spend the rest of his life studying science and other subjects he enjoyed.

But Ben Franklin was never to have the free time he dreamed of. The American people needed him. In 1754 Pennsylvania sent him to the Albany Congress, which was called to unite the colonies against the French and the Indians. Next he had to stay in England for three years to handle other business for Pennsylvania. He returned to England once again when the British began to discuss enacting a new tax, the Stamp Act, on the American people. The tax was to be placed on all newspapers, letters, public papers, and even almanacs. It made Americans exceedingly angry.

Franklin spoke against the Stamp Act in the British Parliament. He warned that Americans would not pay the new taxes. At first the British refused to believe him. But after putting the tax into effect in America, they realized that Franklin had been correct. He continued to argue against the Stamp Act. Finally Parliament voted to end it.

For eleven years Ben Franklin remained in England, trying to keep peace between England and the American colonies. But even he could not prevent a war. He returned to America.

The colonists no longer would obey British laws or pay British taxes. The British insisted that the colonists had to obey. In April 1775 the American Revolution began.

The next year, 1776, the colonists announced that no longer were they fighting merely for their rights as Englishmen. They had decided to form a country of their own, the United States of America. It was a war for freedom from Great Britain.

In the Declaration of Independence, the Americans informed the rest of the world that they were fighting for the rights of free men everywhere. Ben Franklin was a signer of the Declaration, and he was one of those who helped Thomas Jefferson write it.

At first things went very badly on the battlefield for the Americans. Unless they received assistance from foreign nations, defeat seemed certain. In October 1776 Benjamin Franklin, then nearly seventy-one years old, sailed for France to win help for the American cause.

The French were old enemies of the English. If Great Britain lost her rich American colonies she would be seriously hurt. Therefore when the American colonists declared their independence from England, the French were delighted.

An engraving after a painting by Edward Savage and Robert E. Pine shows the vote for independence. Benjamin Franklin is seated in the center foreground. *The Library of Congress.*

The French liked Franklin. They liked his simple speech and manners. They liked his witty sayings. People put his picture in the windows of their shops and houses. They stamped likenesses of him on rings and watches and bracelets. They made copies for themselves of the big fur hat he liked to wear as he walked along the streets of Paris.

But despite Franklin's popularity, King Louis XVI refused at first to help the American colonies. He was reluctant to spend money on a war so far away from France. He doubted, too, that the colonists could win. Finally, after the American army won a great battle, at Saratoga, New York, the king agreed to help.

Without French assistance the American Revolution could not have succeeded. More than anyone else it was Benjamin Franklin who secured that important aid for the colonies.

Franklin helped write the final peace treaty with England and then returned home to Philadelphia. Even then his service to America was not over. In 1787 he was chosen by Pennsylvania to attend the Constitutional Convention.

Planning the government for a new

"Doctor Franklin Crowned by Liberty," a 1778 engraving by Abbé de St. Non after a painting by the French artist Jean-Honoré Fragonard. *Musée Carnavalet, Paris.*

country is scarcely an easy task, and by then Benjamin Franklin was eighty-one years old. He did not agree with everything that went into the Constitution, but he thought the plan had a reasonable chance of success. When other delegates to the convention argued bitterly over elements of the Constitution, Franklin pleaded for understanding, for compromise.

The delegates trusted him. They compromised over disputed points. It was Franklin's wit and good sense that saved the convention from breaking up.

Three years later, in 1790, Benjamin Franklin died. To the rest of the world he was a new kind of person—an American. He was concerned most of all with how to make things work for other people—electricity, for example, and the Philadelphia fire department, and glasses, and the government of the United States of America. If things "worked right," he was convinced, people's lives would be better and happier.

Once, when he was young, Franklin had thought of making his home in England. But he changed his mind. He decided to remain an American. It was, said Franklin, because he discovered that the laws of England were neither just nor honest. The British government showed little concern for the will of the people. It showed equally slight concern for making people happy. And, to Franklin, "the pursuit of happiness" was a central purpose of government.

Perhaps that is why America, a land committed in its founding document to the basic human freedoms—"life, liberty, and the pursuit of happiness"—turned out to be so right for Benjamin Franklin, and he to be so right for America.

PART II

A Search for Freedom and Racial Justice

Sarah Moore Grimké 1792–1873
Angelina Emily Grimké 1805–1879

Southern sisters who were leaders in the fight to free the slaves

Dignified, serious, dressed in simple Quaker gray with a white handerchief framing her delicate features, Angelina Grimké stood calmly at the speaker's stand, preparing to address a committee of the Massachusetts State Legislature.

Outside the State House, men shook their fists in anger. Some hooted and jeered. Others hissed, not the hisses heard at today's sports events, but hisses born of genuine hatred.

It was Wednesday, February 21, 1838. Until that day no American woman ever had addressed a legislative body in this country. The visitors' gallery was packed to capacity. Standees jammed the aisles and the lobby outside the hall. Many in the crowd had come out of curiosity, just to see a woman speak in public, something then considered shameful, even indecent.

Yet as Miss Grimké's powerful voice rang out across the audience, boldly, magnetically, her listeners riveted their attention on her, gripped by the intensity of her message. For there at the lectern stood a white southern woman, born to wealth and aristocratic position, delivering a passionate attack on the South's "peculiar institution"—human slavery.

"I stand before you as a southerner," she declared, "exiled from the land of my birth by the sound of the lash and the piteous cry of the slave. I stand before you as a repentant slave holder.

"I stand before you," continued Angelina Grimké, "as a moral being, and as a moral being I feel that I owe it to the suffering slave and to the deluded master . . . to do all that I can to overturn a system . . . built upon

Angelina Emily Grimké. *The Library of Congress.*

the broken hearts and prostrate bodies of my countrymen in chains and cemented by the blood, sweat and tears of my sisters in bonds. . . ."

In the audience before her some people openly cried. The chairman of the committee, Miss Grimké later wrote, "was in tears almost the whole time that I was speaking." Sarah, her older sister, was to have been the featured speaker that day. But, ill, she had taken to her bed, persuading young Angelina to substitute for her.

No matter. Before long the names of the two sisters became linked, North and South, as leaders in the forefront of the antislavery movement. Other women, until then hesitant to speak out in public against the curse of slavery, followed their example.

In time the leading women of the age—Lucy Stone, Elizabeth Cady Stanton, Susan B. Anthony—all would express gratitude to the Grimké sisters. It was the Grimkés, they said, who first inspired them to join in battle, crusading for the twin causes of women's rights and the abolition of slavery.

The society into which Sarah and Angelina Grimké had been born could hardly have been a more unlikely setting for the development of social reformers. Charleston, South Carolina, led the South in defending slavery. Wealthy planter aristocrats, including

the father of the Grimké sisters, dominated the city's society. The very survival of their gracious and leisurely lifestyle depended on the slave labor system.

It was slaves who planted and harvested their yearly cotton crops—the source of their wealth. It was slaves, too, who built their houses, cooked their meals, cared for their children, stood behind them to fan the flies away as they dined. It was slaves who made possible for the white men their hours of pleasure in hunting and riding, or for the elegant white women the days and evenings filled with tea parties, fancy-dress balls, and an endless round of visits to neighboring plantations.

For young Sarah Grimké, child of the aristocracy, such a life proved, for some reason, not enough to make her happy. Nor did it please the young Angelina, so headstrong, independent, even in childhood, that her mother scarcely could control her. Instead of absorbing the standard school curriculum for girls of the time—music, a touch of French, and gracious manners—the Grimké sisters demanded the right to the same education as their brothers: Latin, Greek, mathematics, philosophy, and law.

Both girls wept at the beatings and other punishments inflicted by slave owners, including even their own parents, to keep blacks humble and obedient. Sometimes Angelina would creep into the slave quarters at night to rub soothing ointment into the open wounds of slaves who had been lashed with the whip.

Sarah, and later Angelina, too, taught the slave girls assigned to them as maids how to read. In most parts of the South such an act was strictly forbidden, but as Angelina admitted with pride in her diary, "The light was put out, the keyhole screened, and flat on our stomachs before the fire, we defied the laws of South Carolina."

In 1819, when Sarah was twenty-seven, her father chose her, instead of his wife or any of her brothers, to travel with him to the North. He was ill and had been advised that a surgeon in Philadelphia might help him, but the illness proved fatal.

The trip was to change Sarah's life. Quakers whom she met in Philadelphia introduced her to their religion. She admired their seriousness of purpose, liked their opposition to slavery. She also approved of the laws passed in Philadelphia to protect free Negroes there.

Although the decision was painful, she decided to leave Charleston and go to live in Philadelphia. Perhaps in the North, she confided to Angelina, a woman might live a life not just of pleasure but of real purpose. In 1829 Angelina, then twenty-four, followed her sister to Philadelphia. Both sisters knew that, hating slavery as they did, the break with their old lives in Charleston could never be healed.

At first the Grimkés tried to live like religious Quakers. They lived simply, dressed simply, and did charity work. But that was not enough for them. Always rebellious, they insisted on speaking aloud in the usually silent Quaker meetings, where they also made a point of sitting in the sections reserved for black women. To them the Quakers were doing too little, moving too slowly, in putting a stop to slavery in America. Just as they had left the Episcopal Church in South Carolina, they also split from the Quakers.

In 1835 Angelina decided to state publicly that all slaves must be freed. She wrote to William Lloyd Garrison, editor of the *Liberator*, America's angriest antislavery newspaper. Abolition of slavery, she declared in her letter, "is a cause worth dying for." Of Garrison himself, she stated that "The ground upon which you stand is holy ground."

Garrison printed Angelina's letter in the *Liberator*. People all across the country read it. Overnight Angelina and her sister became heroines of the antislavery movement. Here were the daughters of wealthy slave owners dar-

Sarah Moore Grimké. *The Library of Congress.*

ing to describe the brutal acts they personally had witnessed and demanding that the slaves should be freed at once.

Next Angelina wrote a pamphlet, *An Appeal to the Christian Women of the South*, urging white women to join the fight against slavery—to put an end to "this horrible system of oppression and cruelty . . . and wrong," even if they had to break the law.

In Charleston the postmaster publicly burned copies of the pamphlet in the city's main square. Authorities warned Angelina and Sarah not to return home or they would be arrested.

The threat succeeded in keeping the Grimké sisters away from Charleston, but it could not stop them from speaking out. In 1836 Sarah published "Epistle to the Clergy of the Southern States." In that letter she urged southern ministers at least to stop giving their support to slavery, even if they could not offend their congregations by opposing it publicly.

Well known by then, the Grimkés decided to give their lives totally to the abolitionist movement. They joined the American Anti-Slavery Society and began to speak, as a team, to small meetings of women in New York City.

Soon these so-called parlor meetings became so popular that many ministers opened their churches to the Grimké sisters, usually on the condition that no men be present. But before long men demanded the right to hear the lectures, even though the appearance of women as public speakers was considered unwomanly. Almost everywhere, the Grimkés found themselves facing mixed audiences—larger and larger ones as their popularity grew.

It was during their triumphant tour of New England in 1838 that Angelina delivered her famous address to a session of the Massachusetts Legislature in the State House at Boston.

Angelina, tall, with piercing eyes and a strong voice, enjoyed meeting an audience. Sarah, more reserved, did most of the writing for the Grimké team. The two worked well together.

At first William Lloyd Garrison and other leaders of the abolitionist movement pleaded with them not to endanger the antislavery cause by linking it with questions of women's rights, especially the right of women to speak in public. Garrison changed his mind, however, as did Theodore Dwight Weld, who had coached Angelina in techniques of public speaking when she first joined the American Anti-Slavery Society.

Instead of avoiding the issue of women's rights, the Grimké sisters spoke out more strongly on it. They demanded not only the right to be heard, but also the right of women to vote, to help make laws, and even to serve as elected officials. Finally they demanded that women be given complete legal equality with men in such matters as divorce and ownership of property.

At one of their speeches a gang of boys threw apples at them. Spectators jeered at them. Newspapermen dubbed them "the weird sisters," or "Devilina and Grimalkin."

Nothing stopped the Grimkés. In the spring of 1838 they spoke at the Odeon Theater in Boston to mixed audiences of men and women numbering two thousand to three thousand. Clearly they had taken center stage in the antislavery movement. No other women in the country were so well known or so frequently discussed.

By now it became obvious, too, that Theodore Dwight Weld's interest in Angelina went beyond her ideas. He continued to give her lessons in public speaking. He accompanied the Grimkés on their tours. But he also had fallen in love with Angelina—and she with him.

In May 1838 they were married. The wedding party included, in the words of one guest, "a motley assembly of white and black, high and low." In direct defiance of "the horrible prejudice of slavery" the bride and groom introduced as bridesmaids and groomsmen six former slaves from the Grimké plan-

tation. Two white and two black ministers presented prayers. At the end of the ceremony William Lloyd Garrison read the marriage certificate aloud and then passed it around the room to be signed by each guest.

Theodore and Angelina insisted that the wedding cake be made with sugar grown by free laborers. The cotton for their mattress, they proudly pointed out, had come from a farm in New Jersey, not "the usual slave-grown cotton ticking."

Two days after their wedding Angelina and Theodore left for a honeymoon. As might be expected, they spent it working for the antislavery cause. Along with Sarah, they attended the opening session of the Anti-Slavery Convention of American Women, held in Philadelphia's attractive new Pennsylvania Hall. The hall had been built especially for such occasions, since reformers, even in Quaker-dominated Philadelphia, had experienced difficulty renting space for speeches on such topics as women's rights and abolition.

On the first night of the convention, Angelina Grimké Weld rose to address a mixed audience of more than a thousand blacks and whites. Outside the hall a mob of whites gathered. As Angelina began to speak they shouted and cursed. They stamped their feet. Then they began throwing bricks and stones at the newly opened hall, shattering the windows. Glass fell to the floor, some of it at Angelina's feet.

"What is a mob?" she continued calmly.

What would the breaking of every window be? Any evidence that *we are* wrong, or that slavery is a good and wholesome institution? What if that mob should now burst in upon us, break up our meeting and commit violence on our persons— would this be anything compared with what the slaves endure?

For more than an hour Angelina spoke on as the mob groaned and roared angrily in the background. Nothing could stop her from delivering her message.

Before the meeting could begin on the next night, the mayor of Philadelphia closed the hall, fearing violence. After he left the scene, the mob surged forward. They burst into the offices of the Anti-Slavery Society there and destroyed many precious papers. Then they set fire to the hall, dedicated to free speech, burning it completely to the ground.

In the months that followed the fire Angelina and Theodore Weld did little public speaking. They began to build a family, eventually having three children. Sarah, now alone, came to live with them, first in their home in New Jersey and later in Massachusetts. She

took special pleasure in caring for the Weld children.

The three also worked together on an important new collection of documents, *American Slavery As It Is: Testimony of a Thousand Witnesses.* Drawing heavily on advertisements and published accounts in southern newspapers, the study offered powerful evidence against slavery. Included were advertisements for the return of runaway slaves, identified by their owners, for example, as "stamped on the left cheek 'R' and a piece is taken off her left ear, the same letter is branded on the inside of both legs"; or, "branded 'N.E.' on the breast and having both small toes cut off."

Harriet Beecher Stowe relied heavily on the Weld-Grimké evidence in writing *Uncle Tom's Cabin*, the novel that, according to some, became a major emotional cause of the Civil War.

In time, illness and age began to limit the involvement of Sarah, Angelina, and Theodore in the antislavery cause. Still, they continued to circulate petitions against slavery. They also became interested in other reforms of the day, such as less confining clothing for women, sensible diet, and better forms of education.

After the Civil War ended the sisters learned that two of their brother Henry's sons, born of a Negro slave woman, were in the North. Without hesitation they welcomed the boys into their home and paid for their education. One son later became a prominent minister in black churches. The other became a leader in the National Association for the Advancement of Colored People (NAACP).

In 1873 Sarah Grimké died. Six years later Angelina followed her sister to the grave. Both had lived long enough to see the end of slavery in America. And although the women's rights movement had not yet triumphed, the Grimké sisters had been early leaders in drawing the nation's attention to that movement, too.

Women of ability and high character, the Grimkés turned their backs, as young adults, on what surely would have been lives of security, comfort, leisure, and wealth. Instead they chose to live lives of struggle but also of great accomplishment and—through service to others—lives filled with meaning.

Dorothea Dix

1802–1887   Pioneer in developing special treatment for the insane
and new techniques for the training of nurses

Pages from the notebook of Dorothea L. Dix, 1842. These are descriptions of "lunatic asylums" she had visited in Massachusetts—places for housing the insane:

Taunton. One woman caged. . . .

Wayland Almshouse. Man caged in a woodshed, fully exposed on a public road. Confinement and cold have so affected his limbs that he is powerless to rise. . . .

Westford. Young woman fastened to the wall with a chair. . . .

January 1843. From a letter by Dorothea L. Dix to the Massachusetts Legislature:

I proceed, Gentlemen, to call your attention to the *present* state of Insane Persons confined within this Commonwealth, in cages, closets, cellars, stalls, pens! *Chained, naked, beaten with rods, and lashed into obedience!* . . .

"Incredible! Incredible!" exclaimed one legislator on reading Miss Dix's letter. Unfortunately, what she had seen was not incredible at all but quite typical of the way in which the insane were treated at the time, not only in Massachusetts but in much of the world.

Why were such people brutalized, treated even worse than animals? And who was the aristocratic-looking woman whose crusade on their behalf would eventually make her name live in memory as one of the great leaders in the cause of human rights?

The early life of Dorothea Dix gave no hint of the contributions she eventually would make to humanity. Her father, born into a well-to-do Boston family, had run away while a student at Harvard and married a woman twenty years older than himself—a woman his family considered "poor, ignorant, and crude." They had gone to live in the woods near Bangor, Maine, an area inhabited mostly by poverty-stricken farmers. In April 1802 Dorothea was born there in a log cabin.

Unable to support his growing family by farming, Dorothea's father became a traveling preacher. Even when crops were good he usually was paid for his services in provisions. When crops were bad, Dorothea, her two younger brothers, and her parents simply went hungry.

Since her father often preached far away from home and her mother frequently was ill, Dorothea had to take care of her brothers. She also spent hours at a time stitching together into books the pages of religious sermons that her father sold to make extra money.

Occasionally Dorothea's grandfather, Dr. Elijah Dix, visited his son's family in Maine. Sometimes he took Dorothea with him to his home in Boston. When she was seven years old, Dr. Dix died. Three years later, unhappy with her lonely, dreary life in Maine, she convinced her grandmother to let her come to live in Boston.

That did not work out well, either. Already a strong-willed person, Dorothea resisted her grandmother's attempts to make her over—to change the way she dressed, the way she behaved, and most of all the way she obeyed; for she absolutely refused to do as she was told.

At twelve Dorothea Dix went to live with an aunt and some young cousins in Worcester, Massachusetts. That event changed her life. For the first time she was happy. She read and studied. After two years, at the age of fourteen, she rented a vacant store and started a school of her own.

To make herself look older she wore long, dark dresses and pinned her hair back severely. Before long she was teaching as many as twenty children, drawn from the most respected families of Worcester.

Teaching students made Dorothea Dix realize just how much she did not know and how desperately she wanted to learn. To educate herself properly she returned to her grandmother's house in Boston, where she read book after book, attended lectures, visited museums. Once again she opened a school. At the same time she also taught at a school for poor children.

At the age of twenty-two she published her first book, an elementary-school science textbook, *Conversations on Common Things*. One year later she produced an anthology of poems, *Hymns for Children*, which included some of her own verses.

Often Dorothea would rise at four in the morning and work until midnight. With such a schedule she had little time for fun. Her engagement to marry a distant cousin ended mysteriously, an event Dorothea refused to explain to anyone. Then, as she was exhausted and overworked, her health collapsed.

Before her illness she had met the famous Unitarian minister Dr. William Ellery Channing. Now Channing and his wife befriended Dorothea. They took her in summer to their home on Narragansett Bay and in winter to St. Croix in the Virgin Islands. For ten years, with their help, she struggled to regain her health.

Each recovery was followed by a relapse. Finally, in 1836, her doctor advised travel abroad and a complete rest. She sailed immediately for England. It was just after her arrival there that she met the Rathbones, wealthy Quaker friends of Dr. Channing. At their estate, where she stayed for eighteen months, she came into contact with some of the leading figures in Britain's reform movement, including Dr. Samuel Tuke. Tuke, deeply troubled by the treatment of the insane in England, had founded a hospital where mentally troubled people were cared for with kindness and love.

Dr. Tuke's ideas changed Dorothea's life. Influenced by him, she determined to do something to help the unfortunate, especially the insane.

When Dorothea returned to America she found that her grandmother's death had left her with a considerable inheritance—enough money to make her independent. Since she no longer had to work to support herself she could make choices about her life. But what would she do?

One day in March 1841, the answer came knocking at her door. A Harvard divinity student asked Dorothea if she would help him find someone to teach Sunday school at a local prison. Instead Dorothea offered to teach the class herself. It was to be the turning point in her career.

When she arrived at the prison she discovered unbelievably wretched conditions. Among the female prisoners the insane were housed together with prostitutes, thieves, and beggars. The cells were filthy, foul smelling, bare, and cold. "Why is there no heat?" she asked a jailer. "Lunatics don't feel the cold like other people," he answered her.

Such ignorance and prejudice about the insane, she soon realized, marked the attitudes of most Bostonians. Few people knew how bad conditions really were. And many who did know believed that only harsh treatment—beating, chaining, torturing—could force the devils out of the insane person's body.

Not everyone agreed with that approach. Dorothea Dix instantly recalled the work of Dr. Tuke in England. In France, Philippe Pinel had written of his success with similar methods of love, tenderness, care. Even in America a handful of hospitals were trying out such ideas, including one in Boston, the Boston Lunatic Asylum.

For the most part, however, a person who suffered from mental illness, especially someone who was poor or uneducated, was doomed forever to a life of misery and terror.

Now, at last, Dorothea Dix had found her cause, the one that would help her find meaning in her own life by helping others. Instantly she leaped into battle.

For the next two years she crisscrossed Massachusetts, visiting every prison, every charity home, every workhouse in the state. She discovered scenes of horror beyond anything imaginable. Sometimes she was greeted with screams, groans, and cries for help. She saw men and women whose hands and feet had been frozen into stumps by the cold. One man was buried alive in a pit, food shoved at him through a tiny hole in an iron grating. In another

case jailers had enclosed their "patients" behind double-thick walls and doors so that the screams would not disturb them in their nearby house.

At last Miss Dix had all the evidence she needed. She gathered her notes and prepared a burning statement for presentation to the Massachusetts State Legislature. In a fierce debate three well-known champions of social reform—Samuel Gridley Howe, Charles Sumner, and Horace Mann—carried her case. They demanded passage of a bill that would require all hospitals in the state to set aside room for the treatment of mental patients. Some legislators feared that the bill would mean higher taxes. Others thought that Miss Dix simply had exaggerated the seriousness of conditions. But the final vote brought Dorothea Dix and her supporters a tremendous victory.

Encouraged by triumph in Massachusetts, she carried her fight to other states. New York voted to build new mental hospitals. So did Rhode Island. After a bitter contest New Jersey agreed to build its first mental treatment center at Trenton, the state capital, even inviting Miss Dix to help design the hospital. She described the building as "my first-born child."

Now the pace of her work quickened. For three years she traveled without stopping, bringing her pleas to the state legislatures of Pennsylvania, Illinois, Kentucky, Tennessee, Mississippi, Alabama, Louisiana, the Carolinas, and Maryland. She pushed from place to place in any way she could: train, stagecoach, steamboat, on horseback. Although she was still in poor health, she refused to rest. Usually she read books on mental health well into the night, often by the flickering light of oil lamps or the dying embers of a fireplace. Once a robber stopped her coach, demanding money. But, recognizing her from one of her prison visits, he returned the money—only to have her insist that he keep some of it until he could find an honest job!

Had she lived today, television would have made Dorothea Dix an instant celebrity. In the 1840s and 1850s fame came more slowly. But gradually Miss Dix's name became known across the nation. Still shy, rarely giving speeches in public, she was heaped with honors. Politicians competed to be seen with her. Railroads gave her free passes. Magazines eagerly published her articles.

One victory eluded her, however. Year after year, for fourteen years, she tried to persuade the Congress of the United States to pass a bill to help pay for treatment of insane poor people. At last, in 1854, her plan passed both the Senate and the House of Representatives.

Dorothea's joy was short lived. President Franklin Pierce, her trusted friend, vetoed the bill. According to Pierce, once the federal government took a first step in providing money to help the poor, there would be no limit to future demands for such causes, regardless of their worthiness. Charitable work, he argued, should be left to the states and to localities, this despite "the deep sympathies of my heart."

Disappointed, Miss Dix set out for Europe, again hoping to recover her health. Yet wherever she went she found it impossible not to work on behalf of her ideas. In England she convinced Queen Victoria to look into problems of the insane in Scotland. Next she visited France, then Switzerland. In Italy Pope Pius IX personally thanked her for bringing to his attention the deplorable conditions at an asylum virtually within sight of the Vatican. Before returning to America she surveyed prison and hospital conditions in Sweden, Belgium, Holland, Hungary, Turkey, and Russia.

Especially in Turkey and Russia she saw new approaches to treating the insane. In those countries she observed the importance to patients of trained nurses, not just sympathetic doctors. As a result she began to inform medical workers and the American public of better ways to prepare nurses for their jobs. At the time nursing was a field that

Dorothea Dix in a photograph taken around 1858. *By permission of the Houghton Library, Harvard University.*

seldom appealed to educated, "respectable" women. Instead some of the least desirable women in society staffed the hospitals. Dorothea Dix, well known and influential, worked hard to change that situation.

In 1861, when the American Civil War broke out, Miss Dix knew she had to do something about the condition of military hospitals. In conflicts of the time, such as the Crimean War, far more soldiers died of infection than from wounds received in battle. Sanitary precautions were almost unknown. Doctors frequently performed surgical procedures they had never seen done before. Sometimes amputated arms and legs simply were thrown into piles outside the flaps of hastily pitched medical tents, directly on the battlefield.

Appointed the superintendent of women nurses in 1861, Dorothea Dix worked to attract and train serious, competent women. All army nurses, she demanded, must be "plain looking women." No nuns or members of religious orders were allowed to serve. Miss Dix visited hospital after hospital and dismissed any nurse who did not meet her high standards. She also reported to the War Department any doctor she found drunk. Using her famous name, she enlisted the help of women's sewing groups across the North in such

tasks as preparing bandages. She arranged for the delivery of raw onions and fresh vegetables at Vicksburg to Union soldiers suffering from scurvy.

At each step of the way she fought for what she thought was right. Officials in the Army Medical Bureau resented the power she had to get her way. They found her short tempered and demanding. So did the volunteers of the United States Sanitary Commission. Dorothea Dix persisted. Still some of the reforms in nursing care she suggested during the Civil War were not put into effect until America's participation in World War II (1941–1945).

At the end of the Civil War she returned to her work with the insane. She pressed for the creation of new mental hospitals and separation of the mentally ill from other prisoners in jails. She also demanded better care for children in orphans' homes.

At last, exhausted and seriously ill, she retired to the hospital she had helped to establish in Trenton, New Jersey, the one she had described as her "first-born." It was there that she died, at the age of eighty-four. Even in her hospital bed she had continued searching for ways to be helpful to those around her.

The life of Dorothea L. Dix was one of single-minded devotion to a cause—

better care for the mentally ill. Always shy and timid in public, she brought to her writing and her hospital visits a burning intensity. She had the force of character, the independence of spirit, to stay with the details of a task until it was finished. Those qualities helped her to overcome the objections of ignorant, uncaring officials.

That she fought on is a tribute to her deep compassion for a group in society that, even today, is misunderstood, neglected, pushed out of sight—the mentally ill.

Frederick Douglass

c. 1817–1895   A slave at birth who became a distinguished spokesman for the rights of his people

Once there was a slave boy. Probably he was born in 1817, but nobody really is sure about his birthday, for he was a slave—and who cared enough to remember the birthday of a slave? For a long time after he was born, few people cared about young Frederick Douglass. One day he would become the best-known black man in America.

Until he was eight years old, life was hard for Douglass. Like many slave children, he worked long hours. He had little time for play. Sometimes he was whipped. Almost always he was hungry. He slept on a damp earth floor with only a flour sack to keep him warm. As each day dawned, the intelligent young Frederick must have asked himself, "Will the rest of my life be like this?"

Then something wonderful hap-

pened. At the age of eight, Frederick was sent to Baltimore to live with his master's relatives, one of whom was Thomas Auld, who was his own age.

It was like a dream. He wore warm clothing and ate good food. He was well treated. Best of all, Thomas Auld's kind young mother taught him to read. She was more than kind, she was brave— because it was against the law to teach a black person to read. Slave owners believed that once a slave could read he would begin to think for himself. He would want to make up his own mind. Then he would not obey their orders.

When Mr. Auld discovered that his wife had taught Frederick to read he was very angry. The lessons stopped at once.

Frederick's happy life in Baltimore

ended when his master died. As a slave he was just another piece of property. He did not know what would become of him.

Seventeen-year-old Frederick was sent to live on a farm. Once again he was beaten and starved. But he would not obey his new owner's commands. Nothing could break his spirit. Nothing could make him do as he was told. His master tried everything. Then he sent Frederick to Edward Covey.

Covey was a farmer who earned extra money as a slave breaker. He bragged that he could train any black man to obey. "With me," he laughed, "either they learn to behave or they pay the penalty."

Day after day Covey flogged young Frederick, beating him with a leather strap until the blood ran. He made Frederick work harder and harder. Then one day, when Covey began to whip him again, Frederick could stand no more.

He grabbed the cruel slave breaker by the throat and threw him to the ground. The two charged each other, fists flying. They fought savagely. Both were hurt. Neither would quit. On and on the black slave and the white farmer pounded and gouged at each other. Then they stopped, totally exhausted.

Frederick may not have won the fight, but things were different afterward. Never again did Covey lay a hand

on him. The brutal slave driver had learned to respect Frederick's courage.

From that day on Douglass dreamed of becoming a free man. Once, he and several friends planned to escape, but another slave betrayed them and they were severely punished.

Finally he succeeded. He borrowed identification papers from a free Negro friend and boarded a train for New York City. All the way he was afraid of being discovered and returned to slavery. But at last he arrived safely in the North. Shortly afterward he married Anna Murray, a free Negro girl he had known before and had grown to love. With her he left for New Bedford, Massachusetts, to start a new life.

Freedom was not easy for him at first. A runaway slave, a black man in a white man's country, he had to take whatever jobs he could find. He worked at handling and loading cargo in a shipyard. His wife took in washing.

Then Frederick Douglass stumbled upon a career. He discovered that he had a gift for speaking to audiences. People listened when he spoke. He held their attention. He was persuasive.

A white minister once heard him speaking to a group of freed slaves about the problems of blacks in America. The minister invited Douglass to address a meeting of well-known white people who were opposed to slavery. Those people had established a group that was known as the Massachusetts Anti-Slavery Society.

Douglass's ability as a speaker was immediately apparent. As he told about his life as a slave, people leaned forward tensely in their seats. He had a splendid voice. Well over six feet tall, he was strong and handsome, with a square jaw and piercing eyes. Wherever he went, people turned to look at him.

Douglass was precisely the man the Massachusetts Anti-Slavery Society needed. He was a remarkable human being. And he had been a slave. Could there be a better person to talk to white men and to show them just how wrong slavery was?

To Douglass's surprise, the society offered him a job. He was to travel in the New England states, speaking out against slavery wherever he could.

More people opposed slavery in New England than in any other section of the country. Yet even there many believed that blacks were less human than whites. Frederick Douglass was forced to ride in railroad cars marked For Colored Only. Many hotels would not let him stay overnight.

When he spoke people sometimes laughed and jeered at him. He was beaten and stoned. Sometimes when mobs attacked him he was lucky to escape with his life. But just as in his fight with Covey, Douglass would not give in.

Meanwhile he was becoming a more accomplished speaker. Soon people were talking about Frederick Douglass, the runaway slave who carried himself like a gentleman. Indeed, he was such a good speaker and used such perfect English that listeners sometimes refused to believe that he ever had been a slave. So Douglass wrote an autobiography, an account of his own life. It was a daring book. In it he named people who had beaten him. He graphically described the horrors of slavery. Many people read the book, even in the South.

Since Douglass was a runaway slave, such a book could be extremely dangerous for him. Now that he was famous, everyone knew where to find him. At any moment he could be seized and returned to his former master.

To avoid capture, Douglass decided to travel to England. There, for the first time, he was treated like a man, not a thing. Nobody said to him, as they sometimes did even in Massachusetts, "We don't allow niggers in here!"

"Someday," Douglass declared, "black people will be treated like human beings in America, too."

After two years in England, Douglass resolved to return to the United States.

Portrait of Frederick Douglass about 1847. *The Historical Society of Pennsylvania.*

"I choose to go home," he told a group in London, "to suffer with my brothers, to toil with them, to lift up my voice in their behalf."

Before leaving for America, he bought his freedom from his old master. The cost was $710.96. Now, according to the laws of the United States, Douglass was a free man. Some antislavery friends thought it was wrong for him to buy his freedom, because to do so meant living by the rules made by slave owners. But Douglass was always a practical man. He knew that he had important work to do. He couldn't do it if he always had to worry about being arrested and sent back into slavery.

On returning to America, Douglass bought a home in Rochester, New York. He transformed it into a station on the Underground Railroad. The Underground Railroad, of course, was really not a railroad. It was a network of routes by which slaves could make their way from the South to freedom in Canada. Runaway slaves were passed from one "station," or hiding place, to another. Rochester was one of the last stations before Canada.

Sometimes escaped slaves would appear at Douglass's home hidden under a load of hay in a wagon or covered with old clothing. One slave came to him sealed in a packing carton marked Open with Care.

Douglass knew he was taking a chance helping slaves to escape. Under the Fugitive Slave Act, anyone aiding a runaway slave could be severely punished. But such a law, according to Douglass, deserved to be disobeyed.

Douglass did not stop with helping others to escape. He acted to end the wicked system of slavery. As one step in that direction, he launched a newspaper, the *North Star*. He called it that because when he had first decided to escape from slavery, he had planned to make his way by "following the North Star."

In addition to publishing his newspaper, Douglass made speeches about ways to end slavery. He tried to get people who hated slavery elected to Congress, where they could win passage of new laws. He wrote articles for magazines. He met with leaders of the antislavery societies. But no matter how much he hated slavery himself, he never asked others to kill slave owners.

One day in September 1859 Frederick Douglass took a train ride. Waiting for him at the end of his ride was John Brown.

Brown was then planning an attack on the federal arsenal at Harper's Ferry, Virginia. He wanted the help of Douglass, who at that time probably was the best-known black man in America. They had been friends for many years. Brown had once been a guest at Douglass's home for several weeks. It was Brown's hope that if Douglass came to adopt his ideas and to promote them, then others—both black and white—would follow his leadership.

Safe in a secret mountain hideout, John Brown showed Douglass his maps. He explained how he would use guns he planned to seize from the arsenal at Harper's Ferry to free slaves in the area. Those slaves, in turn, would fight to free others. Undoubtedly some slave owners would have to be killed in the beginning, but soon most owners would be so afraid of their own slaves that the entire system of slavery would grind to a halt and collapse. There no longer would be a need for killing.

John Brown's eyes flashed like lightning as he described his plan. Tall and lean, he paced back and forth, pointing a finger, waving his arms. Then he stopped and stared intensely at Douglass.

He asked Douglass to go along with him on the raid. Always before, he knew, Douglass had been against violence. But now, explained Brown, things were different. Slavery was spreading to the West. Unless something was done quickly, it would be impossible to stop its advance. America would have people in chains indefinitely.

For a brief moment Frederick Douglass paused. The two peered into each other's eyes—John Brown, the white man who hated slavery so much that he would risk his life to end it, and Frederick Douglass, who knew what it meant to be a slave. Then, quietly but firmly, Douglass gave his answer.

"No, John Brown," he said. "I cannot go with you."

Brown was astonished. "Why not?" he demanded angrily. Was it, he asked, because Douglass was afraid? Or was it that he didn't really care about his people anymore, now that he was a free man?

Brown should know, replied Douglass, that of course he was not a coward. He had demonstrated that throughout his life. And it was precisely because he did care about his people that he could not go with Brown. The attack on Harper's Ferry, he said, was bound to fail. It was foolish to try what John Brown planned with so few men. It would end in disaster. And almost certainly Brown would be killed or captured.

For the good of his own people, said Douglass, he had to live, not die. He had to speak out. He had to lead the black people of America.

That did not mean that Brown should not go ahead with his plan. "The tools to those who can use them," remarked

Frederick Douglass receiving a gun salute of honor on Governor's Island in New York Harbor. *The Library of Congress.*

Douglass. "Let every man work for the abolition of slavery in his own way. I would help all and hinder none."

For two days they argued. But neither could change the other's mind. Finally they parted—John Brown to die for black people's freedom, Frederick Douglass to live for it.

Others learned of their meeting. When Brown's attack on Harper's Ferry failed, the governor of Virginia tried to arrest Douglass, claiming he had helped plan the raid. Douglass fled to Canada. Then he again toured Great Britain, where he spoke to large and friendly audiences.

When the Civil War began, he returned to America, already recognized as the leading champion of his people. Still disliking violence, he understood that the war was a critical opportunity for blacks. If the North won, the slaves undoubtedly would be freed.

Black men, he thought, should have a share in winning their own freedom, so Douglass urged them to join the northern armies. The first to answer his call were his own two sons. Eventually nearly two hundred thousand blacks served in the armed forces of the United States during the Civil War. Some thirty-six thousand were killed in action.

During the war Douglass discovered that black soldiers were receiving only half the pay of whites; they were not promoted to higher ranks as quickly; and, as prisoners, they were often tortured or killed by southerners angry that slaves would fight against their former masters.

Douglass knew that something had to be done. He arranged to visit President Lincoln in the White House. Lincoln listened. Then he promised to raise the pay of black soldiers to that of whites. Shortly after his talk with Douglass, Lincoln warned the South that he would execute one rebel prisoner for each black who was killed in a southern prison.

Lincoln and Douglass immediately liked each other, meeting twice more during the war. Others came to know the president's respect for Douglass. After Lincoln's death, the president's wife sent his favorite walking stick to the former slave, Frederick Douglass.

In the final years of his life Douglass continued to lead his people. He worked with Congressman Thaddeus Stevens and other whites to secure voting rights and education for blacks. He spoke eloquently against keeping blacks separate from whites. Trains, boats, hotels, and other public places were for all the people, Douglass said, and blacks should not be kept out or kept separate from whites. Through his speeches and his writing Douglass tried to help people understand what would be fair treatment of America's blacks.

Famous and respected, Douglass was paid well for his speeches and was able to buy a large, comfortable home within sight of the Capitol building in Washington, D.C.

"There, under that dome," said Douglass, pointing to the Capitol, "is where the power lies to give my people the rights of any other American citizens." He never stopped trying to win those rights.

Nor did he think only of black people's needs. On the very last day of his life, Frederick Douglass spoke at a meeting concerned with winning for women the right to vote. To him equality was important not just for blacks but for all Americans.

When Douglass died in 1895, expressions of sorrow reached his widow from well-known people around the world.

But what would have pleased Douglass even more than the tributes of the rich and the powerful was a memorial fund collected by the poor black people of Americus, Georgia. The words they wrote at the time still have meaning:

"No people who can produce a Douglass ever need lose hope."

Harriet Beecher Stowe

1811–1896   Writer whose antislavery novel, *Uncle Tom's Cabin,* inflamed passions and helped bring about the Civil War

When President Abraham Lincoln was introduced to Harriet Beecher Stowe, he took her small hand in his own broad, strong one and gently said to her, "So you are the little woman who made this great war."

It must have been hard, even for Lincoln, to realize how important the slender housewife from Maine, smiling, with delicate features and soft voice, had been in starting the Civil War. But it was true. Her book *Uncle Tom's Cabin* had stirred hatred between the North and the South over slavery. It had made slavery something that every person was either for or against.

After *Uncle Tom's Cabin* was published, nobody could refuse to choose sides. In that way it speeded up the day when men were willing to kill for what they thought was right and wrong about owning slaves.

Harriet Beecher Stowe had not wanted it that way. A warm, loving woman, she had hoped that her writing would help bring together the North and South. She thought that when southerners learned how evil slavery really was they would want to give up their slaves. Instead her book tore the nation in two.

As a child growing up in New England, Harriet Beecher was deeply religious. She thought often of God and tried hard to live a good life. She hoped to do things as an adult that would make the world a better place, one that was closer to God's purposes. Her father was a minister, and five of her six brothers became ministers.

In 1832 the Beecher family moved to Cincinnati, where Harriet's father had been made head of a school for educating new ministers. Harriet liked Cincinnati. It was there, at the age of twenty-five, that she married Calvin Stowe, a professor in her father's school.

At first Mrs. Stowe used her spare time to write short stories and poetry for magazines. But as her family grew, she had less time for writing. During the eighteen years she lived in Cincinnati, Harriet bore six of her seven children. She had plenty to do just being a mother.

But if she was too busy to do much writing, Mrs. Stowe took every chance she had to listen and to learn. Across the Ohio River from Cincinnati, in Kentucky, people owned slaves.

Frequently she visited plantations in Kentucky. She saw the slaves at their work. Also, she listened to the stories of her brother Charles, who had traveled to New Orleans and seen the cruelty of slave owners and their assistants. In the Deep South slavery was far harsher than in Kentucky.

It was bad enough in Kentucky. Harriet saw with her own eyes a husband and wife torn from each other's arms by a slave trader on an Ohio River dock. Once she begged money from neighbors to buy the freedom of a three-year-old girl who was to be sold away from her mother.

Many Cincinnatians had come to that city from the South. They did not seem to mind when slave catchers from Kentucky raided the part of town where free blacks lived. The "Kentucks" spread fear among the city's blacks. They burned the homes of blacks, sometimes kidnapping black women and children and taking them south to be sold into slavery.

Harriet Beecher Stowe came to believe that all of this would continue as long as the evil of slavery continued.

In 1850 two important things happened to Harriet. First her husband became a professor at Bowdoin College, in Brunswick, Maine. The Stowes left Cincinnati and moved to Maine. It was in 1850, too, that the Congress of the United States passed a strict new law, the Fugitive Slave Act. It gave slave owners the right to go into northern states to bring back runaway slaves. The act required that all police officers provide assistance to the slave catchers.

Northerners were furious. Some states would not allow their jails to be used to hold runaway slaves. Other states allowed jury trials for escaped slaves even though, at the time, slaves were considered "property"—not people—and so were not entitled to trial in court.

It was the Fugitive Slave Act that made Harriet Beecher Stowe at last decide to do something about slavery. Her

Harriet Beecher Stowe and Calvin Ellis Stowe around 1840. *The Schlesinger Library, Radcliffe College*.

anger grew as she listened to one of her brothers, the Reverend Edward Beecher, preach about slavery at his church in Boston. Even in Boston, the birthplace of American liberty in the Revolution, slave catchers were putting chains around the necks of blacks and dragging them back to work in the South.

Edward Beecher's wife wrote to Harriet, saying, "Now, Hattie, if I could just use the pen as you can, I would write something that would make this whole nation feel what an accursed thing slavery is."

To this Harriet answered, "God helping me, I will write something! I will if I live." She had just given birth to her seventh child.

Harriet's chance soon came. A black minister in Boston told her of his escape from slavery and how he had watched his own father lying bruised and bloody on the ground, dying from the blows of a slave owner. She could not get the story out of her mind.

Several days later, as she sat in church praying, the incident that in her book would become the death of Uncle Tom suddenly flashed before her eyes. It was as if she were there herself. She saw before her the dying Tom, the wicked Simon Legree, scowling with whip in hand, and the two slaves whom Legree had forced to beat kindly old Tom. She saw Tom forgiving them for what they had done.

Rushing home after church, Harriet at once wrote down the entire scene, just as it had appeared to her. When she ran out of writing paper, she finished the story on scraps of brown-paper grocery bags.

Everything happened so swiftly that Mrs. Stowe was certain she had been given a message from God and was only doing His will. Her pen, she said, seemed to move across the paper and write by itself.

That evening she gathered her children about her and read to them what she had written. They burst into tears. Henry, her youngest son, sobbed, "Oh, Mama, slavery is the most cruel thing in the world!"

Mrs. Stowe sent her manuscript to *National Era* magazine. The publisher offered to pay her three hundred dollars if she would write about the events leading up to and following the death of Uncle Tom, so that it would be complete. Harriet agreed, preparing the longer story one chapter at a time. Every month another chapter appeared in the magazine. The result was a book, *Uncle Tom's Cabin, or Life Among the Lowly.*

Harriet did all of her writing at a desk in the living room, her children buzzing constantly at her side. Yet she was so involved in the story and its characters that through all the noise she had little trouble concentrating. Like her husband, she was absentminded. Professor Stowe would walk off to teach his classes with a slipper in his pocket. Harriet would forget that she was cooking dinner and burn the stew. It sometimes made her laugh that she was so forgetful.

The principal character in her story, Tom, is a slave. That in itself was unusual. It was the first time that a black man had been the hero of an American story. Tom has good masters and bad ones. But one thing never changes. He is the white man's property, to do with as his master chooses, to sell when hard times come or—as finally happens—to murder.

The book contains scenes that readers even today find unforgettable: the pitiful death of Little Eva; the slave George Harris's joy at becoming a free man; Eliza's terrifying dash to freedom across the ice-clogged Ohio River with snarling bloodhounds snapping at her heels.

But it is the noble Tom whose life shows best what Mrs. Stowe wanted people to understand about slavery—that it was evil. Today when people say that someone is an "Uncle Tom," they mean he is a person who does not fight back or who tries to do what white people expect. But the Uncle Tom in

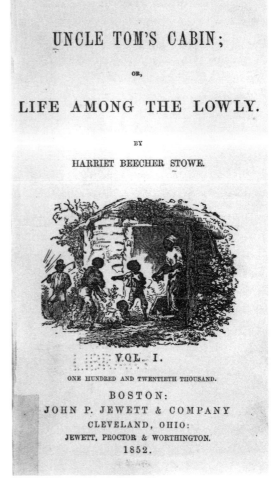

Title page of the first edition of *Uncle Tom's Cabin*. Published by John P. Jewett and Company, Boston, 1852.

Mrs. Stowe's book was a real hero, a man who died rather than betray two runaway slave girls.

Harriet worried that her book was not strong enough, that few would read it. But she was wrong. The first ten thousand copies were sold in a week. In the first year more than three hundred thousand copies came off the high-speed presses that were run night and day to keep up with the demand. In Great Britain and the British colonies, over a million and a half copies were quickly sold, although none of the money from these foreign sales ever went to Mrs. Stowe. Eventually the book was translated into forty languages.

It was set to music, turned into verse, produced as a play. Thousands of people who never before had seen a play went to see it on the stage; many who never before had read fiction read *Uncle Tom's Cabin.*

Overnight Harriet became famous. On a trip to Europe in 1853, she received many honors. Her brother Charles warned her about pride. But there was no danger that she would be spoiled by success. To her, a very religious person, writing was a way to serve God and help the black race— not to become rich and famous.

Mrs. Stowe made considerable money from her book. Unfortunately she and her husband knew little about saving. They knew even less about spending wisely. Despite her vast earnings, Harriet always had to worry about how best to make ends meet for her large family.

Meanwhile *Uncle Tom's Cabin* was creating a storm across the United States. Those who hated slavery were delighted with the book, although some northerners thought Mrs. Stowe had made one of Tom's owners seem too kindly.

Southerners were stunned. They thought *Uncle Tom's Cabin* was both unfair and untrue. They would not allow the book to be sold in their part of the country. Furthermore they were angry that northerners so readily believed that all slave masters were like the horrible Simon Legree.

Harriet soon began to receive unsigned letters in the mail. The writers threatened her. They insulted her. They used vile language. Once she unwrapped a package, and a small object fell out. She screamed when she saw what it was. It was a human ear, sliced from the head of a slave.

In the South mothers told children that Harriet would "get them" if they weren't good. Children sometimes sang:

Go, go, go!
Ol' Harriet Beecher Stowe!
You're nothing but a dirty crow,
So go, go, go!

To prove that what she had written in her book was true, Mrs. Stowe published *A Key to Uncle Tom's Cabin.* She reprinted newspaper clippings, court records, letters, and reward posters for runaway slaves. Still, many would not believe her or were angry that she had dared to tell the truth about slavery.

After the publication of her book, it became virtually impossible to get northerners to return runaway slaves. The tempers of southerners rose to fury when they talked about slavery and abolition. With every passing year each side became more certain that it was right.

Uncle Tom's Cabin prepared the way for the Civil War. It made many in the North see John Brown as a hero for his bloody raid on Harper's Ferry in 1859. Brown said that everything he did—even cold-blooded murder—was necessary to get rid of slavery. And Mrs. Stowe's book already had led some people to believe that Brown was right. Slavery, to such people, was so evil that anything that would end it was acceptable. Violence, bloodshed, the breaking of laws—all were thought right and just.

Harriet Beecher Stowe lived to see the slaves freed. She lived to be old and respected around the world as the woman who had helped to free America's blacks. She gave lectures in many countries and was applauded and honored by kings and queens. Queen Victoria of England admitted that on reading *Uncle Tom's Cabin* she herself had wept bitterly.

Through all her fame Mrs. Stowe remained unchanged—simple, shy, serious, and even more absentminded.

Often she was so deep in thought that she did not hear what people said to her.

As she grew older she continued working for good causes—for the right of women to vote, for an end to drunkenness. But her life had not been easy. One of her sons had drowned in childhood; another had been wounded seriously at the Battle of Gettysburg. The strain of caring for her family, of so much tension over the book, may have been too much for her. Her mind grew weaker.

Little by little she became confused, not able to tell the real world from her dreamworld. Once she was given a gold medal for her good work. She did not understand and thought it was a toy.

In 1896, when she died, *Uncle Tom's Cabin* was still being bought and read. Thousands still jammed into theaters to see it on stage.

Yet, in the very year of her death, the Supreme Court of the United States ruled that in all public places blacks could be kept separate from whites. Blacks did not have the same rights as other Americans. That year hundreds of blacks were lynched by mobs in the South.

Mrs. Stowe was too old, too tired, to understand what was happening. And perhaps that is best, because of the sadness it would have brought her.

William Lloyd Garrison

1805–1879 Publisher of the *Liberator* and uncompromising champion of the antislavery cause

Slavery. People owning other people. In colonial times even southerners considered it "a necessary evil"—something that eventually would disappear.

But it didn't disappear. Instead it grew.

After the invention of the cotton gin, slave labor made the growing of cotton a profitable business, at least for the owners of large plantations. Many poorer whites dreamed of the day that they, too, could live the gracious, easy lives of the wealthy planter class. And for the very poor, the existence of a slave class meant that at least some people were below them on the social ladder.

Even before the cotton gin, some people in both the North and the South understood that slavery would not simply go away. They also realized that owning slaves harmed the slave owner as well as the slave. It forced owners to be cruel, to do horrible things when they needed money—such as selling away the children of their slaves.

One group, the American Colonization Society, tried to raise money to buy the freedom of slaves from their owners. Their plan was to transport the freed slaves back to Africa. In that way the slavery question would be solved. Blacks and whites would no longer have to deal with the problem of living together in America.

Time passed. Each year more and more black children were being born into slavery. Owners encouraged slaves to have many children. Where would the money come from to buy the freedom of so many slaves?

Besides, some people argued, why should blacks be forced to return to Africa? Was not this country started with the "self-evident" truth of the Declaration of Independence that "all men are created equal"? How, then, could it be stated that blacks were not good enough to live in America alongside whites? Finally, as opponents of colonization pointed out, buying the freedom of slaves and then colonizing them was a long, slow process. Meanwhile every day slaves were being chained, beaten, tortured, and killed.

William Lloyd Garrison, a newspaper editor, was one of those who argued that blacks should be given all the rights promised to Americans in the Declaration of Independence. That should happen, said Garrison with ever-increasing fury, not gradually, at some vague time in the far distant future, but immediately—*now!*

When Garrison started his newspaper, the *Liberator*, he left no doubt about his anger that slavery still survived in America. Nor did he intend, like those in the American Colonization Society, to use soft words or moderate language to achieve his purpose—the end of slavery. In the very first issue of the *Liberator* (January 1831) he de-

clared that he was tired of soft words. The time for moderation, said Garrison, was over:

I *will be* as harsh as truth, and as uncompromising as justice. On this subject, I do not wish to think, or speak, or write with moderation. No! No!

And then he concluded:

I am in earnest—I will not equivocate—I will not excuse—I will not retreat a single inch—AND *I WILL* BE HEARD!

In the years that followed, the American public did indeed hear a great deal from William Lloyd Garrison.

Having people notice him, hear him, was an important matter to Garrison. Surely, there is no doubt that he believed in the antislavery cause with a burning intensity. But it is also true that what Garrison always had hated in his life was being ignored.

When he was a child of two, Garrison's father had deserted the family, going off to sea and leaving behind a wife and three other children besides young Lloyd, as they called him.

His earliest memories were of carrying a tin pail from house to house along wealthy High Street in Newburyport, Massachusetts, begging for leftover food from the tables of the rich. He and one of his brothers also had to walk the streets, trying to sell their mother's homemade molasses candy. Often people simply passed him by, pretending not to see him.

Ever afterward Garrison remembered what it was like to be poor, to be ignored. He vowed that when he grew up he would never be ignored. At the same time he came to understand and to sympathize with other people who, like himself, were poor, and who were "nobodys." No group of people better fit that description than America's slave population.

Garrison's mother worked hard. In church she prayed with deep, passionate faith. Yet the family sank deeper and deeper into poverty. To save money, when Lloyd was seven he was sent to live with a woodcutter who belonged to his mother's church.

Somehow he managed to get the bare essentials of an education before being apprenticed at age thirteen to Ephraim Allen, editor and publisher of the Newburyport *Herald*.

It was at the *Herald* that Garrison got his real education. Allen encouraged him to learn grammar and spelling, and also to read economics, politics, and philosophy. It was Allen, too, who taught him to stay calm under pressure. At sixteen Garrison secretly submitted a letter for publication in the paper, signing it only "An Old Bachelor." When Allen discovered that it was his apprentice who had written so fine a letter he promoted him to foreman

of the printing office and invited him to write a regular column.

At the end of his apprenticeship, Garrison became editor of another local paper, the *Free Press*. Almost immediately he announced that if the paper was to have one major theme, "till our whole country is free from the curse—it is SLAVERY."

The *Free Press* failed to win readers. It went out of business in six months. But Garrison was true to his word. He never again let Americans forget about the issue of slavery.

Using the pages of a Baltimore weekly, *Genius of Universal Emancipation*, he sharply attacked the supporters of the slave system. Among his favorite targets were the rich New England sea captains who transported slaves from the port city of Baltimore to coastal plantations in the South. Singling out one shipowner, Francis Todd, Garrison denounced such men as "highway robbers and murderers" who ought to be "SENTENCED TO SOLITARY CONFINEMENT FOR LIFE."

Todd, furious, sued Garrison for libel. The jury took only fifteen minutes to find the young editor guilty. When Garrison could not pay the hundred-dollar fine levied on him he was sentenced to six months in jail.

Instead of regarding it as a punishment, Garrison turned his stay in prison into a triumph. He gave "Baltimore

Jail" as the return address for a flood of letters and newspaper columns he sent out from his cell. The other prisoners applauded him as a hero. Many abolitionist leaders around the country heard his name for the first time.

One abolitionist, the wealthy New York merchant Arthur Tappan, paid Garrison's fine. Thus after only seven weeks behind bars he was a free man. Not only had he made important contacts, he had also thoroughly enjoyed attracting attention to the antislavery cause and to himself.

After his release Garrison, with an old friend, began publishing the *Liberator*, the weekly newspaper that quickly would put him in the forefront of the abolitionist movement. Only four hundred copies were run in the paper's historic first issue, the one ending with Garrison's flaming declaration, "I *WILL* BE HEARD!"

In his second issue Garrison called those northerners hypocrites who, while saying they opposed slavery, still continued to use products made by slave labor, especially those made of cotton. Next he attacked the American Colonization Society. To buy the liberty of blacks only to send them to Africa, argued Garrison, meant accepting the South's view that blacks were inferior, a people incapable of learning to live side by side with whites.

The famous seventeenth issue of the

A lithograph of William Lloyd Garrison by Louis Prang Lithography Company, after a photograph by Alfred K. Kipps. *The National Portrait Gallery, Smithsonian Institution.*

Liberator particularly irritated southerners. On its front page Garrison printed a picture of the United States Capitol building in Washington. In the foreground of the illustration was a black, bound to a whipping post, being flogged. For many weeks the picture appeared on the paper's masthead.

In 1831 a slave revolt—Nat Turner's Rebellion—took the lives of fifty-seven white Virginians. Throughout the South,

A banner used in an antislavery demonstration around 1850. *The Massachusetts Historical Society.*

frightened, angry slave owners looked for someone to blame. For many, the villain was William Lloyd Garrison and his *Liberator*.

The state of Georgia offered a reward of five thousand dollars for Garrison's arrest and conviction. A slave owner in the same state offered three thousand dollars for his ears. The city of Raleigh, North Carolina, promised to jail and flog him if he could be caught and transported there. Hate mail flooded his office, warning him that his death was near. One letter threatened that "poison will accomplish what the dagger may fail to effect."

Garrison was delighted to receive so much attention. Almost overnight he had become a national figure. Each new threat, each new attack on his ideas, gave him greater influence in the antislavery movement. The circulation of the *Liberator* for any one issue never exceeded three thousand copies; yet it quickly became the symbol of the most extreme antislavery position in the North.

In 1833 Garrison visited London, both to raise money and to attend a meeting of the World Anti-Slavery Convention. Two years later the aggressive English abolitionist George Thompson returned the visit. Because he was known to be a friend of Garrison, Thompson's lecture tour of the North-

east was marked by angry demonstrations. Once he had to be rescued from a fist-shaking mob by women abolitionists, who formed a protective ring around him.

Meanwhile a mob of over three thousand in Charleston, South Carolina, publicly burned copies of Garrison's *Liberator*. In Mississippi two abolitionists were accused of encouraging slaves to revolt; they were lynched without a trial. In the North the New York City postmaster announced that he no longer would deliver copies of the *Liberator*. Roaming mobs attacked blacks in the streets of New York and Boston. Even such revered antislavery authors as Ralph Waldo Emerson and John Greenleaf Whittier were forced from the lecture platform by angry crowds.

Garrison would not back down. What happened to blacks in the South, he insisted, most definitely was his business. "Enslave but a single human being," declared Garrison, "and the liberty of the world is put in peril."

Still, public anger at the antislavery movement continued to mount. On October 21, 1835, when the Boston Female Anti-Slavery Society met to hear Englishman George Thompson speak, a mob gathered. They intended to tar and feather Thompson. When Thompson, warned of the danger, failed to appear, the crowd saw Garrison and seized him. Screaming with rage, they led him through the streets of Boston with a rope around his neck, preparing to hang him.

At the very last moment the mayor of Boston, Theodore Lyman, rescued Garrison and placed him overnight in the Leverett Street jail for his own protection.

Garrison later recalled, "I threw myself upon my prison bed and slept tranquilly. . . . In the morning I awoke quite refreshed, and, after eating an excellent breakfast . . . inscribed upon the walls of my cell . . .

Confine me as a prisoner—but bind me not as a slave. Punish me as a criminal—but hold me not as a chattel. Torture me as a man—but drive me not like a beast. Doubt my sanity—but acknowledge my immortality.

For William Lloyd Garrison there could be no compromise. "The early Christians weren't stopped," he said. "Nor shall we be. . . . The Lord won't allow it."

Garrison's certainty that God was on his side could irritate even his friends in the antislavery movement. One of them declared that he was impossible to be with, "a prickly porcupine." Many feared that his broad interest in other reforms would hurt the cause of antislavery. He encouraged the Grimké sis-

ters, for example, to speak in public at a time when women's rights still was a hotly debated issue. He also took a strong stand against war, capital punishment, and the mistreatment of the American Indians.

Finally he came to believe that government itself was evil. Only by total faith in Christ alone, he said, could people be saved. According to Garrison, human government ought to be replaced by what was known then as Christian Anarchism.

On every question he addressed there could be, for him, no halfway measures. His own position was completely right, that of the opposition completely wrong. In life there were no shadings of gray, only deep black and pure white—total evil and total good.

Members of the American Colonization Society might well have considered Garrison intolerant, unrealistic, fanatical, perhaps even crazy. But none of them could deny his ability to arouse people, to influence them, and to agitate. Nor did he mind the hatred he provoked in others. As he put it, "Hisses are music to my ear."

By 1841 Garrison had concluded that it was wrong for the North to continue as part of the United States, living alongside states that permitted slavery. Since the Constitution of the United States clearly allowed slavery to exist,

A mid-nineteenth-century photograph of a slave market in Atlanta, Georgia. *The Library of Congress.*

he said, it must be "a covenant with death and an agreement with hell." Either slavery should be made illegal or the North should secede from the United States.

Events flowed swiftly toward a national crisis. In 1846 the United States annexed Texas and then in the Mexican War added still more slave territory. Garrison, meanwhile, had prayed for "success to the Mexicans and overwhelming defeat to the United States." The Compromise of 1850, settling differences between North and South, included a new Fugitive Slave Act, legally requiring northerners to help return escaped slaves to their owners.

The Fugitive Slave Act angered even northerners who had stayed neutral on the slavery question. Garrison also won sympathy for his cause when a mob forced the closing of the Anti-Slavery Society Convention in 1850, not permitting the abolitionists to speak.

Step by step, northern public opinion began to move toward the antislavery position. Abolitionism was becoming respectable. Editors of major newspapers changed their minds, some of them even speaking respectfully about Garrison himself. Invitations for him to speak at public gatherings cascaded onto his desk at the *Liberator*. As promised, he had not "retreated a single inch." And now he was, indeed, being *heard*.

In a dramatic public ceremony at Framingham, Massachusetts, Garrison lighted a candle and set it to a copy of the Fugitive Slave Act. "Let the people say 'Amen,'" he demanded. "Amen!" roared his audience. Then, lighting another candle, he set fire to a copy of the United States Constitution. "Let the people say 'Amen,'" he demanded. Once more the crowd replied, "Amen!" This time Garrison held up the burning document, dropping it as it burst into flames. "So perish all compromises with tyranny!"

Now event tumbled on event. The Kansas-Nebraska Act led to bloody conflict between proslavery and antislavery forces. The Supreme Court's Dred Scott decision held that a slave was not a person but simply property. John Brown, captured at Harper's Ferry while trying to lead a slave revolt, was hanged.

At the death of John Brown, Garrison at last was forced to choose between two contradictory beliefs: antislavery and nonviolence. Was it right for abolitionists to use violence to gain freedom for the slaves?

Until then Garrison had favored only passive resistance. Now the situation was different. "God knows," he said, "my heart must be with the oppressed. . . . Rather than see men wear their chains in a cowardly and servile spirit, I would, as an advocate of peace, much rather see them breaking the head of the tyrant with their chains. . . . John Brown has . . . told us what time of day it is. It is high noon . . . thank God!"

And the war came.

At first Garrison opposed President Abraham Lincoln, who insisted that the purpose of the war was "to save the Union," not to free the slaves. Finally Lincoln issued his Emancipation Proclamation, declaring that as of January 1, 1863, slaves in territory occupied by the South were to be "then, thenceforth, and forever free."

Year after year the war dragged on. Then with northern victory on the battlefield came the ultimate triumph of William Lloyd Garrison's crusade. One of his own sons led a regiment of Massachusetts troops into downtown Charleston, South Carolina. There the soldiers broke open the slave pens. They ripped apart the wooden auction block, where slaves had been put up for sale to the highest bidder.

The Thirteenth Amendment to the Constitution officially put an end to slavery in the United States of America.

On December 29, 1865—thirty-five years after its founding—Garrison closed the offices of the *Liberator*. Its mission, he said, had been accomplished.

For Garrison, as well as for the newly freed slaves, the years that followed proved disappointing. Without education, skills, or experience in looking out for themselves, the lives of the former slaves became desperate. Thousands died of disease and starvation. Others begged to have their old jobs back on the plantations.

The abolitionists, especially Garrison, had concentrated so completely on removing the problem of slavery— getting rid of the evil—that they had failed to plan for what would take its place.

In 1877 the last northern troops were withdrawn from the South. Once again the white slave masters controlled the region. Blacks were not permitted to vote, even though they were allowed to by law. They were restricted to separate schools, separate washrooms, separate sections of railroad stations, even made to drink from separate drinking fountains and to swear on separate Bibles in courtrooms.

Whites formed a new organization, the Ku Klux Klan, to terrify the former slaves and keep them "in their place." Clothed in hoods and sheets and riding horses with muffled hooves, they tortured and lynched helpless black people.

The struggle to win civil rights for America's blacks was far from over on May 23, 1879, when, old and tired, William Lloyd Garrison lay on his deathbed.

"What do you want, Mr. Garrison?" whispered his doctor, bending over him.

"To finish it up," answered the great crusader for black freedom. That night he died.

In his lifetime William Lloyd Garrison had spoken out. Fearlessly he had aroused the conscience of northerners until they, too, felt guilty for permitting slavery to exist. He had provoked the South into acts that, in turn, had enraged more moderate northerners. In the end the result was a great civil war, the turning point in America's history.

Slavery in America had been abolished.

Through it all, Garrison had not been ignored. Perhaps beyond the wildest dreams of his childhood and youth, people had paid attention to him, listened to him. As he had vowed in the pages of the *Liberator*, he most certainly had been heard.

Elizabeth Cady Stanton

1815–1902   Leader responsible for the beginning of the women's rights movement in America

Elizabeth Cady's father was a lawyer, a judge. The walls of his office were lined with books—large, thick books without pictures. Elizabeth liked to sit quietly in her father's office while he worked. She listened to what he said when people came for legal help.

Sometimes Mr. Cady could help them. But sometimes he could not, especially when the people who needed help were women. In those days women were not allowed to vote or to serve on juries. They were not allowed to practice law or medicine. Only a few colleges admitted them as students. If they were married they could not sign wills or contracts without their husbands' permission. A husband controlled a wife's property and had almost complete control over what his wife and their children did.

Often, when his clients were women, Elizabeth's father would only shake his head and point to the law books on his shelves. As far as women were concerned, he said, the laws were unfair, but there was nothing he could do to help.

Once Elizabeth watched a woman leave her father's office in tears. The woman's case was hopeless, since the law favored her husband's rights, not hers. Elizabeth had an answer. She had a pair of scissors, she told her father. Why couldn't she just cut the bad laws out of the books?

When Elizabeth Cady was eleven years old her brother, Eleazer, died. Deep in grief at the loss of his only son, Mr. Cady declared to Elizabeth, "Oh, my daughter, I wish you were a boy."

Elizabeth never forgot that remark. Soon she began to understand that, to most people, being a boy or a man was better than being a girl or a woman. That realization made Elizabeth increasingly angry. She was determined to prove that she could do anything that boys could do. Her father watched with interest as Elizabeth competed against boys in horseback riding, sports, chess. Often she won.

In her schoolwork she refused to study only embroidery, music, and art as the other girls did. Instead she worked at Latin, Greek, and mathematics, hard subjects usually taken by boys. She won a prize for her mastery of Greek. Still, because she was a girl, she could not attend Union College in Schenectady, New York, where her brother, Eleazer, had been a student. She had to settle for the almost unknown Troy Female Seminary, known today as the Emma Willard School.

For a woman of the time, even attending Troy Female Seminary was something special. Elizabeth was fortunate. Her parents had the money to send her to school and thought it important for her to be educated.

In 1832 Elizabeth graduated. Soon afterward she became interested in the antislavery movement, attending meetings, even helping escaped slaves as they made their way northward to freedom in Canada. She became involved, too, in the other popular reforms of the day: the antiwar movement, the temperance movement (opposition to excessive use of alcoholic beverages), educational reform, and the struggle for better conditions in prisons and insane asylums.

At one antislavery meeting she listened to a fiery speaker. Never before had anyone so stirred her feelings against the evils of slavery. She and the speaker, Henry B. Stanton, came to be close friends. The friendship turned to love. Eventually they decided to marry.

Elizabeth's father did not mind that Henry Stanton was ten years older than his daughter, who then was twenty-four. He objected far more to her marrying an abolitionist—someone who demanded that slavery must be ended at once. In 1840 most people, even in the North, were not yet excited by the slavery issue. It still was unfashionable to demand abolition. Finally, however, Elizabeth's father agreed to the marriage.

On May 10, 1840, Elizabeth Cady and Henry B. Stanton were married. It was an unusual ceremony. Elizabeth insisted that the woman's usual promise to "obey" her husband be dropped from the marriage vows. Henry, also liberal in his views, gladly agreed. Elizabeth announced, too, that she wished to be addressed as Elizabeth Cady Stanton, not Mrs. Henry B. Stanton. In that way she would still be an independent woman, a person with her own identity, not just an extension of her husband.

Immediately after their marriage the couple set sail for a honeymoon in England. There they attended the World Anti-Slavery Convention. To their surprise and anger, they found that women attending the convention were not allowed to take seats as regular members. They had to sit in the audience and were denied a vote. Although William Lloyd Garrison and other Americans objected, the women were not seated as members.

Another young American couple in London for the meeting found it shocking that a "world antislavery convention" would refuse to give representation to women—half of the world's population. That couple, Lucretia and James Mott, came to know the Stantons well. Lucretia and Elizabeth became especially close friends.

On returning to America, Elizabeth Cady Stanton often thought about her long talks with Lucretia Mott in London. Sometimes Elizabeth's friends would ask her what had impressed her most while traveling in Europe. She would answer quietly, "Lucretia Mott." The two ladies had agreed that some-

time in the future there would be another world conference—one on the rights of women.

For several years the Stantons continued to live in Boston, the center of reform activities in the United States. Henry practiced law. Elizabeth became well known in the various reform movements.

Then, when Henry's health demanded a drier climate than coastal Massachusetts, the Stantons chose the tiny upstate New York community of Seneca Falls. Isolated there, Elizabeth missed the bustle and excitement of Boston. She had many things to do: taking care of a large house; being sure that the servants cooked, baked, and cleaned properly; and looking after her rapidly growing family—the Stantons eventually had seven children. In a sense Elizabeth's years in Seneca Falls helped her to understand just how routine and dull the lives of most women could be.

In July 1848 James and Lucretia Mott happened to be visiting in a nearby town. Elizabeth and Lucretia, along with several other women, met and discussed at length the problems being faced by American women. Then, at last, they decided to stop just talking and to do something.

On the very next day, July 14, they placed an advertisement in various

Elizabeth Cady Stanton with her son, Gerritt. *Collection of Rhoda Jenkins and John Barney.*

newspapers, announcing a public meeting on July 19 and 20 to discuss the rights of women.

Only five days later the conference began. The women were astonished by the response. An audience of nearly three hundred appeared, including forty men. Perhaps, they mused, there really *was* an interest in women's rights.

Elizabeth Cady Stanton wrote a statement of beliefs for the convention, a "Declaration of Sentiments." In format her statement resembled the Declaration of Independence. But there was an important difference. While Thomas Jefferson had written in 1776 that "all men are created equal," Mrs. Stanton wrote in 1848 that "all men and women are created equal."

She and her co-authors demanded specific rights. They called for equal educational opportunities, fairer laws about marriage and divorce, and an equal chance with men for jobs. They wanted the same rights as men to speak, teach, and write. Lastly they claimed the right to vote.

On that point—voting—Lucretia Mott disagreed. Cautious, she feared that asking for the vote would make women look "ridiculous" in the eyes of men. Mrs. Stanton's own husband, her strongest supporter in most matters, threatened that if Elizabeth persisted in her demand for voting rights

he would leave the convention. She persisted, and Henry left the meeting. As always, once Elizabeth made up her mind she would not change it just because of harsh criticism—regardless of the source.

A few newspapers published angry comments about the Seneca Falls Convention. Others simply made fun of it. Ministers joined in the ridicule, using their pulpits to voice opposition. Only one newspaper, the *New York Tribune*, took a strongly positive position. Horace Greeley, the *Tribune*'s editor, invited Mrs. Stanton to contribute regular columns for him on the issue of women's rights.

Elizabeth also wrote sometimes for Amelia Bloomer's newspaper, the *Lily*, signing herself "Sun Flower." Today Amelia Bloomer is remembered best for the costume she made popular, a loose-fitting outfit with pantaloons resembling men's pants. At the time most Americans only laughed at the idea of women's wearing such clothing instead of the tight-fitting corsets that they wore to make their waists smaller. Some people became angry, charging that the outfit was not "ladylike." Before long there was so much talk about Amelia Bloomer's pantaloons that they became known as bloomers. Elizabeth Cady Stanton wore them for a few months, hoping to illustrate her belief that women should dress in a comfortable, healthy way rather than merely to please men.

As Elizabeth became better known for her work in the women's rights movement, visitors began coming to the Stanton home. Among them were Frederick Douglass, the former slave who had risen to national fame as a fighter for the cause of black people; John Greenleaf Whittier, the poet; and, of course, on a regular basis, the other leaders of the women's movement.

Undoubtedly, however, Mrs. Stanton's best friend was Susan B. Anthony, or as the Stanton children came to call her, "Aunt Susan." Two people could scarcely have been more different. Mrs. Stanton was round and jolly looking, with dimples, a rosy complexion, and curly hair. She laughed a lot and made friends easily. Miss Anthony, lean, serious, and sharp featured, had a dull, rasping voice. She parted her smooth black hair in the middle and pulled it tightly back over her ears, pinning it in a bun.

Although Miss Anthony often spoke to public audiences, she never really enjoyed writing or speaking. For Mrs. Stanton words came easily. On the other hand, Susan B. Anthony had patience for the hard work of organizing conferences and making arrangements for speeches, matters that Elizabeth Cady Stanton found boring.

Night after night the two women sat beside a fireplace in the Stanton home, writing their speeches and letters to the newspapers. Usually Miss Anthony gave Mrs. Stanton the facts and figures to put into exciting language.

"Our speeches," Mrs. Stanton once said, "may be considered the united product of our two brains."

Once, Henry B. Stanton handed Elizabeth a stack of clippings telling about Miss Anthony's latest articles on the women's rights issue. "Well, my dear," he said, "more notices of Susan. You stir up Susan, and she stirs up the world."

During the Civil War between the North and the South (1861–1865) Mrs. Stanton and Miss Anthony gave less time to winning rights for women, more to winning freedom for Negro slaves. When the war ended, they were certain, men surely would remember all of their hard work on behalf of the northern cause. Their reward, at last, would be equal rights for women.

But that did not happen.

Instead new laws were passed to give the vote to black males. Nothing at all was done for women—black or white. Frederick Douglass, the black leader, urged them to be patient just a little longer. It was important, he said, to get rights for the black man first. As Douglass put it, "This is the Negro's hour, not the woman's hour."

Miss Anthony and Mrs. Stanton fumed with rage. They decided to act at once. When the state of Kansas declared an election to decide the question of votes for blacks and women, the two women immediately set out for Kansas to campaign.

They rode from place to place, covering the state in a carriage drawn by two mules. They spoke in any location where a few voters could be brought together—in churches, barns, log cabins, or outdoors. Once Mrs. Stanton spoke in a mill where she could not even see her audience. The only light was a single candle suspended over her head.

The ladies ate whatever people offered them, usually bacon floating in heavy grease, with black coffee to wash it down. Sometimes they slept in the carriage at night, while pigs noisily rubbed their sides against the carriage steps to scratch at fleas. One night, as Mrs. Stanton slept, a mouse ran across her face.

Despite all their hard work, they lost the election. Kansas decided not to give women the right to vote.

Elizabeth and Susan refused to give up. They returned to New York City and started a weekly newspaper, the *Revolution*. Mrs. Stanton served as editor, Miss Anthony as business manager. The *Revolution* demanded the right of women to vote. But it championed

other social causes, too: the eight-hour day for workers, in place of the then-customary twelve or fourteen hours; easier divorce; the right of women to equal education; better job opportunities—any issue that seemed important.

Mrs. Stanton argued that religion was a major cause of women's problems. She said that religion taught women to obey their husbands instead of making up their own minds. Even Susan worried that attacking religion might prove unpopular. It could make men wonder if women really were wise enough to deserve the vote.

As usual, Elizabeth refused to back down. She believed that women should think for themselves on all public issues, including religion. To her, getting the right to vote was only a first step on the way to freedom for women, not the last step.

As Susan and Elizabeth grew older they continued to work for women's rights. But the days of their close friendship ended. As Elizabeth once put it, "Miss Anthony has one idea [votes for women] and has no patience with anyone who has two."

In her later years Elizabeth's eyesight began to fail. Still she continued to speak out. Women, she said, should wear comfortable clothing and get lots of exercise, such as bicycle riding. In politics, Mrs. Stanton believed that workers, both men and women, should get a fairer share of the wealth that their labor produced. Like those who had begun to call themselves Socialists, she argued that the workers themselves eventually should own the mines, the factories, and the railroads in which they labored.

In 1887 Elizabeth's husband died. After that she moved to New York City and spent time each year in England with her married daughter, Harriot. Later Harriot herself became one of the great leaders of the American women's rights movement.

One day in October 1902 Elizabeth sat down at her desk and wrote a letter to the President of the United States, Theodore Roosevelt, urging him to help women get the vote. Then, having finished the letter, she lay down to rest. She died in her sleep.

Four years later Susan B. Anthony died. Both leaders had worked to free the lives of women. To Miss Anthony, winning the vote was more than just the principal means for achieving equality of the sexes in America; it was an end in itself. To Elizabeth Cady Stanton, too, voting was crucial. But Mrs. Stanton understood that even after women had the ballot they would still have other battles to fight, new victories to win, before—at last—the struggle for equality could be declared at an end.

And, of course, history has proved her right. Even today, long after women gained voting rights, the struggle continues.

Thaddeus Stevens

1792–1868   Congressional leader during the era of Reconstruction who was concerned with winning rights for the former slaves

There was a time when some people thought that a child born with a club-foot—a crippled foot—was a "child of the devil."

On April 4, 1792, in a lonely little village in Vermont, such a child was born to Joshua and Sarah Stevens. Seventeen months earlier, their first child also had been born with a clubfoot. Surely they must have felt themselves under some terrible curse.

As an adult, that second child, Thaddeus Stevens, came to be hated by white southerners more than any man in America. To them he was in every way a true child of the devil.

But to American blacks, Thaddeus Stevens was no devil. He was loved as a hero second only to Abraham Lincoln. He became the greatest defender of the former slaves.

Why did Stevens work so hard to help blacks? Other white men of his time had little interest in them. They thought that blacks never could amount to anything.

Stevens was different. He saw that most blacks were poor and helpless.

Thaddeus Stevens's father was never anything in life but poor. He tried farming, land surveying, and shoemaking, but failed at them all. Discouraged, he turned to drink. Finally he ran away from his wife and children. They learned later that he had been killed in the War of 1812.

Young Thaddeus was quick witted and had an excellent memory. His mother, Sarah, saw that and sent him to school. For many years she worked night and day to pay for his education. She was a maid in other people's houses. It was his mother who taught Thad Stevens to keep on fighting, no matter how great the odds against him—to fight until he overcame his problems.

In later years nothing made Stevens happier than to be able to give his mother a fine farm of two hundred fifty acres and some prize cows, along with occasional gold coins to put in the Baptist church collection box. Stevens never married, and his mother was perhaps the only person about whom he ever spoke with affection and tenderness. Whatever success he had in life, said Stevens, he owed to her.

For the rest of humanity, Stevens felt mostly hatred. He hated his father for running away from the family. He hated anybody who seemed to desert the Republican Party, his party. He hated the South for trying to desert the rest of the United States. He hated the rich for making it hard for poor boys to get an education.

He hated fiercely. And as southerners were to find out, he did not stop hating. He never forgave an enemy. It is said that in his life he never asked for an apology and never gave one.

Stevens was deeply hurt by the cruelty of his schoolmates in Vermont. Because of his clubfoot they laughed at him and called him "cripple." They pointed at him and made fun of the way he limped as he walked. Sometimes when they saw him coming, they limped and pretended that they were crippled, too.

Later in life, Stevens made a habit of putting his twisted foot up on the edge of his desk so that everyone would see it. He knew that it made people uneasy. Sometimes he reminded others that the clubfoot was supposed to be proof that he was one of the devil's children. Then he would smile a dark, sinister smile, as if he enjoyed having them believe the story.

As he grew up Stevens worked hard at sports. He became a fine swimmer, a powerful weight lifter, and a daring horseback rider.

At Dartmouth College he became an outstanding student. Still he felt that others were against him. He was not allowed to join Phi Beta Kappa, a club for school leaders, because he was not well liked by the other college men.

With every passing year, Stevens cared less and less about being well liked. A man is lucky, he once said, to have one true friend. "But he is more truly happy who never has need of a friend." Thaddeus Stevens trusted no one and stayed mostly to himself.

After graduating from Dartmouth in 1814, Stevens became a lawyer in Gettysburg, Pennsylvania. He became well known and successful. People knew that he was intelligent. Even if he was rude and impolite in court, he almost never lost a case.

Despite his success he did not forget his childhood. He told his personal doctor to send him the bill for helping any crippled boys the doctor happened to treat. He fought hard to get free public education for the children of Pennsylvania—and won, almost entirely by himself.

Once, as a young lawyer in Pennsylvania, he spent three hundred dollars that he had been saving for law books to buy the freedom of a black man who was about to be sold away from his family.

Stevens spoke out not only for blacks but for Indians, Jews, Mormons, Chinese, any people that he thought were being wronged by the rest of society or were being "branded" or "marked" as he himself had been by his lameness.

In 1848 he was elected to Congress. At once he made slavery his special target. He called it "a curse, a shame, and a crime." Unlike some northerners, he would not pretend to like slave owners or those who believed in slavery. He spoke of those in Congress who disagreed with him as "men who stuck to their seats by their own slime" or "filthy beasts."

He favored John Brown's raid. In speech after speech, he cried out against the South. And when the war finally came, he was pleased. He saw a war with the South as good, because the North almost certainly would win. The slaves would then have to be freed.

During the war Stevens's main task in Congress was to devise ways for the government to raise revenue. Vast amounts of money were needed to pay for all the guns, food, and clothing used by the northern army. It was Stevens who helped President Lincoln collect enough money to keep the army fighting and winning.

Stevens became the most powerful leader in Congress. Some considered him even more powerful than President Lincoln. Some congressmen trusted him, others feared him, but most did exactly what Stevens wanted them to do. Once, another congressman was speaking against an idea Stevens favored. For a time Stevens listened. Then, snapping his fingers, he ordered the man to be quiet and sit down. Pale with fright, the congressman immediately returned to his seat.

Another time Stevens met a political rival face-to-face on a narrow path. His enemy straddled the path, hands on hips, and declared, "I never step aside

A photograph of Thaddeus Stevens by Mathew Brady. *The Library of Congress.*

for skunks!" Stevens bowed from the waist in mock graciousness and moved to the side of the path with a sweep of his arm. "I always do!" he said purringly.

All through the war anybody who wanted money from Congress had to come first to Thaddeus Stevens, the chairman of the House Committee on Ways and Means. If Stevens thought that something would help win the war he was for it. If not, he refused. Winning would mean an end to slavery. It would mean a chance to punish the slave owners. Winning—and revenge—were all that mattered to Stevens.

In battle after battle northern armies began to triumph. As the South grew weaker there was little doubt that the North eventually would win. But what would be done with the losers? How would the South be treated when the fighting was over and the rebel armies humbled?

President Lincoln wanted to forgive the South and all of its leaders. That, he thought, would be the best way to bring together the two parts of the country as quickly as possible. He even wanted to pay southerners for the loss of their slave property.

Stevens considered the president far too softhearted. To Stevens it was important to punish the southern states for leaving the Union. It was important

to be sure that black men could live safely in the South.

President Lincoln tried to win Thaddeus Stevens over to his side. Stevens listened, but he would not budge an inch. The South, he said, had caused the war and should be made to pay the consequences for all of the bloodshed.

Before Lincoln could put into effect his moderate plan for restoring the southern states to the Union, he was assassinated.

For a while Thaddeus Stevens was the most powerful man in the United States of America.

When the Civil War ended, the South lay in ruins. Most of the battles of the war had been fought there. In some places all the houses were burned to the ground. Only a few lonely chimneys remained standing, heaps of ashes and cinders piled around them. Roads needed fixing; bridges were down; weeds grew in the fields; food was hard to find; sickness was everywhere.

During the war some freed slaves had joined the northern armies. Some had simply stayed on with their old masters as if nothing had changed. Others simply roamed the countryside begging for food, stealing it if they had to.

These "freedmen," as they were called, were in serious trouble. Almost none of them could read or write. As slaves they had not been allowed to learn. They owned no land. They could not vote. Freedom was new to them. When they had been slaves, their masters had fed them, clothed them, housed them. Their masters had made the rules and made most of the decisions in their lives. Now, as free men, they had to do those things for themselves. It was not easy. It was as if they had been in prison all their lives and suddenly were set free.

Many white southerners made the problem even worse. They still treated blacks like slaves. Some states passed strict laws called the Black Codes, regulating such matters as where blacks could work and what time they had to be off the streets at night. Sometimes white mobs attacked and murdered blacks and were not punished.

One group of whites founded a society known as the Ku Klux Klan. Klansmen dressed in white sheets and pointed hoods. They rode at night on horses with muffled hooves. They tried to frighten blacks. But when they found one who still insisted on his right to vote, or who would not step off the sidewalk when a white man passed, they had other ways to treat him. Sometimes they set fire to his house or shot him or hanged him or burned him alive at the stake. Sometimes they tortured his wife or his children.

When Thaddeus Stevens learned what was happening in the South, he was enraged. All that he had worked for in winning the war was being lost. It would have been easy for him to close his eyes to what white men were doing to blacks. Other white congressmen pretended not to know. Trying to help blacks would not win many votes, because few of them could vote, and it was certain to make still more enemies for Stevens.

But he cared little about who liked him or who blamed him. He wanted laws to protect blacks from whites. He agreed with Frederick Douglass that "the man who is whipped easiest is whipped oftenest." Stevens wanted blacks to feel secure about their legal rights. Besides, he was still eager to see the former slave owners punished.

Stevens plunged into the battle. He saw that blacks were ignorant, so he had teachers sent to them. He saw that blacks were hungry, so he asked Congress to send them food. He saw that blacks had no farmland, so he tried to divide up the large plantations and give them land. He saw that blacks were not allowed to vote, so he tried to have new laws enacted that would let them vote.

To make these things work he led Congress into an important step: stationing northern troops in the South. To him, the South was nothing more

Thaddeus Stevens's last speech on impeachment in the House of Representatives. An engraving by T. R. Davis. *Culver Pictures.*

than a conquered country, the "carcass" of a dead animal.

Finally, when Stevens thought that Andrew Johnson, the president who followed Lincoln, cared more for helping former slave owners than former slaves, he tried to remove Johnson from the presidency—to impeach him.

There was a trial. Andrew Johnson was the only president of the United States ever put on trial while in office. And Thaddeus Stevens was the man who did it to him.

But Stevens lost. Johnson was not removed from the presidency.

Shortly afterward, old and disap-

pointed, Thaddeus Stevens died.

In his final days he grew gloomier than ever. He brooded about what the Ku Klux Klan was doing to blacks. He worried that the laws that he had forced through Congress were too weak to protect black citizens.

The North had won the Civil War, and the slaves were free. But Thaddeus Stevens died an unhappy man.

In his will he left money for an orphan home to be open to children of all colors, all religions. None were to be kept out. All the children were to be educated together.

Even in death Stevens stayed true

to his ideals. At the time, most grave-yards were for whites only. But Stevens, before he died, ordered that his body be laid to rest in a small cemetery where blacks, too, were buried.

It was the final act of anger by a courageous but bitter man. Even from the grave he shook his fist at the world and stuck to his beliefs.

Sojourner Truth

c. 1797–1883   A former slave; preacher of a powerful religious message of love, equal rights for women, and civil rights for blacks

Sojourner Truth was born a slave. Slave masters usually did not bother to record the date when a slave child was born, so "Isabella," or "Belle," as she was called, never knew her real birthday. Nor did she have a last name.

Growing up in Ulster County, New York, some eighty miles up the Hudson River from New York City, she was known by white people as "Hardenbergh's Belle," after the master who owned her. Each time she was sold to another master she was given a new name.

The Revolutionary War had ended some fourteen years before Belle's birth. That war, begun in 1776 with Thomas Jefferson's stirring declaration that "all men are created equal," had made America a free country, free of British rule. Yet even in such enlightened northern states as New York and New Jersey, the practice of human slavery lingered on. With it came one human tragedy after another.

Belle's "Ma-Ma," sobbing, told her again and again about the snowy day when a white man, driving a sleigh with tinkling sleighbells, came to the Hardenbergh estate. Ma-Ma had stood by helplessly as the white man took two of her children—Belle's older sister and brother—and put them into his sleigh box, closing the cover over them to keep them from escaping. Then he drove off.

Like two baby lambs, they had been sold and carted away. There was nothing Ma-Ma could do to protect them, her own children. She never saw them again.

Belle grew up knowing that any day the same thing could happen to her. She could be sold to a new white master, wrenched from the arms of her mother, taken away. Belle feared that such a day might come.

Finally that day came. Charles Hardenbergh died. His horses, cows, pigs—and slaves—were sold at auction. Belle never again saw her mother. Her father, too old and worn to be of value, was given his "freedom." He died of starvation and cold, alone.

Because Belle's first master had been Dutch, that was the only language she could speak. Her new master, John Neeley, spoke only English. He never before had owned a slave and took young Belle only as part of a deal that brought him what he really wanted, half a dozen of the Hardenberghs' sheep. The auctioneer included her in the sale package for an extra ten dollars.

Now Belle was "Neeley's Belle." She cleaned and cooked and sewed for Neeley and his wife. But she did not speak English. So, at first, when Mrs. Neeley told her to bring something, like a frying pan, she could not understand. Neeley determined to "beat the Dutch" out of her. Taking her to the barn, he would tie wooden rods together and then, binding her hands behind her back with a rope, he would whip her. And then whip her again.

Belle's mother had told her that there was a God. God would look after her. Even if a master was bad to her, advised Ma-Ma, she should be good to the master, work hard for him, try to love him and forgive him. Still, Belle prayed to God that she would be sold to a new master.

At last her prayers were answered. Martin Schryver, a fisherman and tavernkeeper, bought her from Neeley. For a year, until she was about thirteen, Belle lived with the Schryvers. They treated her with kindness, gave her enough food, put clothing on her back—not just the one discarded cotton dress that had been her only piece of clothing, summer and winter, at the Neeleys'.

Almost overnight she spurted to a remarkable six feet in height, taller than most of the men at Martin Schryver's tavern. Thin and wiry, she began to tie a red bandanna around her head, black girls' sign that they were no longer children but grown women. People began to notice her.

One day a customer in the tavern offered Schryver three hundred dollars for Belle. At first he refused. Then, tempted by the money, he agreed. For three hundred dollars Belle became the property of John J. Dumont of New Paltz, New York.

Within a few weeks Dumont considered her his favorite among the ten slaves on his farm. She worked harder and faster than the others, he boasted. Belle responded to his praise by working even harder, going out into the fields to work after she did the cooking, the cleaning, and the laundry inside the house. Sometimes she worked well into the night to please him. Perhaps, she later remembered thinking, John J. Dumont was the God who lived in the sky that Ma-Ma had told her about.

Then she met Bob, a slave on a nearby farm. She fell in love with him. But Bob's master objected, intending to use the tall, strong young slave to breed children that he, not Dumont, could sell. One day, finding Bob on the Dumont property, he began to beat the fearful black with his cane. When Dumont ordered him to stop, he tied Bob's hands behind his back and led him away. Soon Belle learned that Bob was dead.

Meanwhile Dumont had arranged for her to marry a much older slave, Tom, whose two previous wives had died. With Tom she had her first child, Diana. Then, in quick succession, she had three more children.

In all Belle stayed sixteen years as Dumont's slave, during which time he sold away two of her daughters. In 1827 the state of New York outlawed slavery, so Belle knew that at the end of a two-year waiting period she would be free.

It was at that time that Belle lost whatever respect she had had for Dumont. First he promised to set her free one year early if she worked even harder. Despite taunts from the other slaves of "white man's pet," she worked night and day in the fields and in the house.

At the end of the year Dumont announced that he could not live up to his promise. Business, he said, had fallen off. Next he sold Belle's son, Peter.

Sick with grief, Belle could stand it no longer. One night, just before dawn, she ran away, clutching her baby, Sophie, tightly in her arms.

By sheer luck she knocked at the door of a Quaker couple, Isaac and Maria Van Wagenen, who gave her refuge. When Dumont finally tracked her down, the Van Wagenens bought her services from him for the year remaining until she could, by New York law, be free. For that year of service they paid Dumont twenty dollars, along with five dollars for baby Sophie.

In her own mind Belle knew that, safe from Dumont at last, she already was free.

At the Van Wagenens she heard for the first time such civilized words as "please" and "thank you." She was treated like a member of the family and ate at the table with her masters. In 1827—on July 4, the anniversary of

American independence—she became a free person. On that day, too, reading passages aloud from the Bible as a ceremony, the Van Wagenens gave little Sophie her freedom as well.

Now, as "Isabelle Van Wagenen," fresh out of slavery, Belle took a remarkable step. With help from Quaker friends of the Van Wagenens she sued in the courts for the return of her son, Peter.

The boy had been taken out of New York State, to Alabama, in violation of state law. Astonishingly, Isabelle won! Peter was returned to her. His hands, his legs, his shoulders—all bore scars and welts from frequent beatings. Still, he was back. Only the work of God, concluded Belle, could have brought about such a miracle.

Belle thought more and more about God. She began to attend the services of a Methodist church in Ulster County.

Like many freed slaves, Belle set out for New York City, hoping for a better life.

At first she worked in the homes of white people. Just as before, she cooked, cleaned, washed, and ironed. But now she received wages for her work and could bargain with her employers for a fair price. Still, in the Five Points section of New York's Bowery, near today's Chinatown, she found mostly poverty. Poor people—hungry,

tired, crowded together in the cold of winter and the heat of summer—seemed to be suffering almost as much as the slaves she had known.

Looking for an answer, Belle turned to God. She tried to attend church services, but the white churches had separate times for blacks only, and she refused to believe that God would listen to blacks and whites separately.

Then she stumbled upon the Magdalene Asylum. The asylum's wealthy founder, Elijah Piersen, had dedicated his fortune to helping young women who, because of poverty, were forced to survive by selling their love to men for money.

In exchange for room, board, and a small salary, Belle agreed to work at the Magdalene Asylum. Soon, alongside Piersen and his wife, she took to the streets, preaching the word of God. Together the three prayed. They fasted. And they tried to help "fallen women."

After a time they were joined by Robert Mathews, a strange, bearded man who called himself Matthias, as if he were a prophet from Biblical times. Matthias persuaded them that the time was at hand for the second coming of Jesus to the world.

They must, he said, start a community—a kingdom—to receive the Lord properly. In that kingdom, he argued convincingly, all property must be shared in common. Piersen gave Matthias huge sums of money. Belle gave him all the money she so carefully had been saving to buy a house for herself and her children.

One day, about two years after Matthias first appeared, Belle returned to the kingdom to find him gone. He had taken all of the community's furniture. Even more seriously, Piersen lay dying of a mysterious stomach ailment.

Despite a court's finding that Piersen had died a natural death the press spread wild rumors. One newspaper reporter wrote a book charging that Belle, in reality an evil witch with secret powers, had poisoned him.

Furious at the charges, Belle demanded justice. She convinced another newspaperman to help her. The reporter filed a law suit for libel on her behalf against the author of the book. He gathered statements about her character from as many of Belle's former masters as he could find. They wrote to him about her honesty, her strong sense of truthfulness, and her firm religious faith. As in the case of her son, Peter, the court decided in her favor, awarding her $125 in damages.

For nine more years Belle worked in New York City, cooking and cleaning, not much better off than on the day she first won her freedom. Her son, Peter, had gone to sea, never to be heard from again. Her daughters worked in the homes of white people in Ulster County.

Then one day, while scrubbing the floor on her hands and knees, she had a vision, or as she put it, "a message from God." "I am no longer Isabelle," she announced to her employer. "I have had a message from the Lord, and He has told me to leave. His voice just told me to 'Go east' at once."

That very day, dropping a loaf of bread, a piece of cheese, and a twenty-five-cent coin into a pillowcase, she set off for Brooklyn. It was to be the beginning of an extraordinary new life for her, one that she was to create almost entirely by herself.

On June 1, 1843, the day she left, Belle was about forty-six years old.

At first she just walked, knocking on doors to ask for work and a place to sleep. When a kindly Quaker lady asked her name, she replied, "Sojourner" (meaning "traveler"). And as to her last name? No longer was it the name of some white master. Instead, as she recalled later, it came to her in a flash. God, she said, had told her that her name would be Truth. The name she would carry until the day of her death was Sojourner Truth.

Once, while walking across Long Island, she came on a large outdoor

Sojourner Truth knitting. *Sophia Smith Collection, Smith College.*

religious meeting. Before it ended, some three days later, she had been given permission to speak. She told of her life and her ideas about religion. In those days America was experiencing a religious revival, and Sojourner came to many such meetings. Almost always, she spoke.

Unable to read and write, she had a remarkable memory for passages in the Bible. If she needed to have something read to her she usually turned to a child. Sometimes two or three children would be seen gathered around her, reading aloud.

From Huntington, Long Island, she took a boat to Connecticut, making her way to Hartford, still walking. Everywhere she found people interested in her—this six-foot-tall, unusual-looking woman with skin so jet black it was almost blue.

Attracted at first by her appearance, they usually stayed on to hear her deeply moving story. Growing increasingly confident, she sometimes sang songs to her audiences, songs she had learned from her mother, others she had made up herself. Always her message remained the same—love and hope, combined with faith in a kind and caring God.

In 1843 she found herself in Northampton, Massachusetts. There she became a member of a communal farm and silk factory. The collective society had been founded by George Benson, a brother-in-law of antislavery leader William Lloyd Garrison. It was in Northampton that she came to the attention of Garrison himself, as well as of such prominent abolitionists as Wendell Phillips, Parker Pillsbury, and another former slave, Frederick Douglass. Like almost everyone she met, they were impressed with her intelligence, her wit, her good common sense.

Three years later, when the community's money finally ran out, she stayed on as a maid, but also as a guest, in George Benson's household. By then one of the abolitionists, Olive Gilbert, had taken down Sojourner's life story in the form of a brief book. William Lloyd Garrison wrote an introduction to it, pointing out how evil slavery could be, not only in the South but wherever it had existed.

In 1850 Sojourner set out on a speaking tour. She appeared before large audiences in Ohio, Indiana, Kansas, Missouri, singing her songs, talking about her life. Often the great leaders of the abolitionist movement shared the platform with her—Garrison, Douglass, Pillsbury. In Massachusetts she stayed at the home of Harriet Beecher Stowe, author of the antislavery novel *Uncle Tom's Cabin*. Afterward, in an

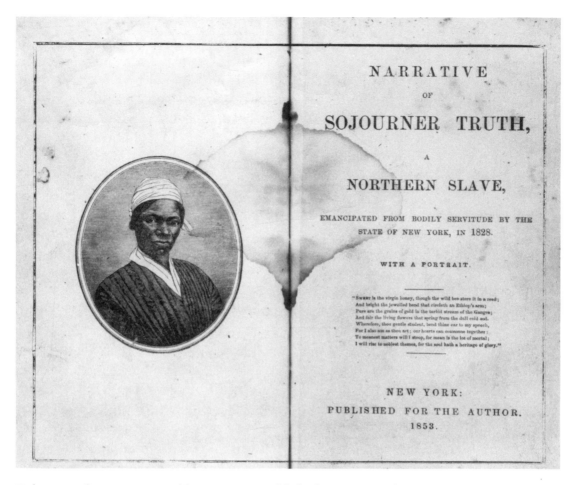

Title page of Sojourner Truth's *Narrative*, published in 1853. *Culver Pictures.*

article for the *Atlantic Monthly*, Mrs. Stowe praised Sojourner with high enthusiasm, describing her as the "Libyan Sibyl."

Sometimes she had to face hostile mobs who threw eggs, tomatoes, and stones at her. Small children taunted her, calling her "nigger witch." Once, local newspapers spread the rumor that, because of her height and deep voice, she really was a man disguised as a woman. The audience demanded that she prove she was a woman by showing her breast. With quiet dignity she opened the buttons of her blouse before the stunned crowd, declaring softly, "It is not my shame but yours that I do this."

To Sojourner, winning rights for women, as well as for blacks, was important. Once, over much protest, she was allowed to address a women's rights meeting in Akron, Ohio. "Ar'n't I a woman?" she demanded.

Look at me! Look at my arm! I have plowed, and planted, and gathered into barns, and no man could head me—and ar'n't I a woman? . . . I have born chilern and seen em mos all sold off into slavery, and when I cried out with a mother's grief none but Jesus heard—and ar'n't I a woman?

Den dat little man in back dar, he say women can't have much rights as man, cause Christ wa'nt a woman. Whar did your Christ come from? . . . Whar did your Christ come from? From God and a woman. Man had nothing to do with him.

Arms outstretched, eyes aflame, she continued in her deep voice, arguing that "If de fust woman God ever made was strong enough to turn the world upside down, all alone, den togedder we ought to be able to turn it back and get it right side up again, and now dey is asking to do it, de men better let 'em."

When she had finished men and women alike rushed to her side, many greeting her with tears in their eyes. Almost by magic she had turned the hoots and jeers of a hostile, angry crowd into respect and admiration.

Unlike Frederick Douglass and other abolitionists, Sojourner Truth hoped that war between North and South would not be necessary to free the slaves. Once, when Douglass declared that "slavery must end in blood," she pointed her finger accusingly at him. "Frederick," she reprimanded him, "Frederick, is God dead?" To Sojourner, love, not war, was the way to change people's minds.

But war did come. And with it, blood.

After the war began Sojourner walked from town to town raising money to help feed and supply black soldiers fighting for the Union. So great had her fame become that in October 1864, President Lincoln received her personally at the White House. Lincoln's autograph, addressed to "Aunty Sojourner Truth," appears in her "Book of Life" alongside the signatures of the leading men and women of her time.

When the war finally ended she worked for the Freedman's Bureau, teaching former slave women how to get jobs in a free economy. By then she was living in Washington, D.C.

In her eighties and bent with suffering, she stood up against separate seating for blacks and whites on the city's streetcars. Intentionally she would sit in sections reserved for whites only. When, with crowds of embarrassed whites looking on, streetcar conductors had to use force to remove such an old woman from their vehicles, putting her out on the street, her point was clearly made.

Once when a conductor slammed her against the door of his car she took the case to the Freedman's Bureau. The conductor was fired and, for a time at least, blacks were permitted to ride with whites on the streetcars of the nation's capital city.

In the period of Reconstruction following the Civil War, Sojourner saw hordes of former slaves crowd into America's big cities. Most lacked education or skills. She urged them to stay away from the cities and, instead, start farms in less settled places like Kansas or Missouri. Although not as many blacks took her advice as she had hoped, a sizable migration to those states can be traced directly to her efforts.

Well into her old age Sojourner continued to address large audiences on behalf of equal rights for blacks and women. In a land where black women so often were treated with cruelty and inhumanity, she still responded with a message of love and faith.

Even on her deathbed, in pain and knowing that the end was near, she told a worried visitor not to be concerned, that God wanted her in heaven. "I'm not going to die, honey," she said comfortingly. "I'm going home like a shooting star."

With her truly remarkable personality—courageous, persistent—her like has seldom been seen in the long history of American social reform.

PART III
Human Rights in an Industrial Age

Booker T. Washington

1856–1915   Former slave who led the movement for industrial education for blacks and their gradual acceptance into white society

"The classroom needs sweeping," the head teacher said. "Take the broom and sweep it."

It was a test, and young Booker T. Washington knew at once that it also was his chance. He swept the room three times. Then he picked up a dusting cloth and dusted it four times. The head teacher inspected the floor. Then, with her handkerchief, she rubbed the woodwork around the walls, the table, and the students' benches.

Finally, when she could find not one bit of dust on the floor or on any of the furniture, she quietly remarked, "I guess you will do to enter this institution."

That incident, as Booker T. Washington later described it in his autobiography, *Up From Slavery,* was nothing less than his entrance examination to Hampton Institute in Virginia.

Having arrived there with fifty cents in his pocket after walking for many days and nights, he accepted a job as janitor to pay for his room and board at Hampton. "Never did any youth pass an examination for entrance into Harvard or Yale," recalled Washington, "that gave him more genuine satisfaction. I have passed several examinations since then," he said, "but I have always felt that this was the best one I ever passed."

Just as Washington had imagined, his admission to Hampton Institute became the turning point in his life.

He had been born a slave, the child of a black mother and a white father whose identity he never learned. As a boy he slept on rags spread on the earthen floor of a windowless one-room log cabin. He ate boiled corn prepared for the cows and pigs.

Yet one day he would win the admiration and financial support of America's richest and most powerful industrialists, including Andrew Carnegie and Henry Ford. He would dine at the White House with the President of the United States. He would become by far the best-known black leader of his era, a model for poor children growing up in this country and in countries around the world.

His life, a fairy-tale success story, also had its costs. In order to achieve so much, he had to make compromises. He had to be patient when he was angry; had to please people he detested; had to dress like, speak like, behave like the very whites who were intent on keeping him and others of his race "in their place." To Booker T. Washington there seemed no other choice, given the realities of the world as he saw it.

In his childhood as a slave Booker had no schooling. In most southern states before the Civil War it was a punishable crime to teach a slave to read. He remembered going up to the schoolhouse door on several occasions to carry the books of one of the girls in his master's family. Looking inside and seeing the children at study made him feel that going to school and learning "would be about the same as getting into paradise." But books, his mother explained, were "white folks' business."

From his childhood Booker remembered never once enjoying a family meal, seated at a table. Each child snatched at whatever scraps could be found in the cabin, a potato one day, a piece of cornbread the next. Not until he was eight did he have shoes, even in winter. His only shirt was made of flax so prickly that his older brother, John, won Booker's lasting gratitude by breaking it in for him.

With the surrender of General Robert E. Lee at Appomattox the Civil War ended. Booker and his family found themselves "free at last" to go wherever they pleased. As they quickly discovered, though, freedom with its many choices is not always easy. Finally they settled in the town of Malden in Kanawha County, West Virginia, where jobs were to be had in the salt furnaces and mines.

As Booker remembered, from the time they arrived in their new home he had an "intense longing to learn to read." Somehow his mother saved enough money to buy him a spelling book. Alone he managed to memorize the alphabet, but without a teacher he still could not make sense of the words.

Then some of the freed slaves, aided by local whites, opened a primitive school in the neighborhood.

Booker's stepfather refused to let him attend, however, arguing that the family needed his wages from work in the salt mines. After many attempts Booker finally persuaded him, promising to work in the mines from four to nine in the morning and again for two hours after school in the afternoon. At that time he was eleven years old.

Several years later Booker decided to leave the family's cabin, located in a dirty, brawling section of town, and become a houseboy to General Lewis Ruffner and his wife, Viola. The move was destined to be an important step in his personal development.

The Ruffners, the leading family of Malden, occupied the town's largest, most elegantly furnished home. They had hired—and then dismissed—a succession of houseboys before Booker. None of them could meet the strict standards of Mrs. Ruffner, a former schoolteacher from Vermont.

At first even Booker found her impossible to please. He ran away, signing on as a cabin boy on a steamboat bound for Cincinnati. But thinking better of the decision he returned from the journey and asked to be taken back. Mrs. Ruffner agreed.

In time Booker came to honor Mrs. Ruffner, describing her as one of the great influences on his life. It was from her that he learned the Puritan ethic—hard work, thrift, and cleanliness. As he later remembered, "She wanted everything kept clean . . . she wanted things done promptly and systematically, and at the bottom of everything she wanted absolute honesty and frankness."

In later years, said Booker, he could never see a dirty yard without wanting to clean it; could never see a loose fence without wanting to nail it back into place. Once, in his adult life, he visited Mrs. Ruffner's former home in Vermont. "For me," he reported, "it was a shrine."

Mrs. Ruffner asked whether, in his spare time, Booker would like her help in learning to read. As she later recalled, it never was necessary to call him a second time for a lesson; he always was ready to begin. She also taught him to grow fruits and vegetables for her and allowed him to collect her profits on their sale. Because he always promptly gave her every cent he collected, her confidence in him increased.

Before long a sense of trust and affection grew between the bright, ambitious black boy and the demanding, intelligent New England schoolteacher. Mrs. Ruffner saw in him the side he wanted people to see—the boy of fault-less conduct, eager to please. But she also saw the other side—the restless Booker T. Washington, desperate to escape the squalor of the poor-white and black society around him and to exchange it for a life like that of the Ruffners.

Sometimes, needing money, Booker found work in the coal mines. It was in the mines that he first heard from fellow workers about the Hampton Institute in Virginia, a school for black boys and girls. What especially interested him was that at Hampton students who could not afford to pay could work their way through.

Eager to get ahead, possibly hoping for a career in law or politics, young Booker T. Washington understood that he needed a good education, certainly a better one than he could get in Malden, West Virginia. In 1872, at the age of seventeen, he packed a small satchel, took leave of his family and friends, and set out on the five-hundred-mile journey to Hampton.

Many days later he arrived, hungry, tired, without friends, without money. For several nights he slept in a hollow beneath the boards of a sidewalk. During the day he worked on the docks, unloading pig iron from ships.

Finally he appeared on the campus of Hampton Institute. And it was there

that the woman principal, a New England Yankee like Mrs. Ruffner, demanded that he sweep and clean one of the classrooms. By then, of course, he knew exactly what was expected of him. Once he was admitted to the school his new job as janitor presented few challenges. His childhood as a slave and then as a houseboy for the Ruffners had prepared him for it.

What the janitorial job did offer was frequent contact with the school's headmaster, General Samuel Chapman Armstrong. One of the youngest generals in the Union army, athletic, soldierly in bearing, General Armstrong became a hero to young Booker T. Washington.

Washington later wrote that Armstrong was "the most perfect specimen of man, physically, mentally, and spiritually" that he had ever encountered. To the former slave, fresh from the life of the mines and now an impressionable adolescent, Armstrong, as Booker later said, struck him as "a perfect man . . . there was something about him that was superhuman."

No wonder, then, that for the rest of his life Washington modeled himself on General Armstrong—his career in education, his views of society, even his choice of clothing. Armstrong, in turn, became Washington's guide, his protector, his promoter. He became, for all intents, the father that Booker never had known and so desperately desired.

The son of missionary parents, Armstrong believed that the principal purpose of education lay not in scholarship but in building character. And the path to character, he thought, could be found primarily in a routine of industrious work habits.

When the Civil War ended Armstrong took a job with the Freedman's Bureau, working on behalf of the newly freed slaves. Then, with the help of the American Missionary Association, he founded Hampton Institute in 1869, intent on using it to prove that his ideas for transforming black people into productive citizens of the United States really worked.

From the "rising bell" at 5:00 A.M. and on through the day students at Hampton were put through their paces: inspection of students, breakfast, prayers, inspection of quarters, roll call and exercises, classes. So it went, through evening prayers, evening study hours, and, at last, at 9:30 P.M., the retiring bell.

Students went through military drill, marched in order to and from all classes, and were assigned demerits for breaking rules. Was it like an army camp? Yes. The difference was in purpose— to be prepared not for battle but for survival in the new industrial America.

For that kind of competition, reasoned Armstrong, black men and women did not need to know Latin and Greek. They needed to know skilled industrial or agricultural trades—ones that would get them jobs. Those skills, combined with the traditional Yankee habits of thrift, hard work, and honor, would turn members of "the unfortunate black race" into useful citizens in the community.

In time, said Armstrong, the race problem would be solved. But before blacks could "learn to run, they first must learn to crawl and walk." If not, they would become a permanent underclass in society, standing on streetcorners without jobs, dependent on charity and handouts.

Hampton Institute proved to be the right place for Booker T. Washington. Earnest, unassuming, he impressed people with his hard work and character. On General Armstrong's recommendation, a merchant from New Bedford, Massachusetts, had sent scholarship money to pay the cost of his instruction. Money for his shoes and clothing came from the "missionary barrels" also sent from the North.

Almost from the beginning Booker showed a talent for public speaking. He joined the debate society, convinced that in later life he would be speaking to crowds, trying to influence them.

Instead of playing games during recreation periods, he read either the Bible or another book that he thought might later prove useful. Following General Armstrong's example, he gave up the idea of a political career. "Patience is better than politics," said Armstrong, "and industry a shorter road to civil rights than Congress has in its power to make."

In 1875 Booker T. Washington graduated from Hampton Institute. His speech at the commencement ceremony was reprinted with praise in *The New York Times*.

In the space of three short years he had traveled from a ragged youth sweeping a classroom to prove his worthiness of an education to the moment of graduation when, as one of his classmates later wrote to him, "You looked like a conqueror."

The rest of Washington's life flowed from his experience at Hampton. "Life at Hampton was a constant revelation," he wrote. "The matter of having meals at regular hours, of eating on a table-cloth, using a napkin, the use of a bath-tub and of the toothbrush . . ."

During the summer after his graduation Booker worked as a waiter and dish-washer at an elegant resort hotel in Connecticut. Then he returned to his home in Malden, West Virginia, to teach in a school for black children.

Again he saw scenes of fighting, drinking, disorder. There were lynchings, sometimes of whites as well as blacks. His faith in civilization—an orderly society based on strong individual character—grew even stronger.

Small wonder that when it came time to create a school of his own it would be a miniature Hampton, founded on personal uplift and on habits of cleanliness and hard work.

In the spring of 1879 General Armstrong invited him to deliver an address at Hampton's commencement ceremonies. His speech, "The Force That Wins," argued that "doing" was more important than just "planning." Labor, he said, was the force that would transform black people.

Enormously impressed with the speech, Armstrong offered Booker a job teaching at Hampton Institute. Washington also became supervisor of the school's new dormitory for Indian boys. His message to the Indians was similar to his message to blacks: "Put away your moccasins" and stop fighting the white man; learn the English language well; acquire a skill such as carpentry or farming that will enable you to earn a living.

In May 1881 General Armstrong received a letter asking him to recommend a suitable white man to head a new school being started in Tuskegee, Alabama. The purpose of the school

Booker T. Washington with his children, Ernest Davidson (left), Booker T. Jr., and his adopted daughter, Laura Murray. Photograph by Frances Benjamin Johnston. *The Library of Congress.*

Booker T. Washington (seated, left) with a group of associates at Tuskegee Institute in 1906. *The Bettmann Archive.*

would be the training of black teachers for service in black schools. Instead of suggesting a white educator, General Armstrong proposed that Booker T. Washington be named the school's founding principal. "I know of no white man who could do better," wrote Armstrong. "I know he would not disappoint you."

Arriving at the tiny town, Washington resolved to make himself "so useful to the community . . . that every man, woman, and child, white and black, would respect me and want me to live among them."

What Washington found at Tuskegee was a section of the country, as he put it, "inhabited almost exclusively by Negroes and mules." What he created over the next thirty-four years was an institution known throughout the nation.

In the beginning some prospective students appeared at the school barefoot. They chewed tobacco, had never used a fork or spoon, had never taken a bath, and had lived mostly on fatpork and cornbread.

Booker went to work. Before long white people came to trust him. When he borrowed money for Tuskegee—to put up buildings or buy more land— they knew he would repay the loans. They knew that Tuskegee graduates would be competent in their trades—

bricklaying, printing, blacksmithing, farming; would be polite and well groomed; would "fit in" to white society.

The years flew swiftly by, years filled with endless hours of labor for Booker T. Washington, who traveled everywhere to raise funds for Tuskegee. Slowly, step by step, the school became a model for educating blacks. By 1915 Tuskegee was preparing students for work in thirty-eight trades and professions; had a faculty of nearly two hundred, all of them black; had more than one hundred buildings on two thousand acres of grounds; and was providing off-campus lessons on farming throughout Alabama and the lower South.

Local and state business leaders had come to expect that graduates of Tuskegee would be well prepared. They had come to trust and admire Booker T. Washington. All of this was just as he had expected. He had won their confidence, calmed their fears about the newly freed blacks. As a result he was able to register tangible, measurable gains for black people.

In 1893 Washington delivered a speech to the Cotton States and International Exposition at Atlanta. That address propelled him into the national spotlight as the outstanding black man in America. Hoping to say something that would "cement the friendship of the races," he uttered the sentence for which he would ever afterward be remembered:

In all things that are purely social we can be separate as the fingers, yet one as the hand in all things essential to mutual progress.

Blacks and whites alike, said Washington, should "cast down your buckets where you are." The reality of life in America was separation of the races, not integration. Change, he advised, must come gradually, through education and hard work, not through politics and agitation.

In his own life Washington received with modesty the honors that increasingly were heaped upon him. He accepted invitations to speak to white audiences or to dine at the homes of whites when he thought that his actions would help Tuskegee or would help his race. Boasting, he knew, would only hurt those causes.

In 1901, for example, when President Theodore Roosevelt asked him to dine at the White House, he later explained, "Mr. Roosevelt simply found he could spare the time best during and after the dinner hour for the discussion of matters which both of us were interested in."

Not surprisingly, many black leaders disagreed with Washington's approach.

The Harvard-educated W. E. B. Du Bois, for example, thought that Tuskegee's emphasis on vocational education was wrong; it would do no more than keep blacks in bondage to whites. Du Bois thought that accepting the separation of the races would lead only to blacks' being humiliated. Why, asked Washington's critics, should blacks be forced to go to separate schools; stay in separate hotels; eat at separate restaurants; ride in separate sections of trains; make use of separate washrooms; drink from separate drinking fountains; even swear on separate Bibles in the courtrooms?

Washington's answer was that, for the present, they had no choice. To him all the rage and tears of Du Bois led nowhere, produced no results. On the other hand, Washington's great autobiography, *Up From Slavery*, was more than just the story of a black man's rise from poverty. It was a set of messages, carefully written to reach different audiences.

To white southerners it said that they had no reason to fear blacks, no need to use all the great power they possessed to crush the black race altogether. To wealthy white northerners, it was a plea for continued financial support from a black man who "knew his place." Finally, to blacks, it was a message of patience and courage: to become

A class at Tuskegee Institute in 1906. Photograph by Frances Benjamin Johnston. *The Library of Congress.*

educated, display dignity in the face of prejudice—and let time take care of social change.

In a famous statue on the grounds of Tuskegee, the sculptor shows Booker T. Washington in a three-piece suit, lifting a sheet off a kneeling young black who holds in his hand a large book. The sheet, of course, represents the veil of ignorance. It is that veil—ignorance—that Washington was committed to lifting from the black race.

At the base of the statue an inscription reads, "I will let no man drag me down so low as to make me hate him." Also on the same statue appears the engraving: "We shall prosper in proportion as we learn to dignify and glorify labor and put brains and skill into the common occupations of life."

Sometimes it is said that the words of Washington, the lesson of his life, were that of a man with the wish not to offend. The odds, as he calculated them at least for that time in history, were against black people. And Washington believed above all in seeing the world as it really was, not as he *wished* it might be.

Hence blacks at Tuskegee were taught to wear clean clothes and to walk with a firm stride and perfect posture. "Shuffling and shambling" were replaced by self-respect. While other blacks throughout the South were turned away from the polls at election time, Tuskegee's blacks, including Washington himself, had no trouble voting. There was always food in the school's cafeteria. The humiliations of prejudice were elsewhere. Tuskegee was an oasis of orderly society.

It is only recently that historians have discovered that, with the utmost secrecy, Washington helped to finance legal action against separation of the races, against juries without blacks, and against the exclusion of blacks from voting—fighting to reverse the conditions he publicly was saying had to be tolerated.

On November 14, 1915, after returning from a fund-raising trip to New York, Booker T. Washington died. He had collapsed on the trip, exhausted from overwork. At the time of his death he was fifty-nine years old. Tributes to his memory poured in from around the world.

Today Tuskegee Institute is in decay. But today, too, blacks no longer are legally denied admission to schools, to hospitals, to baseball parks, to hotels, on the basis of their color. By and large the need for such an institution is gone.

On a shelf at Tuskegee, Washington kept a rack of file boxes labeled Lynching Records. Each card in the boxes told the story of a black who had been taken and hanged by whites without benefit of trial. In 1903 a visitor to Tuskegee counted sixty-three boxes on the rack.

The file boxes reflected "the lay of the land"—the real world of black people in the time of Booker T. Washington. As a child Booker had learned to count. He knew the meaning of those boxes. And he acted accordingly.

That the times have finally changed may, indeed, be the highest tribute to his good judgment—and to his patience.

Chief Joseph

c. 1840–1904   Champion of the Nez Percé Indians against mistreatment by the United States government

Once, in the beautiful Wallowa Valley of Oregon, lived an Indian boy named Joseph. His Indian name was Heinmot Tooyalakekt—"Thunder Rolling in the Mountains."

Joseph's father was a chief among the Nez Percé people. A missionary had given the old chief the English name Joseph, so the white Americans first called the boy Young Joseph and then, after his father died, Chief Joseph.

In 1855, when Young Joseph was about fifteen years old, his father made an agreement with the Americans. He promised that his people would not harm settlers, and the Americans gave their word that the Nez Percé could always live in their beloved Wallowa Valley.

Only eight years later gold was dis- covered on the Indians' land. Greedy white miners rushed to the valley. Some of the Indian leaders accepted gifts and money from the white men. In 1863 some of the Nez Percé signed a new treaty agreeing to give up still more of their land. But Old Joseph re- fused. He and his band stayed in their valley even though the settlers began to move closer and closer to them.

In 1871 Old Joseph died. Just before his death, he made his son promise never to sell the land of his tribe—never to give up the land in which his mother's and father's bones were laid to rest. Young Joseph agreed.

The Nez Percé were peaceful people who sometimes boasted that no Nez Percé ever had killed a white man. They were the friendly Indians who fed the

131

starving Lewis and Clark, two explorers Thomas Jefferson sent west to explore the Louisiana Purchase territory. During the Civil War, while the soldiers were away, the Nez Percé did not raid the homes of white settlers.

Like the Plains Indians, the Nez Percé sometimes hunted buffalo. And like other Indians of the Columbia River area, they also enjoyed fishing. Later, Christian missionaries taught them to farm. The Nez Percé also learned to breed horses. They developed the famous Appaloosa pony, which was known for its great strength and courage in battle.

When he became chief at the age of thirty-one, Young Joseph was a striking figure. He was handsome and strong. Over six feet tall, he stood proud and straight, every inch a noble leader. He seldom smiled, and spoke slowly and clearly, with great wisdom. Among his own people and even among white settlers, he was known for his fairness.

In 1876 the United States government told Chief Joseph that he and his people must leave the Wallowa Valley and go to the Lapwai Indian Reservation in Idaho. There they could farm. But no family was to have more than twenty acres of land. Nor could the Indians roam freely in the countryside.

For a people who made their living mostly by raising horses and who often traveled, the government's order seemed impossible to obey.

Some of the young Nez Percé leaders wanted to fight the white men. Chief Joseph said no. He knew how many soldiers the United States Army could call on to destroy his tribe. It was hopeless to fight. Instead he had his people prepare to leave their land and go to the reservation.

Anything, said Joseph, was better than a war.

Before they were to leave, the Nez Percé decided to meet for one more celebration. It was a mistake. The white settlers used the occasion to steal hundreds of the famous Appaloosa ponies. They killed two Indians.

Already the Nez Percé were sad and angry about having to leave their homeland. Now even their horses had been taken from them. They cried out for revenge. While Chief Joseph was away from his camp, some of his young warriors struck back at the hated settlers. They killed eighteen whites and wounded many others.

By the time Joseph returned, the damage was done. Many of the Indians already had fled to another camp to prepare for war.

What would Joseph do? His wife had just given birth to a daughter. Would he take his family and go to live on the reservation? Would he join the

A photograph of Chief Joseph by Edward S. Curtis. *National Portrait Gallery, Smithsonian Institution. Gift of Jean-Antony du Lac.*

younger tribesmen and lead them in a war that surely would end in death for most of the Indians?

Chief Joseph would not leave his people. He decided to lead the Nez Percé to Canada, which was ruled by Queen Victoria of England. The American soldiers could not follow them across the border into another country. In Canada they would be safe. They would be free.

But the United States would not let them go.

General O. O. Howard, a one-armed hero of the Civil War, was sent to capture Chief Joseph and force the Indians onto the reservation. From June until October 1877, Chief Joseph fought the power of the mighty United States Army, fleeing all the time toward Canada.

Seldom in the history of warfare has there been leadership like that of Joseph. His forces numbered only two hundred warriors, many of them old and sick. He also had the problem of caring for almost six hundred women and children. The government troops attempting to capture him included the First, Second, and Seventh United States cavalries, and the telegraph was used to call additional troops from as far away as Atlanta, Georgia. Joseph's men had a few rifles, most of them taken from dead soldiers, and their bows and arrows. The government troops had the finest modern weapons, including large cannons.

Time and again Joseph managed to escape. He would strike in the night, stealing the soldiers' horses so they could not follow him. He would send his tiny band of cavalry to keep the enemy busy while he moved the women and children. With some American soldiers in front of him and some behind, he somehow slipped loose and made the two enemy columns pursuing him bump into each other. He feinted in one direction and moved in another. Several times the white men caught him and forced him to fight. But Joseph's warriors stunned them with expert riflery, killing so many soldiers that the rest withdrew.

The chase covered over a thousand miles of rugged mountain territory. Chief Joseph and his people hurried on through Montana, parts of Idaho and Wyoming, through Yellowstone Park, and to within sight of the Canadian border.

During the entire retreat the Nez Percé followed the white man's rules of war. Chief Joseph ordered that there be no scalping. There was none. In Yellowstone Park some white women were captured. They were treated gently and then released. Whenever Joseph's little band stopped for coffee, flour, sugar, or tobacco, they paid for the supplies in gold dust or American currency. They destroyed no property. They killed no families of peaceful settlers on the way.

The American soldiers were not so careful. Once, they broke into the Nez Percé camp while most of the Indian warriors were away. They shot and clubbed to death many Indian women and little children before Chief Joseph and his men returned.

Another time, when Chief Joseph was talking peace with the whites, they seized him and made him a prisoner. Only after the Nez Percé struck back by capturing an American army officer did the whites let him go.

The chase picked up speed as Joseph's people came closer to Canada. All across the United States, thousands of Americans followed in the newspapers the story of the gallant Nez Percé and their race for freedom. In the eyes of some Americans, Chief Joseph and his warriors, not the soldiers, were the true heroes.

But the cause of the Indians was doomed. At Eagle Creek in the Bear Paw Mountains, only thirty miles from the Canadian border, Joseph stopped to rest his weary, starving little band. It was a pause he would always regret.

On a snowy, bitter cold day in October 1877, the cavalry stormed into the Nez Percé camp, rifles blazing. Some of the Indians escaped to the north, only to die of cold and hunger. A few managed to straggle into Canada. Most were trapped and encircled, their escape cut off.

The Indians hid behind the rocks. But artillery shells from the white men's cannons rained down on them from above. As the shells exploded, frightened children, including Joseph's own nine-year-old daughter, ran in terror onto the plain. Most of them died from the cold.

Finally Chief Joseph could stand no more. To save the remaining women and children, he decided to surrender.

Mounting his horse, he rode toward the white men's lines. Five brave warriors walked beside him. When the American soldiers recognized him, they stopped firing and waited. Chief Joseph slowly dismounted and walked forward, alone, to meet General Howard and his aide, General Miles.

Joseph came face-to-face with them. He offered his rifle to General Howard, who told him to give it to Miles. Joseph did. Then, folding his blanket around him, Joseph raised his arm to speak. A lieutenant named Wood kept a careful record of everything that was said. It was one of history's saddest, most deeply moving speeches.

"Surrender of Chief Joseph," a lithograph illustration by Frederic Remington for General Nelson A. Miles's *Personal Recollections*, published by Werner and Company in 1896. *Culver Pictures*.

Turning to Miles, Chief Joseph began speaking:

Tell General Howard that I know his heart. What he told me before I have in my heart. . . . My people ask me for food, and I have none to give. It is cold, and we have no blankets, no food. My people are starving to death. Where is my little daughter? I do not know. Perhaps, even now, she is freezing to death. Hear me, my chiefs. I have fought, but from where the sun now stands, Joseph will fight no more forever.

"Then," continued Wood, "he drew his blanket across his face, after the fash-ion of Indians when mourning or humiliated, and instead of walking toward his own camp, walked directly into ours, as a prisoner."

General Howard promised Joseph that the Nez Percé would be sent to the Lapwai Reservation in Idaho. His promise was broken. Instead the tiny band that had survived the thousand-mile dash toward freedom was taken to Indian Territory in Oklahoma. There many of them caught malaria and died. Among those to die were all six of Joseph's remaining children.

Finally Joseph and some of his people

were sent to a reservation in Washington State. They were forced to march all the way, were given no supplies, and arrived in the dead of winter with no food or money.

Still, Chief Joseph was true to his word. He never again fought against the whites. In his final years he tried to educate his people and help them make the best of life on the reservation.

In 1904 he died, brokenhearted, far away from his beautiful Wallowa Valley.

Lieutenant Wood, who saw Joseph's surrender to the Americans, probably best summed up the heroic Indian's life when he said, "I think that, in his long career, Joseph cannot accuse the government of the United States of one single act of justice."

Clara Barton

1821–1912   Organizer of nursing services for troops during the Civil War; leading figure in the founding of the American Red Cross

The story of Clara Barton is well known: the prim New England schoolteacher who gained fame for her deeds during the Civil War as the "Angel of the Battlefield" and later established, over great opposition, the American Red Cross. Calm, kind, and efficient, she knew just how to handle every new situation. She was always confident, always in command, even in the midst of exploding shells and whizzing bullets. Soldiers on seeing her were said to have sighed in relief, "Ah, there is Clara Barton. Now we shall be fed."

The real Clara Barton, though, was very different—and far more interesting.

In the first seven years after Clara Barton's parents were married they had four children, two boys and two girls.

Ten more years passed before, in 1821, Clara was born. Growing up, for her, was a little like being an only child. As she once put it, "I had no playmates, but in effect six fathers and mothers."

From the time of her birth Clara's older brothers and sisters took care of her. They taught her reading and mathematics. They taught her how to handle tools. They taught her how to ride a horse and to swim and to throw a ball.

Her father, a man of wealth who farmed and owned a sawmill in North Oxford, Massachusetts, had fought in the Indian Wars, serving with General "Mad Anthony" Wayne at the Battle of Fallen Timbers. He told Clara exciting, real-life stories about military combat. Later, when she found herself on the battlefield, she claimed that her father's stories had made it easier for her to accept the danger than for other nurses, or even some of the soldiers.

If Clara gained certain advantages from the years separating her from her older brothers and sisters, there were also unfortunate results. She became used to getting her own way. As an adult she found it hard to take orders from other people. She insisted on being in command, making decisions. She cooperated only when cooperation fit into her plans.

Like many children who grow up without a need to compromise with playmates, she tended to be shy, sensitive, perhaps even fearful of being with other people. Some historians have gone so far as to say that Clara Barton was a "spoiled" child.

When Clara was about eleven, her mother became so concerned with her child's shyness that she sought out Lorenzo N. Fowler, a famous phrenologist of the time. Phrenologists, who were popular in the optimistic days from 1815 to about 1850, claimed they could remedy the weaknesses in people's characters by massaging the bumps on their patients' heads. Dr. Fowler assured Mrs. Barton that nothing really was wrong with Clara. What she needed was responsibility. He recommended

that she should become a teacher as soon as possible and be put in charge of a classroom.

Clara liked the idea. At the age of fifteen and totally inexperienced, she plunged into teaching. She set up a school near her father's mill for the workers there and for their children. Despite her youth and lack of experience, she succeeded. Her students liked her. They attended their classes regularly.

Even before teaching she had shown a willingness to accept responsibility. One of her brothers had been injured in a construction accident. He was bedridden for two years. During that time he insisted that only Clara take care of him. She gave him his medicines and read to him. It had been good experience for a career in teaching.

For several years Clara continued to teach. Then, in 1851, when she was thirty, she decided to improve her own education. She attended a school in Clinton, New York, before accepting a teaching position in Bordentown, New Jersey.

Arriving in Bordentown, she discovered that the town had no free public schools. As a result many young people just walked the streets or sat on fences. Their parents could not—or would not—pay the fees necessary to hire additional teachers.

Clara Barton boldly announced to the school board that she would serve for three months without salary if they would make the school free to *all* children. At first they refused, arguing that such a practice, once started, would be hard to reverse. But Clara persisted. Finally she got her way. The school board agreed to the experiment, but only for a three-month period.

She began teaching in Bordentown in a deserted building with six pupils in her care. Two years later she was teaching six hundred students, housed in a brand-new building.

Her students adored her. Barely five feet tall, with sparkling eyes and long brown hair, she had the ability to inspire young people. In her private life she increasingly gave the impression of self-confidence and poise. Three men proposed marriage to her, but each time she refused, so totally involved was she in her teaching career.

Then her school board made a decision. The task of running a school that was so successful, they reasoned, clearly was too much for a mere woman. They appointed a male principal as her boss.

Furious, Clara resigned at once. In her mid-thirties, she decided to put her years of teaching behind her and try something different.

For a time, experiencing nervous tension, she rested. Then the congressman from her home district in Massachusetts arranged a job for her in Washington, D.C., clerking in the U.S. Patent Office. She became one of the first women in America ever to hold a full-time position as a civil servant.

The men in the patent office resented her. They tried to make her uncomfortable, hoping that she would resign. But she hung on, impressing her superiors with her efficiency. She worked harder and for longer hours than her male co-workers.

When the Democrats captured the presidential election of 1856 Clara went home to Massachusetts, out of a job. But with Lincoln's election to the presidency in 1860 she returned to Washington. That city would become her base of operations for the rest of her professional life.

In the spring of 1861 rebel forces fired on Fort Sumter, marking the beginning of the Civil War. The war proved to be the turning point in America's history. It also transformed the life of Clara Barton.

Miss Barton became involved at the very outbreak of the conflict. Soldiers of the Sixth Massachusetts Regiment, making their way to Washington, were shot at and stoned by Southern sympathizers in Baltimore. Many arrived in the capital without their baggage,

A photograph of Clara Barton by Mathew Brady. *American Red Cross.*

wounded and bleeding. Clara placed an advertisement in a Washington newspaper asking for contributions of clothing and supplies for them. She used her own cramped quarters to house the gifts.

After the Battle of Bull Run she watched the battered, discouraged Union soldiers streaming back into Washington, routed by the Confederates. At that point Clara wrote to the popular Worcester, Massachusetts, *Daily Spy,* pleading for bandages, medicines, food, tobacco. With her usual independence, she rented a warehouse to store and distribute the supplies.

When she announced that she would personally deliver the supplies to the battlefield, the War Department objected. But Miss Barton insisted. Finally the department agreed, even providing her with carts and teams of mules to distribute comforts to sick and wounded soldiers. She was given a general pass, extending to any battle situation, along with free transportation for herself. As usual Clara Barton had gotten her way.

She set out at once for the front, arriving in the middle of the night at Cedar Mountain, near Culpeper, Virginia, with wagonloads of supplies. In those days it was unheard of for a woman to appear at the scene of battle.

For Clara Barton that accomplishment was only the beginning. Sometimes she would arrange for the baking of several hundred loaves of bread for a breakfast; serve soup from laundry tubs; ladle out gallons of coffee.

Next she turned to nursing the wounded. Once she saved a man's life by making a tourniquet from a strip of cloth torn from her own petticoat. On another occasion she held a soldier in her arms, raising his lips to a cup, when a bullet whistled past her body and struck him in the heart, killing him. Busy, she never mended the hole in her sleeve made by the bullet. Sometimes she had to stop and wring out her skirt, heavy with blood.

Miss Barton learned to set up nursing stations in tents, in wagons, anywhere. She learned how to start a fire on an open field in the rain. She wrote countless letters home, sometimes for soldiers dying as she watched. After their deaths she would be the one to close their eyes. She prayed for the men, alone and in groups. No wonder she came to be known by Civil War soldiers as the "Angel of the Battlefield."

Often she angered those in power. Refusing to cooperate with the army's own "corps of nurses," she also liked to operate independent of the principal group of civilian volunteers in the North, the United States Sanitary Commission. Moreover, she insisted on her right to treat wounded soldiers of both sides—North and South—despite the outrage such humane behavior caused in the War Department.

In 1865 the Civil War, with all of its horrors, finally ended.

For four years afterward Clara Barton worked to identify the bodies of the war dead and to notify their families. Just a month before his assassination President Lincoln personally had opened the way for her in that task. He also had encouraged her efforts in identifying those men who had been buried in unmarked graves, or who had died at such notorious Confederate prison camps as Andersonville, in Georgia.

After the war Miss Barton spoke out strongly in favor of women's rights. Lecturing around the country on her wartime experiences, she praised Susan B. Anthony, who then was demanding the vote for women. It was, she said, the very same women who now worked for equal rights who had opened the way for her, making possible her mission of saving lives on the battlefield.

Always frail and delicate, Clara Barton finally suffered a nervous breakdown. Worn out, voiceless, she left for Switzerland in August 1869 to rest and recover her health.

The trip proved anything but a rest. In Geneva Clara learned about the International Red Cross, an organization founded ten years earlier to help sick and wounded soldiers in wartime situations. The United States government had refused to join. Dating back to the Monroe Doctrine, the American policy had been "hands off"—avoiding involvement in foreign affairs.

Miss Barton refused to accept the government's decision as final. But before she could do anything about it, the Franco-Prussian War broke out. Rushing to Strasbourg, in Alsace-Lorraine, she joined Red Cross workers in organizing a sewing group for women displaced by the war. That work gave them enough income to stay alive. She also arranged for the collection of clothing at a center in Paris to assist victims of the war. All of her activities were conducted under the banner of the Red Cross.

Again her health failed. Nevertheless, on returning to the United States, she began at once to campaign for American membership in the Red Cross. She contacted President Hayes, as well as the State Department and influential congressmen. She made hundreds of speeches. She distributed pamphlets about the Red Cross.

To appeal to Americans, many of whom believed that the nation never again would be at war, she added the "American Amendment" to the consti-

Danesville, New York, around 1866. The first local Red Cross society in the United States was organized at the Lutheran Church (steeple with clock) on August 22, 1881. *American Red Cross.*

tution of the Red Cross. It defined a peacetime role for the organization— helping the victims of "floods, earthquakes, fires, hurricanes, droughts, epidemics."

On March 1, 1882, President Chester A. Arthur finally agreed to the chartering of the American Red Cross. On that day Miss Barton wrote, "I had waited so long and got so weak and broken I could not even feel glad."

Even then the organization was not truly "national." Most of the group's work was carried on through Red Cross societies in the various states. Still, magazines and newspapers now rushed to print articles about Clara Barton. Artists wanted to paint her portrait. Along with the Red Cross, she was becoming famous.

As president of the American Red Cross she refused to accept a salary, even spending her own small savings when public contributions failed to cover the organization's costs. Miss Barton insisted, however, on keeping tight control over whatever work the Red Cross did.

Over the years she had learned how to convince newspaper writers and her co-workers that, in any situation, she could remain calm, efficient, confident. Privately, in her diary, she expressed many of the same fears, the doubts about her ability, the insecurity, that had marked her childhood and her youth.

Advancing into her seventies, she still refused to slow down, taking on one new project after another. She helped the victims of the great Johnstown flood in Pennsylvania; the survivors of Turkey's massacre of the Armenians; the hurricane that devastated the cabins of blacks on the Sea Islands of Georgia.

During the Spanish-American War, at the age of seventy-seven, she personally rode to the battlefield on a mule-driven wagon to help Cuban civilians and American soldiers. She set up orphanages for Cuban children, served soup to the soldiers, treated wounds.

In time Red Cross workers at home complained that Miss Barton was careless in handling the society's financial records and that she refused to accept advice. Sensitive to criticism, as always, she struck back. At an organizational meeting in 1902 she had herself voted president of the American Red Cross for life. In her diary that night she wrote, "Victory after victory was won through the long, hard warring day, till at length . . . our foes were slain at our feet. . . ."

Eventually it became obvious even to her friends that Miss Barton's strengths were not in directing such a large organization. Money contributions declined. Membership fell off. In 1903 President Theodore Roosevelt withdrew the support of the federal government. At that point, believing herself betrayed, Clara Barton resigned the presidency of the American Red Cross.

She retired to Glen Echo, Maryland. There she confided page after page of memories to her already lengthy diaries. She studied Christian Science and other religions.

As she advanced into old age medals and honors poured in on her from around the world—from Germany, Russia, Turkey, Serbia. Often she represented the Red Cross at international meetings.

Predictably, she was pleased to be noticed. At last, nearing the end of her life, she knew that people appreciated her, the simple farm girl from Massachusetts. They knew of her services on the battlefield, knew how hard she had worked to make the Red Cross one of America's most honored organizations.

Still alert, vigorous, youthful, she died in 1912, at the age of ninety-one. Her remains were transferred to North Oxford, Massachusetts, the place of her birth. There the carriage driver assigned to carry her coffin recalled with reverence that at the battle of Antietam it was Clara Barton who had found his father—a Confederate soldier—bleeding to death. She had bound his wounds and saved his life.

Now, having fought the last battle in a life filled with battles, she belonged to the ages.

Susan B. Anthony

1820–1906   Foremost leader in winning the right of women to vote

Like many eleven-year-olds, Susan kept her eyes open. She saw a lot. For one thing, she noticed that whenever the yarn became tangled or something went wrong with the machinery in her father's cotton factory the foreman, Elijah, called on a woman, Sally Ann, to fix it.

"If Sally Ann knows more about weaving than Elijah," Susan asked her father, "why don't you make her foreman?"

"It would not be proper," he answered her. "It simply isn't proper to have a woman foreman in a factory."

For Susan B. Anthony that incident marked the beginning of a lifetime of work on behalf of equal rights for women: the right to equal opportunity in earning a living; equal opportunity in voting and holding political office; equal opportunity in courts of law. Today Miss Anthony and Elizabeth Cady Stanton, her closest friend and constant companion, are remembered as the greatest leaders in the history of the women's rights movement in the United States. For a time a coin—the Susan B. Anthony dollar—was in general use in the United States, testifying to the importance of her contribution to American life.

Susan's father, a prosperous mill owner, understood how intelligent she was. He sent her to a special school where she could learn not only the "three Rs" (reading, 'riting, and 'rithmetic), but geography and languages as well. She quickly repaid his investment in her schooling when, as a result of the Panic of 1837, he had to give up his mill. Susan took a job teaching school for $2.50 a week to help support the family.

In those days girls had few choices for their adult lives except marriage or teaching. Susan had offers of marriage, but she turned them down. Later she remembered, "When I was young, if a girl married poverty [a poor man], she became a drudge; if she married wealth [a rich man], she became a doll. Had I married at twenty-one, I would have been either a drudge or a doll for fifty-two years. Think of it!"

Instead Susan chose to live a life of struggle, fighting for change. As her father's business improved, the Anthony home at Hardscrabble, New York, became a center for the vigorous discussion of ideas, mostly about the need for changes in American life.

Among her father's guests were such prominent antislavery leaders as Frederick Douglass, William Lloyd Garrison, and Wendell Phillips. A Quaker like her father, Susan joined the Daughters of Temperance Society, working against the hardships brought on by excessive drinking of alcohol.

In 1848 Susan's parents and younger sister returned from the women's rights convention held in Seneca Falls, New York, with glowing stories of Lucretia Mott and Elizabeth Cady Stanton. The convention had called for better education for women; equal pay with men for doing the same work; equal property rights with men; and—most surprising of all—the right of women to vote.

On a visit to Seneca Falls to start a branch of the Women's Temperance Society, Susan was introduced to Elizabeth Cady Stanton. The two liked each other at once, marking the beginning of a lifetime friendship.

At a women's rights convention held in Syracuse, Susan became convinced that what women needed most of all was the right to vote. Only then, she reasoned, would they have the power to win passage of new laws to protect themselves against inequality.

At a teachers' convention in Rochester, New York, Miss Anthony listened patiently to male teachers discussing the reasons teachers were less respected than doctors, lawyers, and ministers. To the shock of the delegates, she rose, demanding the right to speak. After half an hour of discussion on whether a woman should be allowed to speak at a public meeting, the matter was put to a vote. By a narrow majority, Miss Anthony was permitted to make brief remarks.

She addressed the topic of disrespect for teachers. "Do you not see," she said, "that so long as society says woman has not brains enough to be a doctor, lawyer, or minister, but has plenty to be a teacher, every man of you who [decides] to teach tacitly admits . . . that he has no more brains than a woman?"

That was all she said. But from that moment Susan B. Anthony became known as a champion of the rights of women teachers in New York State.

Before long Miss Anthony found that classroom teaching confined her, gave her too little time to work for social reforms, especially the cause of women's rights. So she left teaching. Having at last found a purpose for her life, she threw herself into the struggle totally, completely.

First she arranged a series of state and regional conventions. Next she organized a petition campaign for improvement of the Married Women's Property Law in New York State. Going from house to house despite the bitter snowstorms of winter in upstate New York, she and her co-workers collected six thousand signatures in ten weeks on a petition demanding protection for the right of married women to keep the money they earned.

Her efforts paid off. In 1860 the state legislature passed a law that for many years to come was a model for the nation.

Miss Anthony's principal concern was women's rights, but she also was a leader in New York for William Lloyd Garrison's American Anti-Slavery Society. On that issue, too, she spoke with burning intensity. Pointing out that the Constitution of the United States protected the legal rights of slave owners, she declared fiercely that there could be no compromise with such an evil. "Overthrow this government," she said. "Commit its blood-stained Constitution to the flames, blot out every vestige of that guilty bargain of the fathers. . . ."

Many of the towns she visited never before had seen a woman address a public meeting. At first people came out of curiosity, as if to see some circus animal. Usually they stayed on to listen and found themselves persuaded by her good sense, her intensity, and her wit.

Once a fellow abolitionist, the Reverend A. D. Mayo, challenged her right to speak out on questions of marriage, since she was not married. "Well, Mr. Mayo," she answered, "since you are not a slave, why don't you quit lecturing on slavery?"

Miss Anthony's success, however, usually came less from clever remarks on the lecture platform than from hard work. Thus, when asked why she never married, her answer usually was that marriage and children, time-consuming activities, would distract her from her work in the women's movement.

Susan B. Anthony was often caricatured by cartoonists. *New York Public Library.*

Her raspy voice made her an easy target for newspapermen. They also made fun of her severe facial features and one eyeball that seemed never to move. As a result she never felt entirely at ease on the lecture platform. But her work as a behind-the-scenes organizer and administrator more than made up for the shyness in public that she had to fight off throughout her life.

Even men were forced to admire her

political realism—her ability to see things as they really were, not as she wished they might be. They marveled, too, at her incredible energy, which permitted her to work for many hours without rest.

In almost all of her activities, Miss Anthony cooperated closely with Elizabeth Cady Stanton. Mrs. Stanton put her ideas into writing quickly and easily. Miss Anthony found it hard to write, but she was good with facts and figures. She gave the facts to Mrs. Stanton, who then wrote them in language that would excite people. As Miss Anthony once described their teamwork, Mrs. Stanton "loads the gun" when she writes a speech. Then she, Susan, "pulls the trigger and lets fly the powder and ball."

The two worked hard together to win freedom for America's slaves. When the Civil War ended and slavery was abolished they both hoped that women, along with black males, would get the vote. But it was not to be. "Be patient," they were told. "This is the Negro's hour, not the woman's hour."

Not accepting that judgment, they campaigned hard to get women's suffrage (the right to vote) enacted into law.

In 1867 Miss Anthony learned that the state of Kansas was going to have an election to decide the question of votes for blacks and women. Despite her distaste for lecturing before audiences, she spoke everywhere she could in Kansas. While Mrs. Stanton had to rest and bathe every evening before meeting an audience, Miss Anthony sometimes spoke without even stopping to eat first.

As usual, though, her greatest contribution was her efficiency in handling the details of the speaking tour. She rented the halls, put notices and advertisements in the newspapers, gave interviews to reporters, wrote ahead for ushers and janitors.

The vote in Kansas was close, but in politics "close" is not good enough. Susan B. Anthony and Elizabeth Cady Stanton had fought hard and lost. They settled into deep gloom.

Still, they refused to give up. Together the two published a newspaper, the *Revolution.* In it they championed not only the cause of women's rights but such causes (radical for the time) as an eight-hour day for workers and the right of mistreated women to receive divorces, with money from the husbands to support them and the children of the marriage.

The *Revolution* stirred people up. In fact, it became so controversial that advertisers finally refused to support it. Again and again Susan borrowed money to keep the paper going. Before long she owed ten thousand dollars.

Finally a friend of the two women agreed to take over the *Revolution,* along with its debt. To make everything legal she gave Susan a token payment of one dollar.

After paying for her train ticket home from New York City, Miss Anthony had little more in her purse than some change and the one-dollar payment. Then, in the railroad station at Rochester, New York, a thief stole the dollar!

Paying back the ten-thousand-dollar debt of the *Revolution* became a matter of honor for Miss Anthony. She lectured to every audience that would listen, usually receiving seventy-five dollars or one hundred dollars for her appearance. On one occasion she spoke at a home for the insane. Once she even spoke to a group that could not hear her: people at a home for the deaf. Her words had to be repeated in sign language.

It took six years, but Susan B. Anthony paid back every penny of the ten thousand dollars.

Through all of those years Miss Anthony never forgot her central purpose—getting the vote for women. When the election for president took place in 1872 she tried a new approach. She, along with fifteen other women, simply walked into a polling place and *voted.*

Two weeks later the police stepped in. A deputy United States marshal arrived at Susan's home. It was his duty, he notified her, to take her to court, where she must stand trial. Because it was against the law for a woman to vote, she had committed a crime. Susan demanded that she be handcuffed, but the deputy refused. At the courthouse, a date was set for her trial: June 17, 1873.

It was a memorable trial. Justice Ward Hunt, presiding as trial judge, would not allow Miss Anthony to testify in her own defense. He instructed the all-male jury to return a verdict of guilty and would not even allow the jurors to retire to consider the evidence.

Susan had lost the battle, but in the end she won the war. Asked if she had anything to say before being sentenced, she rose to speak.

"Yes, Your Honor, I have many things to say, for in your ordered verdict of guilty you have trampled underfoot every vital principle of our government. My natural rights, my civil rights, my political rights, my judicial rights are all alike ignored."

Judge Hunt, impatient, interrupted Susan. He ordered her not to go on. But she would not stop speaking. "The prisoner must sit down—the court cannot allow it," bellowed the judge, banging his gavel.

As her sentence, Judge Hunt imposed a fine of one hundred dollars.

"May it please Your Honor," began Miss Anthony, "I will never pay a dollar of your unjust penalty." Instead, declared Susan, she would continue to do just what she had been doing—educate all women "to rebel against your man-made, unjust, unconstitutional forms of law, which tax, fine, imprison, and hang women, while denying them the right of representation in government. . . .

"And," she continued, "I shall earnestly and persistently continue to urge all women to the practical recognition of the old Revolutionary maxim, 'Resistance to tyranny is obedience to God.' "

Since Susan refused to pay the hundred-dollar fine, Judge Hunt could have sent her to jail. But then she would have had the right to appeal her case to the United States Supreme Court. Instead he announced that he would not commit her to prison. Miss Anthony, of course, never paid the fine.

The trial was a high point in the history of the women's rights movement as well as in the life of Susan B. Anthony. From that moment on, as she advanced into old age, Susan became the leading figure in the movement, even better known than Elizabeth Cady Stanton. She was revered almost as a saint.

Newspapers, which so often in the past had ridiculed her plain looks and

Susan B. Anthony at her desk, surrounded by photographs of women's rights leaders. *The Library of Congress.*

dull speaking voice, now praised her. They spoke of her snow-white hair and erect posture, her grandmotherly qualities, her wit. People came to think of her as the very symbol of the women's rights movement.

Wherever she went she was the center of attention. Just the mention of her name drew applause. When she was introduced at one conference, the cheering lasted for fifteen minutes. Men threw their hats in the air, women

their handkerchiefs. At women's rights conferences in London (1899) and Berlin (1904) she was described as "Susan B. Anthony of the world" and, more simply, as "our Aunt Susan." More than anyone else Susan B. Anthony laid the groundwork for passage in 1920 of the Nineteenth Amendment, giving the vote to women.

She did not live to see that victory. In 1906, at the age of eighty-six, Susan B. Anthony died. Less than a month earlier, at a women's convention in Baltimore, she had given her last speech. In it, with the courage and single-minded spirit that marked her life, she had urged her listeners that in the future of the women's movement there was only one certainty: *"Failure is impossible."*

Andrew Carnegie

1835–1919   Donor of much of his fortune to work on behalf of world peace, the improvement of teaching, and the construction of public libraries

If you knew that every month for the rest of your life you would receive at least $1 million, what would you do with the money?

In 1901 Andrew Carnegie sold his giant Carnegie Steel Company. Interest from his share of the sale price would bring him no less than $1 million a month, for life. What did he do with the money? He gave it all away! Indeed, during the last eighteen years of his life he gave away nearly $350 million.

The lives of rich men, said Carnegie, are divided into two parts. The first part is for getting money. The second should be for giving it away.

Carnegie thought that men who became rich were very special people. Like the tiger in the jungle, they were the strongest, the quickest, the most intelligent. That was why they were rich. But they should not keep the money for themselves. That would be selfish. They owed it to the rest of humanity to make the world a better place in which to live. By giving away their money carefully, rich men could make a better world.

Andrew Carnegie did not always have money to give away. In 1848, at the age of thirteen, he came to America from Scotland. He came with his father, mother, and younger brother, Thomas. His mother borrowed the money from friends to pay for their passage. In Scotland times were so hard that Andrew's father could find no work.

Young Carnegie's first job in America was in a cotton mill near Pittsburgh. He was one of the bobbin boys, who changed spools of thread on the machines. For working six days a week from sunrise to sunset his pay was $1.20.

Carnegie did not stay a bobbin boy for long. He was quick witted and had a good memory and a fine sense of humor. He got along well with people. Soon he was an engine tender. Then he became a telegraph messenger, at $2.50 a week. His bosses noticed how fast he worked and how he thought of better ways to do whatever job he had.

Carnegie did not waste a minute. As he waited for telegraph messages to deliver, he read the plays of William Shakespeare and the poetry of Robert Burns. Although he did not believe in God, he read the Bible carefully, since he thought it was an important book. He read about the ancient Greeks and Romans. Every Saturday night he borrowed books from a man in Pittsburgh. That man had his own library of four hundred books, which he lent to working boys. Before long Carnegie was writing letters to the *New York Tribune* about politics, especially about slavery, which he detested.

The habits of reading and study stayed with Carnegie all his life. He taught himself so much that, later, he could be comfortable with men who had far more formal schooling than he.

Carnegie also taught himself Morse code, the telegraph operator's alphabet of dots and dashes. At the age of sixteen he was a telegraph operator at a wage of four dollars a week.

One man who watched young Carnegie's work with interest was Thomas A. Scott, an official of the Pennsylvania Railroad. Scott hired the youngster as his private secretary and telegraph operator. The pay was thirty-five dollars a month. To Carnegie it was a fortune. But he was such a good worker that Scott considered it a bargain rate.

Two years later William Carnegie, Andrew's father, died. Andrew was now head of the family, supporting his mother and younger brother. At that time he promised to take his mother back someday for a visit to their native town of Dunfermline, Scotland. She no longer would be poor, as she was when they left, but dressed in silks, riding in a carriage of her own.

Margaret Morrison Carnegie lived to see her son become one of the richest men in the world. He kept his promise to her, and much more. She could have anything she wanted. Few ladies in the royal families of Europe lived as well as she. Andrew did not marry until after his mother died.

Step by step Carnegie worked his way to better jobs with the Pennsylvania Railroad. Thomas Scott boasted to friends about his "clever little white-haired devil." Meanwhile, with Scott's help, Carnegie began to buy stock—shares in companies. First he spent small amounts of money, then more and more. If he made any extra money, he used it to buy more stock, or he put his cash to work in ways that would make still more money.

During the Civil War, Carnegie organized the telegraph service of the United States Army. It was a great success. In that way Carnegie played an important part in winning the war for the North. He also helped to start Pullman sleeping-car service for the Pennsylvania Railroad. His Pullman Company stock brought him a handsome profit.

After the war Carnegie made an important decision. He gave up his job with the railroad. He decided there was more money to be made in the iron business. Railroad trains were getting heavier and faster. The old wooden railroad bridges needed to be replaced by iron ones. New iron railroad tracks were being laid all across the country.

Carnegie joined with a few friends to establish the Keystone Bridge Company. In 1867 he built the Eads Bridge across the Mississippi River at St. Louis. At the insistence of engineer James B. Eads, Carnegie used only the finest iron and steel parts, producing a truly magnificent bridge. People marveled that the bridge's slender steel arches could support such a great weight. After that, new orders poured in.

Carnegie and his brother, Tom, set up their own ironworks near Pittsburgh. But Andrew had the good sense to let others look after the business of making the iron. He himself was a supersalesman. Among his old friends were the presidents of such railroads as the B & O (Baltimore and Ohio) and the Pennsylvania. He convinced them to let the Keystone Bridge Company build their iron bridges and make their rails.

Business boomed. At the age of thirty-three Andrew Carnegie was making fifty thousand dollars a year.

It was at that time that Carnegie wrote to himself a now-famous note, declaring that in just two more years he would have enough money to retire. Then he planned to attend Oxford University in England and gain a sound education. With that background he would buy a newspaper and be active in public affairs for the rest of his life.

Nothing like that ever happened. Instead, on his business trips to England, Carnegie learned about a new way to make steel. The discovery changed his life. Until about 1870, steel was very

Andrew Carnegie with his dog. *Culver Pictures*.

Andrew Carnegie (left foreground) in 1885 at a Pennsylvania Railroad tunnel. *Culver Pictures*.

expensive. But then an English inventor, Henry Bessemer, found a way to turn iron into steel cheaply.

No time could have been better for the discovery. Good, tough steel had a thousand uses. It could be used for buildings. Steel, in fact, made possible the tall, new buildings known as skyscrapers. It could be used for railroad bridges and tracks. Navies and steamship lines could use it for the new metal ships that were fast replacing wooden sailing vessels. America was growing. It gobbled up all the steel that could be produced.

Carnegie decided to abandon all of his other business interests. The choice, as he described it, meant "putting all of his eggs in one basket and then watching the basket."

Having made his decision, Carnegie at once plunged into action. He bought the best ore lands near Lake Superior, in the Mesabi mountain range, so he always would have his own supply of iron. He built his own fleet of ships to carry iron from the mines to his furnaces. He bought coal fields. Watching every penny of expenses, he slashed his costs and sold steel cheaper than anyone else. Between 1875 and 1900, he dropped the price of his steel from $160 to $17 a ton—and still made a profit.

One rival after another gave up the fight against Carnegie. His profits grew. In 1900 the Carnegie Steel Company made a $40 million profit, $25 million of that amount going to Carnegie himself. His steel was used in the Brooklyn Bridge, in the Washington Monument, in the New York City elevated railroad, and in thousands of buildings across the nation.

One reason for Carnegie's success was his ability to hire the right men. In his words, he looked for men "far cleverer than myself." In the end Carnegie had about forty partners in the business, even though he kept most of the stock himself. Each partner was given a share in the company according to how good a job he did. That incentive made his partners redouble their efforts.

It also made them drive their own workers harder. Day laborers in Carnegie steel mills worked twelve hours a day, seven days a week, firing the blast furnaces and lifting heavy steel balls into molds. Steelworkers, most of them Italians, Poles, and Slavs, were tough. To survive the noise and heat of the furnaces, day after day, they had to be.

Carnegie left most of the problems of handling his workers to a close assistant, Henry Clay Frick. In 1892 a strike broke out at the Homestead, Pennsylvania, mills. To force the strikers back to work, Frick called in private armed guards known as Pinkertons. A bloody battle took place. Many on both sides were killed. Even though Carnegie himself was away on vacation at his castle in Scotland, the public blamed him for the trouble.

Carnegie denied nothing. He showed no sorrow for what had happened at Homestead. But he and Frick soon split up after a bitter quarrel. Years later, secretly, without using his own name, Carnegie gave pensions to the Homestead strikers or to their widows and orphans.

Some of Carnegie's most trusted partners started out as common laborers. Charles M. Schwab, his right-hand man, started as a stake driver at one dollar a day. Every man tried to do his best for Carnegie, knowing the possible rewards.

Another reason for Carnegie's success was his optimism. Even during hard times in the United States, particularly during the depressions of 1873 and 1893, he remained confident of recovery. As a result he kept all of his workers at their jobs, bought new equipment, improved his buildings. He did all of this when prices were low. Then when prosperity returned—as he was sure it would—Carnegie was ready and could sell steel for lower prices than any of his rivals.

By the year 1900, he was master of the United States steel industry. He could make steel at lower cost than anyone in America or Europe. He had helped establish the United States as the largest producer of steel in the world. And it was steel that made the United States the leader among all the world's industrial nations.

Just then—at the peak of his success—Andrew Carnegie retired. In 1901 he sold all of his properties to J. Pierpont Morgan and a group of men who had founded the United States Steel Corporation. The sale price was almost half a billion dollars. After signing the papers Carnegie turned to Morgan with a sigh of relief. "Well, Pierpont," he said, "I am now handing the burden over to you."

For nearly twenty years afterward, Carnegie did the things he most enjoyed. He read, traveled, listened to fine music, collected art, wrote books

A 1903 cartoon in *Judge* magazine depicts Carnegie's donations to the public.

about his ideas—and gave away money.

At the age of sixty-five, Carnegie was more certain than ever that his success was due not to luck but to hard work. Like the scientist Charles Darwin, he believed that all of life was a struggle. Only the fittest—the strongest and most clever—survive; the weak die. In the business jungle, Carnegie had survived. He had made millions of dollars, so he must be one of the "fittest." He must be one of the "best."

But being one of the fittest was not

enough, said Carnegie. For the human race to advance and become stronger it must always seek out the fittest people and help them to become leaders. As leaders they could do the most good for humanity. Indefinitely into the future, argued Carnegie, things would continue improving for the human race, if only the "fittest" were left free to succeed.

Therefore Carnegie did not give money away to just anyone. If he had simply distributed his money among the poor, each person would have received only a few cents. Instead he gave with great care. He helped, for example, to pay for twenty-eight hundred libraries in the United States and the British Empire, at a cost of $60 million. Boys like himself, he said, could improve their minds by reading, even if they could not stay in school very long. Those with the most ability would then fight their way to the top in life.

The same reasoning characterized the $30 million Carnegie gave to American and British universities. He directed his gifts mostly to smaller, less well-known schools, not the schools of the rich. He wanted the children of poor workers to have a chance for a college education, too. Without a college education it would be hard for them to compete against rich boys. The

rich could pay for good schooling in the best colleges. The poor could not. Carnegie wanted all the players in the game of life to have an equal chance. He was sure that, if they did, the "fittest" would win.

Carnegie also gave large amounts of money for pensions for teachers and for his steelworkers. He gave money for a college in Pittsburgh—Carnegie Institute—which was to be especially concerned with science. He made possible the Carnegie Hero Fund, which gave medals and sometimes cash for bravery in time of peace. Finally, he gave $125 million to the Carnegie Corporation of New York to carry on his work after his death.

Through the years Carnegie came to know many of the world's great men. He was friendly with the British prime ministers William Gladstone and David Lloyd George and with such American leaders as James G. Blaine and Theodore Roosevelt. But his favorite friends were writers—Mark Twain, Matthew Arnold, Herbert Spencer. Carnegie himself wrote many books and articles. He called one book *Triumphant Democracy*. In it he explained why life in a republic like the United States was better than life in England or any other country ruled by a king.

Yet Carnegie never forgot his love for England and Scotland. In 1898 he built a magnificent home in Scotland, Skibo Castle. He and his wife used to spend six months of every year there. At Skibo Castle he flew from the same flagpole both the American Stars and Stripes and the British Union Jack. He always believed that the two great English-speaking nations should work together for a better world.

Throughout his life Andrew Carnegie hated war. During the Civil War he had helped to load wounded Union soldiers, their bodies broken and drenched in blood, onto railroad cars to be taken to hospitals. He thought it senseless for men to kill each other "like wild beasts." It especially pained him to see steel used to make guns and bullets—the tools of death. To him, steel should be used only to build greater civilizations.

Carnegie gave $10 million to the Endowment for International Peace, which hoped to do away with war. He built the Peace Palace at The Hague, in Holland, where he hoped nations would settle their problems by talking instead of fighting.

In 1898 the United States went to war with Spain and, as a result, occupied such territories as Cuba, Puerto Rico, and the Philippine Islands. Andrew Carnegie spoke out strongly in protest. He feared that owning lands overseas would draw the nation into still other wars. Americans would become a warlike people who would come to love the idea of armies and navies.

In 1907 Carnegie visited with Kaiser Wilhelm II, the leader of Germany, in the hope of keeping Europe at peace. But in August 1914, what he most dreaded happened. A great war, World War I, began. Carnegie never was the same after that. Before the war he had been happy and still bursting with energy despite being nearly eighty years old.

As the war continued, he knew that steel bullets were killing the "fit" as well as the "unfit." The bullets could not tell the difference. Carnegie kept more and more to himself, saw few of his many friends, and stopped work on the story of his life, which he had been writing. In August 1919 Andrew Carnegie died.

Historians have not always been kind to Carnegie. They speak of him as hardhearted and shrewd. They point out that he paid low wages to his workers. Through cutthroat competition he ruined his rivals in business. But Carnegie never saw the world of business as a Sunday-school class. It was a jungle. And, as in the animal kingdom, beasts such as the dinosaurs, which were not strong, clever fighters, simply died out. Carnegie intended to survive.

There were other sides to Carnegie,

too. Contemporaries described him as fascinating, exciting. A bouncy little man—only five feet two inches tall, with flashing blue eyes and white hair—he loved conversation. He talked fast, thought fast, made up his mind fast. It was hard for him to sit still. Constantly walking, he would throw his arms about, sometimes even jumping as he talked. But he knew when to stay quiet and listen, and always was willing to let others speak up, convincing him if they could that he was wrong.

Today new laws make it impossible for one person to monopolize an entire industry the way Carnegie controlled the steel industry. Taxes take some of the profits. Nor are Americans so willing to trust the business community as they were in Carnegie's time. They have seen too many scandals, too many examples of greed and corruption in business. So—for good or ill—it is doubtful that the nation ever again will see the likes of Andrew Carnegie.

Samuel Gompers

1850–1924   Fighter for higher wages, shorter hours, and better working conditions for union members

Samuel Gompers was a leader of workers. He organized one of America's great labor unions, the American Federation of Labor (AFL), and spent a lifetime attempting to win for workers a fairer share of what they themselves had produced.

From his early boyhood he knew what it was like to be a worker and to be poor. Born in London, until the age of ten he attended a Jewish day school in the city's East End. Then he had to drop out of school and go to work, helping his father, a cigar maker.

Even with Samuel's help the family could not meet the basic expenses of food and shelter. A children's song that Samuel would sing told of America, a land of opportunity. Samuel's father, listening to the song one day, made up his mind to leave England.

In 1863, when Samuel was thirteen, the family sailed for America, settling in New York City, the nation's great center for cigar making.

Having hoped for a better life, the Gompers family found Manhattan's Lower East Side not very different from London's East End. They worked in their tiny apartment, rolling and shaping large brown tobacco leaves into cigars. Day after day, that was all they did. Their rooms were dark and cold, with no running water. When they needed water, they trudged to a barrel in the street and carried some back.

More than anything else, Sam Gompers wanted an education. At the end of a day's work, he was exhausted, eager for nothing more than to drop into bed and fall asleep. Instead he attended Cooper Union, a school with free evening classes for workers. There he listened to lectures. He studied.

Cigar making was difficult to learn. Yet once a worker mastered the technique he could do it almost without thinking. The most expensive cigars were not made in people's homes but in special shops and factories. There, highly skilled workers sat next to each other on benches and worked at long, low tables. While they worked swiftly away with their fingers, one of the men would read aloud to the others from a book or newspaper. Afterward the reader sometimes would lead a discussion of what he had read. In that way the workers filled the long hours and learned at the same time. Since the men were paid for the number of cigars they made, each worker made a few extra cigars to pay the reader for his time away from work.

Samuel Gompers was blessed with a fine, deep voice. He read well. The men in his shop often gave him extra turns at reading. They were not disappointed. He chose books that interested them, books about politics and labor unions.

As he learned more, Gompers began to believe that the cigar makers should formally organize a union. By joining together, they could ask for higher pay and shorter hours. As Gompers explained, the union also could collect dues and establish a reserve fund. In that way, when a man became sick or injured and unable to work, his family would not starve. The union would be capable of caring for its members in good times and bad.

Many of the cigar makers were afraid to form a union. They feared that the company owners, threatened by the possibility of having to pay higher wages, would respond in anger and fire them. Also, the bosses of cigar factories often owned the apartment houses where their workers lived. They could force the men and their families out onto the streets.

Gompers kept trying to bring all cigar makers into the union. He felt sorriest for the unskilled workers. Usually these were whole families who worked in cramped and dirty apartment buildings, called tenement houses. They received even lower pay than cigar workers in the shops. In such homes the children, some as young as five or six years of age, could not go to school. They were needed for the income they contributed to the family. The children awoke at dawn and did nothing all day but cut and roll the tobacco leaves. They had no time for school or play, only work.

In the late evening they often just fell asleep on the floor, too tired to move. The next day they had to begin all over again.

In 1877 the Cigarmakers' International Union went on strike for higher pay and better housing. By then Samuel Gompers had become the union president. He spoke to cigar makers at meetings and in their homes. "Join the union," he said. "We are all in danger."

Gompers was right. Because of the strike, the bosses decided to teach the workers a lesson. They made some workers move out of the tenement buildings. They refused to buy cigars from any of the families still working at home. Then they stopped paying the skilled workers in the shops and factories.

The union set up soup kitchens where workers could get food. It tried to find housing for those with no place to live. The union even tried to set up its own shop and make and sell cigars.

But the bosses were too strong for the cigar makers. The bosses could hold out longer than the workers, who had to take care of their families. One by one the cigar makers began going back to work in the dirty, run-down tenement buildings at their old pay, discouraged and beaten.

Losing the strike was a serious blow for Samuel Gompers himself. All the bosses in New York knew he was the leader of the strikers. None of them would hire him. He went from place to place looking for work. Always the answer was "No!"

At the age of seventeen Gompers had married a working girl named Sophia. The Gomperses' first child was ill, and Sophia was expecting a second child. Sam Gompers sold everything he owned to buy food and pay the rent. He even sold his winter coat. Sophia made soup out of water, salt, pepper, and flour.

Gompers knew that if he quit the union he could get work. One owner offered him thirty dollars a week—much more than he had ever made before—if he would leave the union.

As a man with a family to support, he was tempted by the offer. Was the union really that important to him? Gompers weighed the choices. Then he turned down the offer. From that time on, he was certain that working with unions would be his career.

Gompers had learned much in losing the cigar makers' strike of 1877. He now saw the importance of a reserve fund saved from the workers' union dues. Then, when the next strike came, the union would have a better chance to win. With more money in reserve it would be possible to hold out longer.

Gompers also learned that for a strike

to succeed, every worker had to be a union member. If all the skilled workers did not go out on strike together, the factory owners always would win. The owners would have no difficulty finding skilled workers to replace just a few strikers.

Gompers had still another problem to consider. What if all the cigar makers in New York City belonged to the union, but cigar makers in Philadelphia, Boston, and other places did not? During a strike the owners could transport workers from those cities to take the place of strikers. Every cigar maker in the nation had to belong.

In 1879 Gompers founded a new union. It included all the cigar makers in the United States. When one local branch called a strike all the other "locals" supported it. Because of the fine leadership of Sam Gompers, the cigar makers' union became one of the strongest unions in the nation.

Gompers did not stop there. He began putting together a union that would unite all skilled workers of every trade in the entire country. It would join together the plumbers, electricians, carpenters—all workers with skills—into one big union.

He wanted only skilled workers. That was because in time of strikes it was relatively easy to replace the unskilled. Two great unions in America had tried

to include all workers, no matter what their skills. But both had failed. Some said it was selfish of Gompers to think only of the needs of the skilled workers, who least needed help. He answered that it was important to start someplace and win victories for labor. The skilled workers were more likely to win.

When he started putting together his "union of unions," Gompers was only thirty-two years old. To make himself look older, he grew a large walrus mustache. He was an amusing little figure as he went around the nation, barely five feet four inches tall, with short legs and a barrel chest, yet speaking with a deep, resonant voice. So great was his energy that he could travel and speak to crowds for several days at a time with only snatches of sleep in between.

Gompers was proud of his strength, saying in his old age, "I never got tired and never gave any thought to my body. The Gomperses," he remarked, "are built of oak."

He needed every ounce of his strength and energy to build the great national union he dreamed of heading. Month after month he worked away. Finally, in 1886, the leaders of twenty-five unions met in Columbus, Ohio, and agreed to form the American Federation of Labor, the AFL. Sam Gompers was elected its first president and given

Samuel Gompers photographed in West Virginia around 1890 during an organizational drive among striking coal miners. *The George Meany Memorial Archives.*

$160.52 to set up a national office for the union in Manhattan.

The AFL, which was to become America's strongest union, started in one room on the East Side of New York. The Gomperses' kitchen table was the main piece of furniture in the office. Wooden grocery crates served as file cabinets. And President Gompers himself sat on a box, working at his daughter Rose's little writing desk. Sometimes there was not even enough money for a bottle of ink, and Gompers's son, Henry, had to borrow a bottle from a neighborhood public school.

With Gompers as its leader, the AFL grew rapidly. Often using his own money to travel from place to place, Gompers wrote and spoke tirelessly in an attempt to build union membership. He met with workers. He dealt with management. He absorbed existing unions into the AFL.

In working with member unions he never tried to force them to adopt his policies. Instead he suggested ideas and relied on his powers of persuasion to win them over. Usually they accepted his reasoning.

In every year except one, for the rest of his life, Samuel Gompers was elected president of the AFL.

The union was a success mainly because Gompers understood American workers. He knew what they wanted.

One thing they wanted was shorter hours. He was able to win a reduction in the hours of skilled workers from ten hours a day to nine, then to eight, the standard workday even now.

Gompers persuaded many companies to buy insurance for workers who might be hurt on the job. Then, if a man was injured, the insurance paid his medical bills. It paid all or part of his salary, too, so that his family would have food and a place to live.

For men who became too old to work, Gompers won pensions. The workers could retire and not have to depend on their children to support them, or die in a poorhouse.

Gompers helped show Americans how terrible it was to let little children work in mines and factories. He argued that children should be learning in schools and playing in the fresh air.

Most important, Gompers helped the workers in his union get higher and higher wages for their work. Whenever he was asked what the union wanted, he answered, "More! More! More! Now!" By this he meant more money, more free time, more pleasant places to work, more of the good things of American life for the workers—and right away.

Not everyone agreed with the policies of Samuel Gompers. Some still believed that the union should include

Samuel Gompers in a 1919 parade in Washington, D.C. *Brown Brothers.*

unskilled workers. Others were angry
when Gompers began working to end
immigration to the United States. They
reminded him that he himself had been
an immigrant from Great Britain. Was
it right to stop others from sharing the
opportunity of America? Gompers
replied that jobs were scarce and immigrants would work for very little money.
Since that made it hard for people already in America, said Gompers, the
doors to the United States had to be
closed. In part because labor leaders
such as Gompers spoke so strongly,
immigration was almost completely
halted.

Other critics charged that Gompers
was wrong to spend so much of his time
talking with rich and powerful men,
such as President Theodore Roosevelt
or John D. Rockefeller, the owner of
the Standard Oil Company. Gompers
answered that, if necessary, he would
"talk to the devil—if it would help labor." He would do anything to get more
money and better conditions for his
men.

Gompers's greatest enemies were the
Socialists. Socialists such as Eugene V.
Debs said Gompers did not go far
enough in trying to fight the owners
of factories. The factories should belong

to the workers, said Debs. The government of the United States should be run by the workers. Then the country would be farther along on the road to perfection.

To Gompers that was foolish talk. He was not interested in perfection. That might never happen. He did not want to hurt anyone—not even the factory owners. He only wanted workers to have a better life each and every day. That, he said, was what labor unions were all about. Workers did not have to run the government to win more money and better housing. Their unions would get those things for them. America didn't have to be destroyed and rebuilt on the ashes, only reformed—changed. Socialists, declared Gompers, were only starry-eyed dreamers.

By 1920 the AFL included on its rolls more than four million members. It was powerful. People listened when labor leaders spoke. And Gompers was the best-known labor leader in America. He even traveled with President Woodrow Wilson to the peace conference that ended World War I. He helped to found the International Labor Organization (ILO), which was concerned with the problems of labor in every country of the world. He personally began working on a union of all skilled craftsmen in Latin America.

But Gompers was getting old. He was hurt in a taxicab accident. His eyes grew weak. Still he refused to slow down. He kept on traveling. In 1924 he was elected president of the AFL for the last time. A few weeks before his seventy-fifth birthday, he died.

In his last speech he once again showed his confidence in American workers, saying, "We shall never stop. Some of us may and will pass over to the Great Beyond, but there are others who will rise and take our place and do as well if not better than we have done."

Perhaps, as Gompers's enemies charged, he was not sufficiently interested in radical change in the United States. Perhaps he was too exclusively interested in winning union demands for higher pay and shorter hours.

In Gompers's mind there never was any real question that he might be wrong. He was absolutely certain that he was right. To the end of his life he stuck to his one great aim for American workers—"More!"

Jane Addams

1860–1935   Leader in America's settlement house movement; founder of Hull House in Chicago

Halsted Street, Chicago. 1889. A blistering hot summer day.

Garbage is everywhere. The broken pavement is covered with spoiled fruits and vegetables, papers, bottles—rubbish of every kind. In places the garbage is several inches deep. The alleys running off Halsted Street, near Polk Street, smell like open sewers. The few real sewers are not attached to the broken-down wooden houses and dark, dirty tenement buildings that line the street. There are no toilets in the houses. Courtyards are thick with cockroaches—and crawling babies. Rats dart to and fro. In some of the basements, sheep are slaughtered. The smell hangs in the air. Oily rags collected from the city dump line the walls of rooms, covering cracks. There are no fire escapes.

In dirty cellars under the sidewalk, bakers make bread. Tubs of milk stand uncovered to buzzing swarms of flies.

It was to this neighborhood that two well-dressed, attractive young ladies first came during the summer of 1889. Both of these young ladies were in their late twenties. They hoped—of all things—to rent a house on Halsted Street. Most well-dressed people wouldn't even go near such a street. Who were these women?

One was Jane Addams. The other was her good friend, Ellen Starr. As they made their way along the crowded sidewalks of Halsted Street, people scarcely noticed them. The two listened silently to the shouts and busy chatter of voices in many languages—Polish, Greek, German, Russian, Yiddish, Italian. At the time, three of every four Chicagoans were immigrants. Settlers from more than twenty nations lived in the Halsted Street neighborhood. There, on Halsted Street, the two ladies found a large old house that was just right for their purposes.

They were going to start a settlement house. It would be a place where poor people could learn to help themselves. If the idea worked in Chicago, it could work in other cities. And then America would be a better place.

Jane Addams and Ellen Starr called the house they had chosen Hull House. Along with the many women who later worked there, it would become famous throughout the world.

What was it that brought Jane Addams to Hull House? Why did she decide to spend her life helping others?

As a child Jane Addams often was ill. She was born with a crooked back and walked with her head to one side. It was painful for her to ride horseback, and she could not run and play with other children. Instead she read much and thought much. Early pictures show her as a serious child with sad, dreamy eyes.

Still, she had a comfortable childhood. Her wealthy father owned a flour mill and a sawmill in a small Illinois town. A well-known man in the state, Addams served in the state legislature and at one time even was considered for the governorship.

Jane adored her father. She believed everything he said. She even tried to copy his ways of speech. Since he awoke before dawn to read for several hours, so did she. Thinking herself ugly, she did not want to be seen in public with her father. Jane did not like to feel that "strange people should know my handsome father owned such a homely little girl."

As early as the age of six, Jane Addams thought about her responsibilities in life. Again and again she dreamed at night that she was the only person left on earth. Nothing could be done to start the business of the world again until someone made a wagon wheel. She knew it was a job that only she could do, but she did not know how.

Also at the age of six, she saw poor people for the first time. She learned that being poor had something to do with housing. It was then she promised herself that when she grew up she would go to the city. She would have a big house like her own. But it would not be alongside other big, beautiful houses. She would put it right in the middle of all the "horrid little houses."

Very few six-year-olds think the thoughts Jane Addams did. She was a very "different" kind of child.

At Rockford College in Illinois, Jane

Jane Addams with her mother and brother George around 1876. *Jane Addams Memorial Collection, Special Collections, The University Library, University of Illinois at Chicago.*

graduated with the highest grades in her class. But she did more than just study. She took part in almost every school activity. Although she was shy, she taught herself to be a good public speaker. Once she participated in a speaking contest with students from other colleges. Among the other contestants was a young man about whom the United States would hear much. His name was William Jennings Bryan. Neither Miss Addams nor Bryan won the speaking contest.

At Rockford Jane had a romance with a young man named Rollin Salisbury. He asked her to marry him. She refused. Later he became a famous professor at the University of Chicago. For many years he worked only six miles from Hull House in Chicago. Legend says that he never once stepped inside the door.

After graduating from college Jane Addams enrolled in medical school. She hoped to become a doctor and work among the poor, but after one year she had to drop out because of poor health. Her doctor suggested that travel and relaxation might help.

Miss Addams traveled through Europe. But she did not relax. She visited the slums of London. There she saw starving women and children clawing at each other to get at rotting food already marked "not fit to eat." It was a horrible sight. She never forgot it.

While in London she visited a settlement house called Toynbee Hall. Workers could go there at night for classes. Children could play games. Students from Oxford University were in charge of Toynbee Hall. Even though the Oxford men were from wealthy families, they wanted to do something for less fortunate people.

That seemed important to Jane Addams. As the daughter of a wealthy man she had been allowed to get an education. But as a woman she was not really expected to do anything with it.

Was her life worth much, she asked, if she could not do anything with her knowledge? Suddenly, while watching a bullfight in Madrid, Spain, she decided to stop just thinking about helping the poor and actually do something. She would fight!

At that moment in Madrid, she saw in her mind exactly what she would do with her life. She would give other wealthy young women a chance to use their educations, just as the Oxford men had used theirs at Toynbee Hall in London.

Miss Addams returned to America. Just before her twenty-first birthday, her father had died. He had left her an inheritance. She saved all of that money and still had enough extra of her own to begin looking in Chicago for the house she needed to begin her work.

The house she found was Hull House. It had belonged to a wealthy real-estate man named Charles J. Hull, who once had been a penniless orphan boy. He had never forgotten the days of his childhood and had always tried to help the poor. When Jane Addams and Ellen Starr discovered Hull House, the ground floor was being used as a saloon, the second floor as a furniture factory.

At his death Charles Hull had willed the house to his niece. She first rented one floor of it to Jane Addams, then later leased the entire house to her, free of charge.

In September 1889 Jane Addams and Ellen Starr joyfully moved into Hull House, bringing with them their own furniture and works of art.

At first the people of Halsted Street were suspicious of the two well-dressed women. Why would wealthy young ladies want to live in such a slum? Gradually Miss Addams and Miss Starr

Ellen Starr and Jane Addams at Hull House around 1902. *Jane Addams Memorial Collection, Special Collections, The University Library, University of Illinois at Chicago.*

proved that they wanted only to be good neighbors and friends.

They began by setting up a reading room and a kindergarten. Many years later one of the first "guests" remembered "the soft words of the women of Hull House, the only soft and kind words we immigrant boys heard in those days."

Before long, Jane Addams busied herself with many things—washing newborn babies, taking care of children, nursing the sick, arranging for funerals, helping single working girls find clean, safe places to live.

Ellen Starr loved art. Because of her work, a wealthy Chicago merchant presented a gift of five thousand dollars to Hull House for the building of an art gallery. That was important to Jane

Addams, too. She and Miss Starr both believed that human beings could not live in the ugliness of factories and slums. Surrounded by all that ugliness they would become less human, more like animals, unless somehow they could keep their love of beauty. Art was not just a frill. It was at the heart of what they were trying to do.

Shortly after the art gallery was built, the ladies opened a public kitchen. There the people of the neighborhood could buy good, nourishing food at low prices. They learned how to cook better and how to spend their food money wisely. But the immigrants were far more interested in books and paintings than in the kitchen. They flocked to the art gallery. They came in great numbers to the reading room.

One immigrant boy who later became a writer remembered that Hull House "was the first house I had ever been in where books and magazines just lay around as if there were plenty of them in the world."

It was hard for people living on Halsted Street to remember the beauty of nature. All around them they saw concrete and ugliness. So Jane Addams arranged for the children to go to camps along Lake Michigan. She also planned trips to the country for the adults. Some of the adults did not know there were lovely places in America. They thought the whole nation was like the streets of Chicago.

As the newspapers began to write about Hull House, many wealthy young women were drawn there. Like Jane Addams and Ellen Starr, they wanted to do their share in making a better world. And they had the education and free time to do something about it.

With more helpers the activities of Hull House grew. There was a playground for children—the first one in Chicago—so that youngsters would not have to play in the streets. There were clubs and classes for young people who had to work and could not go to high school. There was a music school. There was a nursery where working mothers could leave their children during the day. People were asked to pay a small amount of money for these services so they would not feel they were taking charity. The idea of Hull House was not to give charity but to help people to help themselves.

Older immigrants had a particularly hard time in America. What could they do in a country where so much of the work was done by machines? At Hull House Jane Addams gave them rooms where they could work on the crafts of their native lands—spinning, weaving, carving, metalworking, rug making. Then they could sell their products.

Before Miss Addams ever launched

her work at Hull House, she underwent surgery to straighten her back. At that time the doctor told her she would never be able to have children of her own. Perhaps because of that, she always had a special place in her heart for the children of Halsted Street. Often she told of an incident when several little girls surprised her by refusing to take candy she wanted to give them. She learned that they had been working for weeks in a candy factory, six days a week from 7 A.M. to 9 P.M., and could not stand the sight of candy. Miss Addams fought hard to win passage of a law putting an end to child labor. Finally, in 1903, she won. The law that halted child labor in Illinois was almost entirely the work of Jane Addams.

She also attacked the problem of children in the prisons. Children accused of even minor crimes customarily were thrown into jail with tough, hardened criminals. Instead of learning to be better citizens, the children often emerged from prison ready for a life of crime. Jane Addams helped establish special juvenile courts, just for youthful offenders. Often she convinced judges not to send children to jail but to put them in her care.

Hull House became a place where anyone in trouble could come. And they came by the thousands—murderers and thieves, or simply young girls who could not afford to buy "proper" wedding dresses. Jane Addams and the women who worked with her never turned anyone away.

The story of Hull House became known throughout the United States, as did the reputation of Jane Addams. Miss Addams often was asked to help with other causes in the field of human rights. She helped, for example, to win passage of an amendment to the Constitution giving women the right to vote. Leaders such as Susan B. Anthony and Carrie Chapman Catt led the way, but Jane Addams also played an important part in winning adoption of the amendment.

Always she was interested in the problem of war. She hated war and thought that women could do much to put an end to it. In this she was disappointed. But she never stopped trying. Even after the United States entered World War I, she refused to admit that the purpose of the war was just. To her, peace was more important than winning any war—no matter how right the reasons for fighting might appear.

At the age of sixty-five, she still worked fourteen, sixteen, even eighteen hours a day. She traveled and gave speeches throughout the world. Every day she worked until she became too dizzy to work anymore.

In her old age she received many

Jane Addams at Yale, where an honorary degree was conferred upon her in 1910. *Brown Brothers.*

honors. Fourteen universities gave her honorary degrees. She received cash awards of as much as twenty-six thousand dollars in a single year, but she kept none of the money for herself. Finally, in 1931, a telegram arrived, telling her of the greatest honor of all—the Nobel Peace Prize. She gave the entire sixteen-thousand-dollar prize to the International League for Peace and Freedom, a group that was trying to put an end to all wars.

The years that followed were quiet ones for Jane Addams. One by one, the women of Hull House died. Then, finally, on May 21, 1935, Jane Addams herself, by then aged and ill, died peacefully in her sleep.

For hours thousands filed past her coffin to say good-bye to the small woman with the crooked back. One little child was heard to say, "Are we all Aunt Jane's children?" And in a way, they were.

In her lifetime Jane Addams had made few personal enemies. She tried to understand even those who opposed her. She shamed politicians into having the garbage cleaned from the streets of Chicago. Factory owners were certain they would go broke if they could not hire children to work for only a few pennies an hour. Jane Addams tried to understand even those men.

Some people consider the methods of someone like Jane Addams too slow in "ridding the world of evil." Change, they think, must be rapid, sweeping. But Jane Addams always knew that even "evil" people do not think they are evil. That is why she was willing to listen, to learn, and to understand the other person. Her way of working for a better world, although perhaps less dramatic or exciting, often achieves more lasting change in people's lives.

William Jennings Bryan

1860–1925   Champion of the rights of farmers

Summertime in Chicago means heat—sweltering heat. Inside the Chicago Coliseum in the summer of 1896 the heat seemed almost too much to bear. From all over the country, delegates to the Democratic National Convention had come to choose their candidate for President of the United States.

The delegates fanned themselves with newspapers. They drank gallons of lemonade. They turned to each other and said things like, "Hot enough for you?" Some even tried to doze.

One dull speaker followed another. Each had his own ideas about what should be done to end the hard times in America. Each claimed to know who was to blame. The speeches droned on and on. People milled in the aisles,

bored. Nobody listened. The chairman pounded his gavel for silence, but the buzzing continued.

Then, suddenly, as if by magic, the crowd became silent. All eyes turned to the tall, slim man at the speaker's stand. His hair was coal black, his nose beaked like an eagle's. His black eyes flashed. His arms reached out as if to bring the entire audience close to him. When he spoke the words rang out clearly. His voice resounded, deep and musical.

No microphones helped him. Yet even in the farthest gallery of the gigantic coliseum, his message could be heard. He seemed to speak easily, effortlessly.

He spoke of the wrongs done to the

poor by America's rich men—the bankers and railroad owners, the stockbrokers and moneylenders.

The audience began to stand and cheer. Even those who did not agree were spellbound. They could not stop listening. As the speaker began each new sentence, the room became as still as a church. Then the stillness would be broken by applause and thunderous shouts.

As he finished, the speaker was swept up in the arms of his listeners. They carried him off on their shoulders. A band played the "Battle Hymn of the Republic" and then "Onward, Christian Soldiers."

The next day the convention chose the handsome young speaker—William Jennings Bryan of Nebraska—as the Democratic party's candidate for president.

Speechmaking was nothing new to William Jennings Bryan. Even as a ten-year-old boy, he had played make-believe "U.S. Senate" with his friends. In Illinois, where he grew up, the public schools often had speaking contests and debates. In a formal debate, speakers from two teams compete against each other in the discussion of a question, such as "Should there be one government for the entire world?" Judges decide which team has argued most effectively. Bryan loved to debate.

After finishing high school he enrolled at Illinois College, a small school. He was on the college debate team. He did not always win his debates. Judges were looking for good ideas. But Bryan cared less about ideas than about pleasing his audiences. He thought that people made up their minds according to their emotions, not their thoughts. So he tried to make the audiences laugh or cry or become excited. At some debates, even though it was against the rules, his listeners stood and cheered him.

Meeting college expenses was hard for Bryan, since his family could not afford to send him much money. To pay for his meals he had to clerk in a hat store. Still, one year he spent all of his clothing allowance on speaking lessons.

Bryan also had to struggle to make good grades. Somehow, however, he managed to graduate at the head of his class. During his college years he thought seriously about religion. At first he was a Baptist; then he became a Presbyterian. Yet he took time to visit all of the local Protestant churches and sometimes even attended Catholic and Jewish services. He also escaped from his studies long enough to court the woman he would later marry.

Busy with so many distractions, Bryan signed out a total of only eigh-

William Jennings Bryan at age twenty-one, the year he entered Union College of Law. *Nebraska State Historical Society.*

teen books from the college library in his four years as a student. Most of those were novels. Aside from reading the Bible he never became much of a reader.

In 1881 he graduated from Illinois College. At the time one of his classmates wrote that twenty years later Will Bryan would be living in the White House. It very nearly happened.

Bryan went to a law school in Chicago and then moved west to Nebraska to open a law office. He started practic-

ing law and won almost all of his court cases. Juries listened to him and believed him. He used simple words that were easy to understand. People trusted him.

But Bryan did not want to be a lawyer for the rest of his life. He had bigger things in mind. He decided to go into politics and run for Congress.

It was easy for Bryan to become a politician. He honestly believed that he could help the people. And as a religious man, he thought that the people were the "children of God." The people spoke through their political leaders— the men they elected. Politics, he reasoned, was therefore a way of making a living while also pleasing God. He could serve the people and serve God at the same time.

In 1890 he ran for the House of Representatives—and won. Two years later he won again.

By this time Bryan thought he knew which ideas were right. He believed in God, hard work, and a life of farming. He thought that the wealth of a nation came from its workers and that when the workers—the common people— suffered hard times, the whole nation suffered.

Bryan knew what hard work meant. He had pitched hay, built fences, dug wells, threshed grain, plowed. He had been poor, too. In his speeches to Congress, he said that farmers and factory workers were tired of being poor. They were tired of having to fight to keep their homes from the banks. They were tired of not being able to feed their families while rich men grew richer.

All through the early 1890s, farmers watched the prices of crops go down, but the prices they had to pay for farms and machinery went up. The prices they had to pay for seed and fertilizer and fencing went up. They borrowed from banks. When the time came to pay back the loans, they discovered that they had to sell more wheat or cotton or corn than they could grow to make the payments.

When the farmers could not pay back their loans, the banks sometimes foreclosed their mortgages. After years of backbreaking work, farmers did not even have roofs over their heads.

Who was to blame? More and more the farmers came to believe that it was the bankers on Wall Street in New York City. Farmers thought there was not enough money in the United States. If only the money supply were increased, they could pay off their debts more easily. But the Wall Street bankers, they charged, refused to permit the United States government to make any kind of money but gold.

Some farmers clamored, quite simply, for the printing of paper money in large quantities. But most western farmers, particularly those from silver-

mining states, thought that silver should be converted into money—as much silver as the mines could produce.

Gold, said the farmers, was the money of the rich. Silver was the money of the poor. Silver would be the answer to their problems.

William Jennings Bryan was not sure at first. Then he decided. The common people were right. Gold was bad. Silver was good. It was as simple as that. Once Bryan made up his mind about something, nothing could make him change. He came to believe completely in silver. He declared one day that anyone who did not agree with the people of the West about silver was either a fool or a criminal—and that was that!

By the time of the Democratic National Convention of 1896, Bryan was well known. People had heard his speeches defending the poor and favoring silver money. His ideas had been printed in the newspapers. But almost nobody thought that the convention, meeting at Chicago, would choose him to run for president. Nobody, that is, except Bryan himself. He was sure that he was going to win.

On the evening of July 8, 1896, as he waited for his turn to speak, Bryan closed his eyes and prayed. Then he squeezed his lucky rabbit's foot. His suit was wrinkled from the heat. His black string tie dangled loosely.

His forehead and even the legs of his trousers were moist with sweat.

But when he began to speak, he forgot all of that. The audience was his. He had practiced the speech for months while traveling through the West. Yet at that moment in Chicago, the speech seemed fresh and new. The anger of the poor — the "have-nots" — spilled from his lips.

His target was the rich—those who wanted only gold dollars. They were the ones who crushed the dreams of poor people. They were the ones who took for themselves what farmers and laborers had sweated to produce.

Bryan came to the end of his speech: "We have entreated and our entreaties have been disregarded. We have begged and they have mocked us when our hour of calamity came." He paused for an instant, then continued, "We beg no longer. We entreat no more. We petition no more."

The applause was deafening. Bryan waited while it slowed, and then—at just the right moment—he added firmly: "We defy them!" Again, applause rolled from the audience.

Who was strong enough to challenge the rich? Bryan punched the air with his fist as he answered his own question: "[T]he producing masses of the nation . . . the laboring interests . . . and toilers everywhere."

He paused again. Then his voice rose to a crescendo. His arms reached skyward and then slashed down to the podium as he declared, "We shall answer their demands by saying to them, *You shall not press down on the brow of labor this crown of thorns, you shall not crucify mankind on a cross of gold!*"

For a few seconds the audience sat in stunned silence. Then there arose a tremendous roar. The crowd went completely wild. People lifted Bryan high and carried him away in a great wave. With the band playing loudly, the crowd, now a mob, marched around the coliseum, madly cheering the new leader of America's poor.

That moment in Chicago was the high point of Bryan's life. At the age of thirty-six he had come from nowhere to win the leadership of the Democratic Party. He had even been forced to borrow one hundred dollars to go to the convention. After paying the hotel bill for himself and his wife, he had had only ten dollars left in his pocket. Today candidates spend millions of dollars to win the nomination of their party.

Bryan did not win the election of 1896. He ran again in 1900 and in 1908, losing those elections, too. But for the rest of his life he was a hero to millions of poor people.

That was not all. One after another of the ideas Bryan fought for were made

William Jennings Bryan speaking at Telluride, Colorado, in 1902. Photograph by Byers and St. Claire. *The Denver Public Library, Western History Department.*

into law—often by the very men who had defeated him in elections. Among those laws were the income tax; direct election of United States senators by the people instead of state legislatures; and voting rights for women. In Bryan's own lifetime gold remained the main kind of money in the United States, but in the presidency of Franklin D. Roosevelt that, too, was changed.

As he grew older, Bryan came to accept his many defeats and even to joke about them. It is possible that he did not really expect to win. After all, he had been only a poor farm boy. To run for president three times may have seemed to him enough of a reward. He was always in the public eye. He had an audience whenever he wanted one. Having an audience was important to Bryan.

As the life of farmers in America became easier, Bryan grew fat, good natured, and rich. He was paid high fees for lecturing. He bought and sold land in Florida, and was paid well to convince people to "Come to Magic Miami." When he died in 1925 the great champion of the American poor was a millionaire.

Bryan was a leader because he understood the people. He knew what the common people of America were thinking because he was one of them. If they had prejudices, so did he. In many ways he was an average American.

But there was a difference. Bryan could put their feelings into words. He could speak in a convincing way. He would listen to what people believed and then become the voice of those ideas. In that way Bryan really was more a follower of the masses than their leader.

Unlike Thomas Jefferson or other great American statesmen, Bryan did not have a fine mind. He had read a little about science, but he still refused to believe in scientific ideas because he thought they made the Bible seem less true. He did not believe in war, either, but he enlisted in the United States Army as soon as war was declared against Spain in 1898. He did not believe in taking land from other countries, but he did more than any other person to win congressional approval for America's seizure of the Philippine Islands from Spain.

Admittedly he had many limitations. And few historians have considered him a "great man." Yet even Bryan's enemies knew he was a person of courage, a man who believed what he said. What he lacked in brainpower he made up for in heart.

It was in touching people's hearts that Bryan did most to change the country. He awakened the nation's sympathy for the poor. Like Jefferson and Jackson, he believed in fair play—an equal chance for all. At the time he delivered his famous "Cross of Gold" address, the poor did not have that chance.

At the time of his death, millions mourned. And no wonder. Few American leaders ever have been more loved by the simple, hardworking people of the nation than William Jennings Bryan.

PART IV

New Frontiers in Human Rights: The Twentieth Century

Emma Goldman

1869–1940   Anarchist and defender of women's right to economic independence

Pug nose, light brown hair falling loosely over her forehead, saucy blue-gray eyes, soft manner. Passersby who noticed Emma Goldman eyeing the shop windows along Fourteenth Street, on the rim of New York's Greenwich Village, might have dismissed her as just another high-school girl, a shopper out for a stroll.

Her real purpose was far more sinister. Emma Goldman was looking for a way to make money—quickly—in order to buy a pistol for her companion, Alexander Berkman, or, as she called him, "Sasha."

She succeeded. With the money she mailed to Berkman, waiting in Pittsburgh, he bought a revolver, as well as a dagger that he dipped in poison. Forcing his way past a porter, he con-fronted Henry Clay Frick, chief assistant to Andrew Carnegie at the Carnegie Steel Corporation.

It was Frick who had turned Pinkerton men—privately paid soldiers—against the striking steelworkers at Carnegie's Homestead steel plant, causing blood to flow like water among the strikers. Now Berkman would take revenge on Frick.

Without a word Berkman pumped three bullets into Frick's body and then, to be absolutely certain of the steel magnate's death, plunged the poisoned dagger into his thigh.

Did Emma Goldman have any regrets in helping Berkman in his plot to kill Henry Clay Frick? Only one: that he had not allowed her to go along with him to do the deed. As she later wrote, she had pleaded with him, " 'I will go with you, Sasha,' I cried; 'I must go with you. I can be of help. I could gain access to Frick easier than you. I could pave the way for your act. Besides, I simply must go with you. Do you understand, Sasha?' "

Miraculously Frick survived. Berkman was sentenced to twenty-two years in prison. Emma Goldman, never implicated in the assassination plan, soon afterward was sentenced to a year in prison for another kind of "crime"— urging hungry people to demand that the government give them work, and if they did not get it, to demand bread. And if they did not get either work or bread, she had cried out, "Take bread! It is your sacred right!"

Emma Goldman was an anarchist— a person who believes that most of the problems of society come from too much government, too much authority. According to anarchists, individuals should be free to think for themselves, should be free to live life without interference from government.

In her own lifetime Emma Goldman came to hate the revolutionary "communist" government of the USSR as much as she hated the capitalist governments of the United States and other Western countries. To her, the Russian Revolution had been betrayed. It had become a tyranny. True freedom, she always insisted, would come only when people were free to shape their own lives according to choices they made for themselves.

How had Emma Goldman, or "Red Emma," as the press liked to call her, gotten her ideas? Why did she devote her life to trying to destroy all governments as a way of helping people?

Born to Jewish parents in Russian Lithuania, Emma suffered through a stormy childhood. At the time of her birth her mother already had two children by an earlier marriage and considered her only an extra burden, another child to care for. Her father, eager for a boy, resented her. He often beat her.

Not only did Emma's family suffer from poverty, they also had to bear the burden of most Jews in Russia—vicious prejudice against them in getting education and jobs, along with periodic violence in bloody attacks known as pogroms. Emma and her family finally escaped to East Prussia, in Germany.

In Germany she received a rigorous but superb education from teachers she came to admire for their intelligence but hate for their brutality to students. Often the teachers whipped their pupils, not only for making mistakes in their studies but also for the sheer pleasure of watching the children suffer.

When Emma was a teenager the

The Goldman family in St. Petersburg, Russia, 1882. Emma is standing at left. *Emma Goldman Papers, Manuscripts and Archives Section, New York Public Library.*

Goldmans returned to Russia, settling briefly in the nation's capital city, Saint Petersburg, today's Leningrad. There Emma read the works of socialist and anarchist writers such as Kropotkin. She met with other young people who held those views.

As a result of her reading she took as a model for her own life the character of Vera Pavlovna in *What Is To Be Done?* Like Vera Pavlovna in Chernyshevsky's novel, Emma found herself embittered by her experience with society and determined to fight for change.

In 1885, when she was sixteen, her father arranged for her to marry a much older man, whom she did not love. Instead Emma fled. She escaped to America, settling in Rochester, New York. At first the only work she could find was in a clothing factory, earning $2.50 a week.

After two years she married a fellow worker. Almost from the beginning the marriage proved to be a failure. She won a divorce. Then, thinking she had been too harsh with her husband, she agreed to remarry him. But the marriage failed again, and she had to go through the pain of a second divorce.

Hoping to start a new life for herself, Emma moved in 1889 to New York City. There she quickly fell under the influence of the two men who were to shape her life—Johann Most, the editor of a radical newspaper, and young Alexander Berkman, a fiery anarchist.

Most and Berkman impressed her at once. Although Most was considerably older than Emma, she found herself attracted to him romantically. She admired his knowledge and the way he showed that, despite his poise and years of experience in radical politics, he needed her. Meanwhile her affection for Alexander Berkman—her "Sasha"— also grew steadily.

Because of the harsh treatment she had received in her childhood and as a factory worker in America, she already distrusted people in authority. Still she had been deeply moved by the high idealism and morality of her Jewish upbringing, as well as by her readings in radical literature.

After meeting Alexander Berkman she grasped eagerly at the anarchist political philosophy he presented to her. It was her way of rebelling against au-

thority, yet remaining hopeful for the future.

According to anarchist teachings, the state (meaning the government) eventually will be replaced by a society of equals—all people working cooperatively, with perfect harmony and peace, for the good of all others.

Most important, anarchists believe that people will behave with love and caring—voluntarily—just as soon as the cause of their misery—government— is removed. That is because, declared the anarchists, people are basically good. It is power—the power of governing—that corrupts them.

Emma Goldman believed in the importance of the "collective" (the community) in bringing about the final state of affairs, the condition of perfect equality. But until then, she believed that individuals had a crucial role to play in winning social justice. Individuals— including individual women—had to be strong and independent.

Her faith in the individual often caused her to disagree with other radicals, especially socialists, who believed much more firmly than she did in collective or group action in achieving human equality.

Early in her career as an anarchist Emma considered violence an acceptable way to bring about change. She claimed to have no regrets about helping Alexander Berkman in his plot to assassinate Henry Clay Frick. When the murder attempt failed, Johann Most, until then a hero to Emma, turned against Berkman. Perhaps Most was beginning to doubt the use of violence—even murder—to create a new society. Perhaps he was only jealous of Emma's love for her Sasha.

Whatever the reason, Emma Goldman was furious with Most. She was especially angered by the newspaper articles he was writing that charged Sasha with acting out of self-interest in trying to kill Frick, not on behalf of the anarchist cause.

Emma bought a horsewhip. Then, at an anarchist lecture, she sharply questioned Most, demanding proof of his charges against Sasha. When his answers failed to satisfy her she pulled out her whip and leaped at him. Again and again she lashed him across the face and neck. Then she broke the whip over her knee and threw the pieces at him.

Johann Most and his supporters never forgave her, and Emma showed no remorse for what she had done. Gradually, however, her own views about violence started to change. She served her year in prison for declaring that workers had a "sacred right" to take bread if they were starving. During her term she worked as a prison nurse.

After her release she studied nursing in Vienna, Austria. She became increasingly interested in *saving* lives rather than *destroying* them.

By 1901, when an insane young man shot President McKinley, Emma Goldman expressed sympathy for the stricken president. She was cleared completely of any involvement in the assassination. Later in her life she declared that acts of violence generally had proved useless in bringing about a better world. Rather, she said, society must be "reconstructed" peacefully.

Miss Goldman eventually became a magnetic, appealing lecturer. Historian Richard Drinnon has described her as "perhaps the most accomplished woman speaker in American history." Despite attempts by the police to silence her, she spoke out on the topics of anarchism, organized religion (which she opposed as a tool of the state), free speech, and women's rights.

On the subject of women's rights, she struck sharply at the practice of marriage. To her it seemed unnecessary for people who respected and loved each other to have to go through a ceremony to prove their affection. And if their love ended, she said, they should simply stop living together. Marriage, she said, paralyzed women, making them dependent on men. As with an "insurance policy," the buyer—a wo-

Emma Goldman in later life. *Culver Pictures*.

man—entered into an economic arrangement in order to protect herself. In exchange she gave up her self-respect and privacy. By holding that the proper relationship between men and women was one of love, Emma Goldman was different from the many feminists who considered themselves "man haters."

From 1906 to 1917 Emma Goldman and Alexander Berkman published the anarchist journal *Mother Earth*. In it they agitated openly against the United States government and the capitalist system. When the United States entered World War I, the two revolutionaries suggested that men stay out of the army or, once enrolled, refuse to fight. In June 1917 both Emma and Sasha were arrested for speaking out against the military draft. Convicted, they spent the next two years behind bars.

At the end of the war a "Red Scare" hit the nation. Communists, Socialists, and anarchists were hounded and persecuted for their beliefs. In December 1919 Miss Goldman and Alexander Berkman, along with 247 other "leftists," were deported to the Soviet Union aboard the transport ship *Buford*, known to the press as the "Red Ark."

In the Soviet Union Emma Goldman quickly became disillusioned with the new communist government. She came to believe that the Bolshevik leaders who had made the Revolution of 1917 had in fact betrayed their followers, not given them the freedom they had promised in overthrowing the old czarist government. Instead, there was brutal repression.

Although Emma spoke out vigorously against the Bolshevik leaders—Lenin, Trotsky, Stalin—most of her radical friends in America did not. They refused to hold the Soviet government to the same high standard that they expected of capitalist governments. Always they seemed to find reasons to excuse what the Soviet leaders did.

Unhappy in the Soviet Union, Emma went to live in Sweden, then Germany, and finally England. To obtain British citizenship she married an Englishman, her third marriage, and lectured extensively in England and Canada. In 1931 she published her autobiography, *Living My Life*.

Five years later, in 1936, Alexander Berkman committed suicide. Just days before the famed anarchist leader shot himself Emma had tried to rouse him from his despondency over his illness and his sense of failure in life. "No one," she wrote to him, "ever was so rooted in my being, so ingrained in every fiber, as you have been and are to this day."

Profoundly shaken by Berkman's death, Emma Goldman plunged into a new cause. She tried in vain to rouse the world to help forces struggling in the Spanish Civil War against the Fascist General Francisco Franco. In the spring of 1940, as the forces of German and Italian fascism ominously massed in Europe, she was living alone in Toronto, Canada, a bitter, lonely woman.

On May 14, 1940, she died suddenly of a paralytic stroke. The United States government, which had expelled her as unworthy of living in America, allowed her body to be returned for burial. According to her wishes she was buried alongside the anarchists executed in 1887 for their supposed part in Chicago's Haymarket Riot.

Emma Goldman, never a "saint," lived the life of a thoroughly liberated person. She is perhaps the most important example in America's history of a woman who looked for her liberation not to *more* governmental action, but *less*. True freedom, she urged with passion, could come only in the total triumph of the free individual.

To her the concept of human rights was, above all, a personal matter.

Jacob Riis

1849–1914   Reporter and lecturer who publicized the wretched
conditions of tenement dwellers in New York City

One Christmas Day, in the town of
Ribe, Denmark, when Jacob Riis was
thirteen years old, his parents gave him
a present: a silver coin.

Unlike many thirteen-year-olds, Jacob chose not to spend the money on
himself. Instead, he took it to a poor
man living in a run-down tenement
house—a slum building—in Ribe. That
tenement, built over an open drain, was
infested with rats. Rats were everywhere, scurrying through all the apart-
ments of the building. The adults of
Ribe knew all about the rats. But they
had done nothing.

Jacob told the poor man to use the
silver coin to get rid of the rats—to
buy whitewash for the walls and to clean
out the rats' nests in the open drain.
Meanwhile Jacob set about killing all

the rats he could find. Before long the
job was finished. The building was free
of rats.

Jacob Riis's family had no way of
knowing that their son's achievement
in clearing the rats from a tenement
would foreshadow his mission in life,
a triumph to be acted out in a distant
land, America.

Young Jacob Riis was destined to become a hero in adulthood as a newspaper reporter and lecturer combating the
terrible conditions in New York City's
slums. Armed only with pencil and cam-
era he would make the American public
aware of "how the other half lives." He
would describe the filth, the crime, the
disease visited on poor people, especially children, by greedy landlords and
uncaring public officials.

Because of him, new laws were passed and new organizations were founded to do something about the evils of city life. His formula for conquering slum conditions became the rallying cry of a whole generation of American reformers. The answer, as he put it, must be "not charity, but justice."

Riis did not follow a straight path to a career in journalism; he zigzagged to it. At age fourteen, while still in Denmark, he dropped out of school and became apprenticed to a carpenter. Four years later his sweetheart's parents refused him when he asked permission to marry her. What future would it be for her, they asked, married to a humble carpenter?

Then and there Jacob Riis decided to come to America, "the land of opportunity," to make his fortune. Later, he promised himself, he would return to Denmark and claim Elizabeth, the woman whose love had been denied him.

Like so many immigrants, Riis soon discovered that the streets of America were not, as rumored, "paved with gold." Success took hard work. For Jacob Riis, that was no obstacle; he was willing to work. Still, life proved anything but easy for him at first.

Arriving in the spring of 1870, he found that there was no work to be had, not even for someone highly skilled with a hammer and saw. He tried his hand as a coal miner in Pennsylvania but hated working underground. Next he found work in a brickyard in New Jersey, pushing a cart loaded with heavy bricks. He did that until the weather became too cold for brickmaking and caused the yard to close.

In New York City again, he wandered the streets looking for work, any work. At night he often slept in doorways, sheltered from rain and snow only by the overhangs of storefronts.

One night, cold, wet, and shivering, he stood on a pier overlooking the dark waters of the river, considering suicide. But at the last minute a little dog nestled up close to him for warmth. Feeling needed, at least by something, he decided to keep on trying.

That night he slept in a crowded, steamy lodging room for tramps, run by the police. While he slept someone stole the gold locket he had brought from Denmark and wore on a string around his neck.

Riis once again left Manhattan, this time finding work with other Danes making cradles in a furniture shop in upstate New York. At night he polished his English-language skills, having already studied English for several years in Denmark. It was clear to him, as to so many other immigrants, that learning his new country's language would be the crucial step in really becoming an American.

For three years he worked at whatever jobs he could find. Then, at last confident of his English, he won a job working for a small newspaper in Manhattan. Often he would work for fourteen or fifteen hours a day, finally dropping off to sleep totally exhausted. In spare moments he tried to read and study.

In a few months he took a job for higher pay, working for another small newspaper, this one in Brooklyn. Eventually he came to run the entire paper himself, writing the news items, setting up the presses, and hiring newsboys to sell the paper on street corners.

More confident of his earning power, he wrote to Elizabeth, his boyhood sweetheart in Denmark, asking her once again to marry him. This time her parents agreed to the match, and Elizabeth accepted.

Soon after returning to America from the marriage ceremony in Ribe, his Danish hometown, Jacob got his big break. He found work as a reporter on the *New York Tribune*, at the time one of New York's great newspapers.

His assignment was to be a police reporter, covering the action at police headquarters on Mulberry Street, a street on Manhattan's Lower East Side with the highest rate of murders, robberies, and fires in the entire city. In time, Riis would find his life's work in dramatizing for the public what he saw on Mulberry Street, using it as a case study in crusading for change in America's slum communities.

Often he walked until well past midnight through the filthy alleyways and among the tenement buildings of Mulberry Bend, where, in Riis's words, Mulberry Street "crooks like an elbow."

On any one night he might see a shooting, a stabbing, a robbery, or a gun battle among competing street gangs. Usually, because he looked like a physician with his thick eyeglasses and rumpled hat, slum dwellers called him Doc and left him alone. Many of them thought they might need a doctor someday. On occasion Riis found himself called on by ambulance crews to help them tend to victims of street violence.

From the beginning Riis not only got the news but cared about the people of Mulberry Street. Angered by their condition, he wrote about them in vivid personal stories. He described old men and women starving to death on tenement stairways; landlords taking for rent more than half of some families' weekly earnings; fires shooting up in the middle of the night from spilled fat in bakeries located in tenement basements, burning all of the inhabitants to death before they could escape.

Once, after Riis had moved his family into the suburbs, his own small children gathered armfuls of flowers from the fields. They presented them to him and pleaded with him to give them to "the poors." To his surprise, many children on Mulberry Street had never even seen a flower. They begged him for even one small blossom. As he described it, some children who did not receive a flower "sat in the gutter and wept with grief."

After Riis wrote about the incident in the *Tribune* he was astonished to find that people from all over New York deluged the newspaper office with flowers and flower boxes. Office workers, policemen, even reporters from rival newspapers, helped him distribute the flowers. According to Riis, the flowers were a first step in making the street more "neighborly."

Riis became a major figure in organizing settlement houses in New York's slums. These were places where people could come to learn English or to learn about nutrition. Children could play in a playground or gymnasium, or perhaps join a club.

Over the years Riis's newspaper column built up a devoted following. His popularity soared. Offers came for him to write magazine articles. In 1890 he wrote his first book, *How the Other Half Lives*, describing what he had seen on Mulberry Street. The book became known across the country, bringing home to many Americans for the first time the unhappy circumstances of slum dwellers.

One of Jacob Riis's special concerns was the children of the slums. His stories helped to prove a point: that if we fail to help a poor child at the beginning of life—if we do nothing—we run a strong risk that such a child will grow into a life of crime. Later we may find ourselves beaten, robbed, or even murdered by that child.

A better way, according to Riis, was to *educate* children, teach them skills, and give them a stake in society. The result, then, would be more law-abiding citizens and, moreover, taxpayers. According to Riis, playgrounds, schools, and decent housing were infinitely better—and cheaper—than prisons.

In his second book, *Children of the Poor* (1892), Riis told story after story of children he had seen on the streets. He told of Giuseppe, an Italian newsboy who, looking for a warm place to sleep on a winter night, crawled into a ventilator chute and burned to death when a fire broke out in the chute. He told of a crippled boy who, when Riis asked him if he had ever laughed in his life, thought seriously before finally replying, "I did wonst."

Jacob attracted many friends. They liked his sometimes rough sense of humor, his phenomenal energy, his will-

"Street Arabs in Sleeping Quarters," a photograph by Jacob Riis, from *How the Other Half Lives*, published in 1890 by Scribners. *The Museum of the City of New York.*

ingness to express himself openly, to laugh or to cry. One of his friends declared that even when Riis behaved with the rough manner expected of a police reporter everyone knew "he had the tenderness and sensitivity of a woman."

In 1894 New York City elected a reform-minded mayor. He appointed as police commissioner a man who would become Riis's closest friend of all, Theodore Roosevelt. From the day they first met, "Teddy" and "Jake" took a delight in each other's company. Day after day, night after night, Riis walked with Roosevelt through the slum district. Together they stepped over drunks sprawled in alleyways. They trudged through sweatshops where whole families worked for pennies a day making clothing or rolling cigars.

It was Teddy who helped Jake establish sixteen Good Government Clubs all over New York City to provide an outlet for middle-class people who wanted to work for reform. When Roosevelt became governor of New York, Riis often visited him in Albany, the state capital. Even then the two sometimes made surprise visits to the slums at night. Nobody was closer to Roosevelt than Jacob Riis.

One of Riis's greatest triumphs came when, one by one, the tenement buildings of Mulberry Bend were torn down, with most of the occupants being moved into better housing. In 1897, largely through pressure from Riis, the rubble from the demolished buildings finally was removed and a park, Mulberry Bend Park, was constructed on the site where once the filthy slum had stood. Later Riis would proudly point to the "spot of green" where children played in the sunlight. The park's creation, he said, gave him more pleasure than any other accomplishment of his career.

In 1901 Theodore Roosevelt became President of the United States. Often he invited his friend Jake to visit the White House or Sagamore Hill, the Roosevelts' home in Oyster Bay, Long Island. Teddy considered him "one of my truest and closest friends," someone "like my own brother."

At about the time that Roosevelt began his presidency Jacob Riis decided to give up newspaper work. Instead he devoted all his time to writing and lecturing, preparing books and articles and speaking around the country.

One of his most popular lectures, "Tony and His Tribe," was about a slum child, Tony. According to Riis, when he first encountered Tony the angry little boy was about to throw mud in the face of another child. But when Riis offered him a handful of flowers he dropped the mud and, rushing home, put the flowers in a cup. It was perhaps the first thing of beauty the boy had ever owned.

From hundreds of such experiences Riis drew his own conclusions about poverty and the poor. "The people," he said, "are alright, if we only give them half a chance." Further, it is the *prevention* of poverty that society must concentrate on, not its effects.

Like Clarence Darrow, the great criminal lawyer, Riis believed that it was the accident of one's birth and the environment that a person grows up in that produces criminal behavior, wasted lives. Change those conditions through better health care, better education, better housing, and the whole society will benefit.

As Riis grew older he suffered from heart disease, but he refused to slow down his efforts to give poor people "a chance." Even after a serious heart attack he continued to write and lecture. As he put it, "Let us wear out if we must, but never rust."

In 1914 Jacob Riis died. The achieve-

A late nineteenth-century photograph of Jacob Riis. *Brown Brothers.*

ment he left behind him is prodigious. Through his newspaper columns, for example, he had called the public's attention to serious pollution of the Hudson River at Croton, New York, the source of New York City's water supply. As a result, the city purchased the watershed there. His books and articles helped push through new laws regarding light and ventilation in tenement buildings.

He had played an important role in winning passage of child-labor laws, limiting the hours that children could work. He had exposed the dens of crime in city slums and forced police action to close them down.

Through all of those spectacular successes Riis had remained true to his faith in the people. To the end of his life he believed firmly that poor people, given a fair chance, would help themselves.

What they needed was "not charity but justice."

Clarence Darrow

1857–1938   Leading defense lawyer of his day, known for his championship of unpopular clients, especially the "underdogs" in society

Do you think you will be a criminal when you grow up? Will your friends become criminals? Why do some people live lives of crime whereas others do not?

What pressures make us behave the way we do? How much real control do we have about the direction of our lives, for good or for evil? If people commit crimes, what should society do with them? Will punishment reform a person, change the way that person behaves?

Clarence Darrow, known to history as "attorney for the damned," asked questions like those. In a legal career that spanned more than fifty years he brought to the American scene a passion for justice and a belief that the criminal might not be the enemy of society, but rather its victim.

Using the courtroom as his classroom, Darrow taught the nation to seek out the underlying *causes* of crime. He argued, too, that society has a responsibility to protect the underdog and the oppressed—the laborer, the small businessman, the political outsider, the black. Few American lawyers have devoted themselves so completely to defending the defenseless.

Darrow believed that three factors influence a person's life, setting some people in one direction, other people on a different path. Those factors are heredity, environment, and chance—the physical and mental traits passed on from parents, one's surroundings, and, finally, pure luck. With those elements in mind, it is interesting to observe the influences that shaped Darrow's own life.

He was born in 1857, shortly before the Civil War began, in the village of Kinsman, Ohio, the fifth of eight children. His father, Amirus Darrow, was a furniture maker and undertaker. Trained at first to be a Protestant minister, Amirus had lost faith in God. To his neighbors in Kinsman, mostly farmers, he was known as an atheist—"the village infidel."

Amirus read the works of Tom Paine, which questioned formal religion. On most of the burning issues of the day, such as slavery, he liked to make up his own mind, regardless of what his neighbors believed. Very early in the antislavery crusade the Darrow home became a station on the Underground Railroad, which helped escaped slaves on their way to safety in the North or in Canada. At the time most northerners cared little about the problems of slaves.

Amirus taught his children never to accept an idea in politics or religion without question. Instead they should always think for themselves and depend on reason to make up their minds, no matter what other people thought. Amirus also believed that every human being on earth has a responsibility to help the less fortunate.

Growing up in the slow-paced life of Kinsman, young Clarence Darrow at first showed little interest in such profound issues. He considered school something of a waste of time, made up mostly of just memory work with little thinking. Instead of arithmetic, grammar, and spelling, his greatest interest was baseball.

Darrow especially remembered one game he played in his youth for the town of Kinsman against a neighboring team. He was at bat with two outs and two runners on base in the last of the ninth inning. The visiting team led by a run. After missing the first two pitches he slammed the ball over the roof of a nearby clothing store for a home run. For weeks afterward he was the town hero. Even as an adult, nationally known, he remembered that home run as a high point of his life.

To young Clarence fun and games were important. Similarly, he couldn't understand why cake and pie—things he liked—had to come last at dinner, after the meat and vegetables. Since life was short, he reasoned, people should have the things they enjoyed first, because if they waited too long for their "pie," death might cheat them out of it.

After high school Darrow attended the University of Michigan for a year. Then one of America's periodic depressions struck: the Panic of 1873. To help his father, whose business was badly hurt, Clarence took a job teaching.

He was the only teacher in a one-room schoolhouse near Kinsman. Some of the students were as young as seven, others even older than Darrow. On the first day of school Clarence announced that he would not use paddling as a means of discipline. Young people, he said, should not learn through fear of punishment. He also lengthened the lunch period and the recess.

Finally he joined the students in their games, especially baseball. When some of the parents protested, Clarence managed to persuade them that his methods worked and that the children actually were learning more.

On weekends Darrow liked to participate in the debates at the Kinsman Literary Society. Like his father, he usually took the unpopular side of issues, but because of his gentle, easy-going style and sense of humor, people liked him. After hearing his arguments, they often would change their minds. Remarkably, in a community where his neighbors disagreed with him on most topics, Clarence was respected, even admired.

Tall and lanky, dressed in rumpled clothes, Darrow developed a reputation much like that of Abraham Lincoln for simplicity, honesty, and high intelligence.

Whenever he could, Clarence listened to political speakers campaigning in the vicinity. Most of the really good speakers, he noticed, were lawyers. He also noticed that the lawyers dressed in better clothes, owned fancier carriages, and spoke with an authority and confidence he found attractive.

Besides, lawyers didn't have to work with their hands. After helping in his father's furniture store for several years Clarence had decided that, above all, he would never choose a career requiring mechanical ability.

At the end of his third year of teaching he enrolled in law school at the University of Michigan, having finished his undergraduate work at Allegheny College in Pennsylvania. After a year in law school Darrow returned home to Kinsman and began studying for the bar examination on his own. In 1878 he passed the examination and began practicing law.

Step by step the ambitious young Darrow moved his law practice to bigger settings: first to Andover, Ohio; then to Ashtabula; then, in a daring leap, to Chicago. Meanwhile he had married and become the father of a son, Paul.

If Darrow's family was growing, so was his mind. To gain time for reading he usually ate lunch at his desk, often just a piece of fruit. He read history, philosophy, psychology, poetry, fiction—anything that would help him to understand the world and why things happened as they did. Two books particularly influenced him: Henry George's *Progress and Poverty* and John P. Altgeld's *Our Penal Machinery and Its Victims.*

Henry George warned that in America the rich were becoming richer, the poor poorer. For a while Darrow believed that George's solution—a single tax on land—might succeed in restoring equality in the United States.

Altgeld's book argued that injustice came in part from the way society treats criminals: punishing them instead of removing the *causes* of crime, especially poverty. Like Henry George, Altgeld suggested new approaches to the serious problem of inequality in society.

Once Darrow was settled in Chicago he began speaking at political rallies. After one of his speeches Henry George himself came to the platform to congratulate him. Soon afterward Darrow went to see John P. Altgeld, then a judge in Chicago, carrying a copy of Altgeld's book under his arm. The two liked each other at once and became good friends.

From the beginning Darrow idolized Altgeld, working hard in the judge's successful campaign in 1892 for the governorship of Illinois. Altgeld, in turn, helped Darrow to rise rapidly in Chicago's legal circles. It was through

his influence that Darrow climbed, by the age of thirty-three, from unknown attorney with a few clients to head of the legal department for the city of Chicago.

Despite his solid successes Darrow suffered from bouts of depression. He began to despair of success in his search for a "perfect" political system, a system that would distribute wealth fairly among the world's people. Governments, he concluded, would always help some people and hurt others. At best, society could only encourage citizens to become more tolerant in dealing with each other. But even that modest goal, he feared, might be impossible to attain.

Moods of deep gloom were not new to Darrow. As a youngster he had tried to escape from them through sports, especially baseball. Now he turned to his new friends in Chicago, mostly lawyers and writers. They talked and played poker well into the night. But for Darrow it was not enough. Again like Abraham Lincoln, Darrow's deep thinking about life and death—his questioning—led him to unhappy conclusions.

Still, he continued to smile and to work hard for the people he thought were suffering most in life. Among the most unfortunate Americans in the final years of the nineteenth century were industrial workers. Rich factory owners paid their workers only pennies a day. When they protested the owners often crushed them with brutal force.

After one such incident, workers held a protest meeting in Chicago's Haymarket Square. Someone—to this day it is unclear who—threw a bomb into the ranks of policemen trying to break up the meeting. Both sides began shooting. When it was all over seven policemen lay dead, many more injured. The workers dragged away the bodies of their own dead and wounded.

After the so-called Haymarket Riot a wave of antilabor feeling swept Chicago. Influenced by that mood, a court sentenced to death seven workers, including a number of anarchists—people who opposed all governments. Some of those condemned to die had not even been in Haymarket Square at the time of the violence.

Despite appeals to the courts, by 1893 only four of the prisoners remained alive; the others had been hanged. Darrow was in the middle of the legal fight to save the remaining four. It was at Darrow's urging that John P. Altgeld, then governor of Illinois, pardoned the surviving Haymarket defendants, giving them their freedom. That act of mercy produced such public anger that it destroyed Altgeld's political career. One of the few public figures to stand behind him afterward was Clarence Darrow.

Darrow became known as a champion of the labor unions. At the time of the Pullman strike (1894), he defended Eugene V. Debs, leader of the American Railway Union. In 1902 he was counsel to the coal miners' union in the Pennsylvania anthracite coal strike. Later he successfully defended William ("Big Bill") Haywood of the "Wobblies" (Industrial Workers of the World) against charges of murdering the governor of Idaho.

While defending a worker in one well-known labor case, Darrow addressed the jury in a remarkable summary. He was not, he explained to the jurors, speaking only for that particular defendant: "I speak for the poor, for the weak, for the weary, for the long line of men who, in darkness and despair, have borne the labors of the human race." When he had finished, many of the jurors and spectators were in tears.

Darrow probably gained his greatest fame not as a labor lawyer but as a criminal lawyer. His unusual strength in defending clients came from an ability to show juries the special reasons behind a crime—the forces in society and in each defendant's mind that somehow could bring him to do a terrible deed.

In 1924 he defended two brilliant

teenagers, Richard Loeb and Nathan Leopold, Jr. The sons of millionaires, the two had kidnapped and senselessly killed a fourteen-year-old in an attempt to commit "the perfect crime." The public, angered in part by the boys' wealth, demanded the death penalty for them.

Darrow insisted that they plead guilty. He himself then described the terrifying crime in all of its gruesome details. But he also portrayed the murderers as "immature" young people with "diseased brains." In part, he said, they had killed because of their environment—not because of poverty, but because they were too rich, too neglected by their parents.

Besides, Darrow advanced, capital punishment was wrong. The crime of Leopold and Loeb had been barbaric, cruel. But it would be equally barbaric of society, out of revenge, to execute the boys. The state must not lower itself to the level of such monsters by "public bloodletting." To do so, said Darrow, would only increase the hatred and sickness we see in the world. "I am pleading," he summarized, "that we overcome cruelty with kindness, and hatred with love."

The trial judge, deeply moved by Darrow's words, sentenced Leopold and Loeb not to death but, as Darrow had pleaded, to life imprisonment.

One year later, in 1925, Darrow came to the aid of a biology teacher in Tennessee, John Thomas Scopes. Scopes was accused of breaking a Tennessee law against teaching evolution in the schools, evolution being the scientific theory that humans developed gradually from lower forms of life, such as the apes. Always fascinated by science and determined to defend the rights of free thought and free speech, Darrow came face to face with religious fundamentalists, people who believe that the words of the Bible were literally true—to be taken exactly as they were written.

The high point of the so-called Monkey Trial came when Darrow called to the stand to testify the opposing lawyer in the case—William Jennings Bryan, by then the Democratic party's unsuccessful candidate for President of the United States in three election campaigns.

To Bryan it was a simple matter of science versus religion, and he, Bryan, had chosen religion. Darrow, too, believed that it was not Scopes who was on trial, it was civilization itself—the right of people to think, to investigate, to express their differences freely. As Darrow put it, once government can silence an educator's ideas, can burn books, it was but a simple step to the next act, the act of burning people.

Because of the summer's oppressive

An early twentieth-century photograph of Clarence Darrow. *International Museum of Photography at George Eastman House.*

Clarence Darrow pleading at the Scopes trial, July 10, 1925. John T. Scopes (in white shirt, arms interlocked) is seated behind Darrow. *Culver Pictures.*

heat, the judge moved the trial outside, onto the courthouse lawn. There Darrow, with his shirtsleeves rolled up, thumbs tucked characteristically under the suspenders of his trousers, paced as he spoke. He used no notes.

Did a whale, he asked Bryan, literally swallow Jonah, just as the Bible said? Was the world created in exactly 4,004 B.C., as some fundamentalists calculated? Did God punish the serpent in the Garden of Eden for tempting Adam by making it, forever afterward, slither along on its belly? And, if so, how had the snake gotten around before?

Darrow's witty questions made Bryan look foolish, ignorant. Nevertheless the trial judge found Scopes guilty of breaking Tennessee's law against teaching evolution, and fined him one hundred dollars.

On appeal, the case against Scopes eventually was dismissed because of a technicality, but because of the national

publicity given to the trial Darrow succeeded—at least for a time—in stem-
ming the attacks of religious extremists
on the nation's public schools.

In the great stock market crash of
1929 Darrow lost nearly all of his savings. Until then fully a third to a half
of his professional practice had been
devoted to clients from whom he collected no fee. Now, advanced in age,
he had to take on new clients just to
pay his living expenses. He also lectured throughout the nation on a wide
variety of topics: evolution and religion;
the abolition of capital punishment; the
proper limits on free speech; prohi-
bition of alcohol; the League of Nations.
With his rumpled clothing and a sense
of humor both charming and biting, he
became a favorite on the lecture circuit,
making enough money to ease the final
years of his life.

As the end approached, Darrow still
wrestled with the truly great puzzles
of human existence. He wondered
whether people had any control over
their lives—had the power to make
choices by free will. Or were most
things determined by the accidents of
birth and environment?

He wondered how much power
should be given to government to improve social conditions, as the Socialists, for example, hoped to do. And,
on the other hand, how could the individual be protected against *too much*
government? What, in fact, was the best
possible balance between liberty and
order? He wondered, too, about human
lives, each one of them so completely
different.

In his own law practice he had tried
to help jurors understand his own thinking about these complex yet basic questions. His ability to do so accounts in
large part for his enormous success as
a criminal lawyer.

Darrow had managed to introduce
on the "stage" of the courtroom—and
to a larger national audience—the essential tragedy that he saw in human
life, a drama without purpose, without
plan. The principal actors in that
drama—individual men and women—
appeared to him to be puppets, helpless
participants in deeds of both good and
evil.

Still, despite his underlying pessi-
mism, Darrow never completely lost
hope, never stopped dreaming that the
human condition might somehow,
someday, be improved.

He died in Chicago at the age of
eighty. A complicated man, he also re-
tained the simplicity of his youth—his
love of baseball, of cakes and pies, and,
as he grew older, of the beautiful view
of Lake Michigan from his apartment
window.

Darrow's own life, so richly productive, disproved some of his own ideas, especially the belief that people could do little to shape their own existence. Indeed we find in Darrow the example of a man who kept on trying, kept on crusading, never stopped fighting. In doing so, he acted not only for himself, but in the cause of all humanity.

Dorothy Day

1897–1980 Radical journalist and upholder of women's rights who lived a life of voluntary poverty on behalf of those victimized by society

Dorothy Day was pregnant. But she was not married.

When she told the father of her unborn child that she intended to have the baby baptized as a Catholic and to become a Catholic herself, he told her that if she did, he would leave her. "You can't be a radical and a Catholic, too," he said. "That's the church of the rich. . . . People are starving, and they put money into elegant buildings and fancy robes for the priests."

Dorothy Day knew that he meant it. If she had the baby baptized as a Catholic he would abandon her.

And he did.

But that didn't stop Dorothy Day. "To become a Catholic," she later wrote, "meant for me to give up a mate with whom it was the simple question of whether I chose God or man."

For the rest of her life she tried to combine the ideas of the Catholic Church with her political beliefs. She tried to live exactly as the Bible said that people should live—caring for the poor and the sick and working for peace. The result was one of the truly remarkable stories in the history of the human rights movement in America.

Dorothy Day was born in Brooklyn in 1897, the third of five children. Neither of her parents was Catholic, or for that matter very much concerned with religion. Her father, a sports writer who specialized in horse racing, actually disliked organized religions, often ridiculing them.

Until the San Francisco earthquake of 1906 the Days lived in Oakland, California. Dorothy Day later remembered the earthquake and the great fear she felt for the powers of nature, as well as her own feeling of helplessness. "If I fell asleep God became in my ears a great noise that became louder and louder, and approached nearer and nearer to me until I woke up sweating with fear and shrieking for my mother."

The earthquake destroyed the newspaper building where her father, John Day, worked. As a result he accepted a job as a sports writer with a newspaper in Chicago. At first the Days lived in a drab six-room apartment above a saloon. To prevent his daughter from coming in contact with what he considered "bad influences," John Day would not let her make friends with other children in the neighborhood or at school. Instead he surrounded her with books —those works he considered "the best" of all time, produced by writers of fiction such as Dickens, Poe, Cooper, Hugo, Scott. By the age of eight she had become "hooked on books," reading in every spare moment, never seen without a book in her hand. Moreover she remembered what she read and loved to discuss her reading with other people.

As Dorothy Day grew into adolescence, she added reading choices of her own: the scientists Darwin and Huxley, along with the complicated ideas of philosophers—Spencer, Kant, and Spinoza. Finally she discovered the classics

of religion—the Bible, the *Confessions* of Saint Augustine, the Anglican prayer book, and the sermons of Jonathan Edwards.

At age twelve she visited an Episcopal church in Chicago with a friend, and from that time began learning prayers by heart. In her autobiography she says, "I had never heard anything so beautiful as the *Benedicite* and the *Te Deum*. . . . The Psalms were an outlet for the enthusiasm of joy and grief."

Her parents, hostile or at best indifferent to religion, found her fascination with the subject puzzling. For Dorothy Day, the world of religion offered a way to show her independence. Also, growing up in a home where it was considered improper to let one's feelings show, she found religion to be a way to express herself.

Not only did Dorothy Day read, she also enjoyed writing. Often alone, she began to keep a diary at an early age, even though her brothers sometimes found it and teased her by reading parts of it aloud. At twelve she helped start a neighborhood newspaper, writing stories and poems for it. In school she often wrote about the poverty she saw around her. Writing about people's suffering, she discovered, made her feel that perhaps she could do something about it.

By the time she graduated from high

school Dorothy Day had decided to become a writer. But what would she write about? At first she wrote about God, who she said spoke directly to her.

More and more, however, she wrote about the poverty she saw around her. It was the age of progressivism in America, the beginning of the twentieth century. Writers such as Jack London, Upton Sinclair, and Frank Harris were introducing Americans to the darker side of the nation's life—the slums, the hopeless search for jobs, the scandals in the packaging of meats and other food products, the bread lines.

By the age of sixteen Dorothy Day had come to believe that things could be different—that society could be changed, "reformed." It was at that age that she entered a scholarship contest and won it, enrolling at the University of Illinois as a freshman.

In part, Dorothy Day was going to college to escape the strictness of her life at home. She also looked forward to free time to read and study. But her college experience disappointed her. The courses struck her as lifeless, unrelated to the real world she saw everywhere around her.

Soon she began cutting classes to read and write on her own, according to her own schedule. She attended meetings of the University's Socialist Club. She wrote articles about some of her fellow students who had barely enough food. To show sympathy for them, she went without food herself.

In college she turned against religion. Like many of her friends, she came to see religion as a tool of the rich to keep poor people "in their place." She started to swear, perhaps cursing God as a way of pushing religion out of her life.

Jesus, she pointed out, had said, "Blessed are the meek." But, declared Dorothy Day, "I could not be meek at the thought of injustice. For me Christ no longer walked the streets of the world. He was two thousand years dead and new prophets had risen up in his place."

After two years of college Dorothy Day dropped out. She moved to New York's Greenwich Village, a section of Manhattan that attracted many free-thinking artists and writers. There she joined with a whole generation of young men and women, idealists rebelling against what they considered an outdated set of middle-class moral standards.

In place of the capitalist goal of making more and more money, this group demanded greater freedom for individuals: freedom to experiment in literature and art, and freedom from repression in relations with the opposite sex. Many young people drawn to Greenwich Village at that time admired Karl Marx, whose *Communist Manifesto* had cried out, "Workers of the world, unite! You have nothing to lose but your chains!"

People who remembered Dorothy Day when she first lived in the "Village" described her as tall and beautiful, with high cheekbones and slightly slanted blue eyes. She soon had many admirers. Young, bright, eager to learn all she could, she won a job on the *New York Call*, a Socialist newspaper. She covered strikes and protest marches. She interviewed members of the "Wobblies" (the Industrial Workers of the World), along with personalities as widely different as Communist leader Leon Trotsky and the butler of Mrs. Vincent Astor, one of America's wealthiest women.

Dorothy Day's articles, written from the heart, featured specific examples: children without food; mothers trying to live on the five dollars a week that public charity gave them; and the horrible smells coming from the alleyways and halls of New York City's slum buildings. Dorothy Day always had been conscious of smells; now they became a regular part of her descriptions of poverty.

In 1917, after a period of uneasy neutrality, America entered World War I.

Dorothy Day left the *Call* and, now twenty years old, took a job as book reviewer with *The Masses*, a daring, controversial magazine.

Writing for *The Masses*, she met some of the leading radicals of the twentieth century—persistent critics of the American social system. Among her co-workers were Max Eastman, Elizabeth Gurley Flynn, and John Reed.

Using sarcasm and wit, *The Masses* opposed America's participation in the war. The U.S. Department of Justice, disturbed by the magazine's attacks, finally had the post office refuse it the use of the mails. Before long *The Masses* was forced to shut down.

Without work, Dorothy Day joined a protest march in Washington, D.C., sponsored by women demanding the right to vote. While picketing the White House she and the other women were arrested. They were thrown into Occoquan jail, where some were subjected to beatings and forced feeding. Dorothy Day was one of the women placed in solitary confinement. Thoroughly frightened, she found herself, to her surprise, turning to the Bible to quiet her fears.

Back in New York, Dorothy Day again plunged into the wild, rebellious life of Greenwich Village. She came to know Eugene O'Neill, the playwright. The two became close companions. Often they smoked and drank together at a famous Village saloon, sometimes known to regulars as the "Hell Hole."

Dorothy Day usually joined in the noisy laughter and conversation of the saloon's back room. Sometimes she would have to help the drunken O'Neill return to his apartment and put him to bed. Then, for a moment of quiet, she would slump into the rear pews of St. Joseph's Church in the Village. She found herself comforted by the silence, the soft lights, and the reverence of the worshippers.

Unsure of her purpose in life, Dorothy Day returned to Chicago, where she worked on the *Liberator,* a Communist newspaper. Once, not having a place to stay, she decided to spend the night at a free hostel run by the International Workers of the World. When the police raided the hostel she was arrested as a prostitute and put in jail. For a time she was enrolled in nursing school, hoping for a career in that field. But she found the routines of a nurse's work dull, unstimulating.

Still seeking meaning for herself, she twice fell madly in love. First there was Mike Gold, a Communist propagandist who later wrote *Jews Without Money.* Next came a love affair with a Jewish newspaperman, Lionel Moise. After living with Moise for several months she found herself pregnant.

Moise refused to marry her. Wanting to have the baby but uncertain how to support it, she arranged for an abortion.

Then a few months later, lonely and desperately unhappy, she married a forty-two-year-old literary promoter and sailed away with him for Europe. In less than a year the marriage collapsed.

Confused, uncertain, she walked the streets of Manhattan. She tried to revive her love affair with Moise, but that, too, failed. Finally, she considered suicide.

Instead Dorothy Day threw herself into her writing. The result was a novel, the thinly disguised story of her own unhappy life. To her surprise, a Hollywood film studio liked the book and paid her five thousand dollars for it. With that money she bought a small beach cottage on Staten Island. There she entertained some of her old friends, including writers who soon would become well known—John Dos Passos, Hart Crane, Malcolm Cowley.

One of the friends who came to her cottage was Forster Batterham. Batterham, an anarchist, distrusted all governments, all churches. But he did like Dorothy Day. Daily they fished, talked, and studied species of sea life they found while walking together on the beach.

In the summer of 1926 Dorothy Day discovered that once again she was pregnant. Remembering her unhappiness after having to abort her earlier child, she was overjoyed at the news. She decided to go ahead with the birth no matter what Forster Batterham said.

At the same time she had been finding increasing comfort in the Bible. She had begun to attend church services regularly. Like most of her radical friends, she believed that churches had done too little to help poor people win equal justice in society. Churches, she thought, had convinced people not to struggle, but to accept inequality, waiting for a reward in heaven after death. Or as the Communists put it sarcastically, "There'll be pie in the sky by and by!"

Dorothy Day had tried the life of Greenwich Village and found it unsatisfying. Now, at the age of thirty-five, she decided to find a deeper understanding, a more profound meaning in her life.

In March 1927 she gave birth to a daughter, Tamar Teresa. With the help of a nun she had met on the beach she had the baby baptized in the Catholic Church. She, too, was baptized and became a Catholic.

At that point Forster Batterham left her. Dorothy's own father angrily stormed at her for joining the church of "Irish cops and washerwomen." Her Greenwich Village friends laughed at her; some thought she had gone crazy.

Dorothy Day shrugged off the criticism. In the Catholic Church she finally discovered the sense of order and certainty that always before had eluded her. She found a mystical—that is, a direct—relationship with God.

Still unsure of how to make a living, Dorothy Day returned to newspaper work. With the coming of the Great Depression of the 1930s she described what she saw everywhere around her. She wrote about the struggles of the poor to survive. For her newspaper columns she covered strikes, protest meetings, conferences of intellectuals.

In December 1932 she witnessed a hunger march of the unemployed in Washington, D.C. Afterward she went to pray at the National Shrine of the Immaculate Conception at Catholic University. "There," she later wrote, "I offered up a special prayer, a prayer which came with tears and with anguish, that some way would open up for me to use what talents I possessed for my fellow workers, for the poor."

Returning to New York, Dorothy Day found waiting on her doorstep a short, shabbily dressed man who spoke to her in a thick French accent, scarcely giving her time to reply. He preached to her about his ideas, developed over many years of working, thinking, talking. His name was Peter Maurin. And what she must do, he told her, was to start a Catholic newspaper to educate the public about the situation of the poor, the unemployed.

To Dorothy Day it seemed that her prayer in Washington had been answered. From Maurin's idea grew a newspaper—*The Catholic Worker*—which projected her onto the national scene. From Maurin, too, came the overall solution she had been looking for, the answer to her problem of how to be a religious Catholic and also a worker for social change in America.

Dorothy Day was not a Communist. It is true that, like Peter Maurin, she believed that the capitalist system—a society based on getting and spending money—was a dead end. Being rich, as she and Peter Maurin already had learned, did not make people happy.

Still, she did not think that the answer to humanity's problems lay in destroying the system of private property and then building something new on the ashes. Nor did it mean, as most Communists of the 1920s and 1930s believed, using the Soviet Union (USSR) as a model. To Dorothy Day, nationalism—love for one's country—led too easily to war. And war, like poverty, led only to human misery.

The solution that Dorothy Day worked out, with Peter Maurin's help, was highly personal. It was based on changing society by changing the lives of individuals. To succeed she would have to teach people to cooperate instead of competing. She would have to help people to search out the spirit of God in their daily lives. It was that holy spirit, not some notion of "class struggle," that had rescued her from the emptiness, the meaninglessness of her earlier life.

God, she now was sure, could be found among the poor: in the breadlines, in the jails, in the hopeless lives of white tenant farmers in the South and of blacks suffering in the slums of northern cities. Dorothy Day now made it her mission—her "pilgrimage"—to help the poor and, by doing that, to change society.

On May 1 (May Day, celebrated as a workers' holiday in many countries), 1933, Dorothy Day distributed the first issue of *The Catholic Worker*. The first press run was 2,500 copies. Within two years the paper's circulation had grown to 150,000. Its price always remained one cent.

The Catholic Worker had as one of its main goals the establishment of "Houses of Hospitality." These were places where poor, homeless men and women could go to get help. Dorothy Day, as usual more practical than Peter

Maurin, started by renting an apartment on Charles Street in Manhattan. There hundreds of people lined up each day for a place to sleep or a meal of soup, bread, and coffee.

Swiftly the idea spread across the country. Within ten years more than forty Hospitality Houses operated to feed and shelter the poor. When people applied for help they underwent no test of race or religious belief. Anyone who came to the door was welcomed. Later Dorothy Day and Peter Maurin established six farming communes. These were aimed at doing in the countryside what the Hospitality Houses accomplished in the city. They also had the purpose of sending people back to the land, where they could grow their own food and more easily support themselves.

Always the aim of Dorothy Day and Peter Maurin was to decentralize society—to make people less dependent on government and more dependent on themselves. For that reason they often were considered anarchists—opponents of all government. Actually they believed that government was important, necessary—but that governments should serve people, not the opposite.

The beginning of World War II posed a serious dilemma for Dorothy Day. Always before, *The Catholic Worker* had spoken out firmly against war. As Dorothy Day pointed out, Jesus loved even his enemies and had preached against violence. Therefore Christians were obliged to believe that *all* wars were bad, not just some wars.

Yet she could not just stand by and accept the horrible deeds of Adolf Hitler, including the mass murder of Europe's Jews. *The Catholic Worker* condemned Hitler's acts. Dorothy Day personally challenged the vicious anti-Jewish statements of an American priest, Father Coughlin. She worked ceaselessly to save Jews by having them admitted to the United States. She also reminded her Catholic readers that Jesus himself had been a Jew.

Nevertheless Dorothy insisted that a war to defeat Hitler and his Japanese allies would, in the long run, bring terrible results to humanity. Later she cited as proof the deaths of thousands of civilians in air raids on Hamburg, Dresden, and Tokyo. America's dropping of atomic bombs on Hiroshima and Nagasaki represented to her only the beginning of still greater horrors if people did not turn against wars as a way of settling disputes.

In the 1950s she was jailed for her opposition to the peacetime draft of men into military service, as well as for her protests against civil defense practices. High officials in the Catholic Church, including Cardinal Spellman

Dorothy Day with her grandchildren. *Dorothy Day-Catholic Worker Collection, Marquette University.*

of New York, considered taking action against her but always backed down. One Church leader advised caution because, in Dorothy Day, the Church might be dealing with a future saint.

In the 1960s Dorothy Day became a leading opponent of America's involvement in Vietnam. She and other members of her community tried to block the entrances to submarine bases and missile bases. They supported men who burned their draft cards. They urged people not to pay income tax, because the taxes helped finance the war.

Gradually, in the next two decades, many more priests, nuns, and lay Catholics came to accept her beliefs about war. They started to use the kinds of protest methods she had pioneered.

As she grew older Dorothy Day still insisted on living the kind of life she suggested for others—one of "sacrifice, worship, a sense of reverence." Part of her worship was the voluntary choice of poverty. Traveling around the country, she stayed in the communities of the Catholic Worker movement. She ate the humble food her "guests" ate, and, like them, wore cast-off clothing. True, she continued to read good books, enjoy classical music, and go to the theater. That was another side of her life, the private side. It was just as much a part of her as the Dorothy Day who

gave her strength to build a humane community.

Even in old age, crippled by arthritis, she remained amazingly young and free spirited. Abbie Hoffman, a fiery radical leader of the 1960s, called her "the first hippie," a term she enjoyed enormously.

Surely, however, her life was drawing to a close. Peter Maurin had died in 1949. Her daughter, Tamar Teresa, or "Bubbie," had made her a grandmother several times over. Confined to her room at Maryhouse in Greenwich Village, she remained close to the scene of her earlier searching, close to the bittersweet memories of her old friends in the Village.

From around the world tributes came pouring in: *Life* and *Newsweek* magazines produced flattering biographical sketches of her. In a cover story *Time* referred to her as "a living saint."

Men and women she had encouraged continued to show their gratitude. From the slums of Calcutta Mother Teresa sent greetings. So did the great writer and priest Thomas Merton. In 1973 Dorothy Day had gone to prison for the last time, arrested while picketing on behalf of the nonviolent action of Cesar Chavez and his United Farm Workers union. Chavez considered her, along with Gandhi, his greatest source of inspiration.

Dorothy Day is led to jail by a policewoman after having picketed with United Farm Workers in Fresno, California, in 1973. *Religious News Service Photo.*

Dorothy Day died in November 1980, shortly after her eighty-third birthday. Her grave is on Staten Island, overlooking the ocean. It lies very close to the place where her daughter was born— the place where she took on her new faith and made her fateful decision to live a life devoted to healing and to hope.

Bayard Rustin

1912–1987   Labor union leader who played a major role in America's civil rights movement

In 1931 Bayard Rustin graduated with his high-school class in West Chester, Pennsylvania, as valedictorian—the student with the highest grades. He had also been an athlete, competing in track, tennis, and football. As a young man excelling in both academics and athletics, he must have forgotten sometimes that he was supposed to be "inferior"—not as good as other people. For Bayard Rustin was black.

When he graduated from high school many Americans actually believed that blacks were an inferior race. That was true not only in the South, but also in northern states such as Pennsylvania, where Rustin grew up. Almost everywhere customs and laws reminded blacks to "stay in their place"—a place separate from whites.

Once the bus carrying Bayard's high-school football team stopped at a restaurant in Media, Pennsylvania. All of the other members of the team were served, but because he was black Bayard was refused service.

"I sat there a long time," he remembered many years later, "and eventually was thrown out bodily. From that point on, I had the conviction that I would not accept segregation."

Eventually Bayard Rustin became one of the great leaders in the civil rights movement in America. It was Rustin, along with such figures as Martin Luther King and A. Philip Randolph, who sparked the epic struggle to gain equal rights for blacks.

Rustin, however, developed an even broader vision, a more ambitious goal.

He hoped that injustice would end eventually not only for Americans, but for all people everywhere. Only then, he believed, could those who worked for human rights finally declare their victory.

Rustin was born in 1912. His father and mother had never married, and his father, from the West Indies, played no part in bringing him up. Instead his grandparents gave him most of his guidance. His grandmother, a Delaware Indian by origin, had been educated by Quakers. Like them, she opposed violence of all kinds, including war.

His grandfather, the son of a Maryland slave, worked part-time as a caterer, preparing food for the parties of wealthy white people. Bayard like to recall good-naturedly the experience of so many blacks who cooked for whites. "We lived on a rich diet of party leftovers—turtle soup, Roquefort cheese, lobsters, pies, and cakes." In later years Rustin may have been able to laugh about the poverty of his youth, but at the time it hardly could have been funny.

Along with poverty came the humiliation of racial segregation. Before he enrolled in a racially mixed high school, every school he had attended in West Chester had been segregated—blacks and whites in separate schools.

After high school he attended Wilberforce College in Ohio, a black institution. Soon he transferred to another black college, Cheney State Teachers College in Pennsylvania. Finally he studied at City College of New York and lived in Manhattan's black community, Harlem.

To help pay his college expenses he sang with a quartet, the Charioteers, a group later to become famous for its recordings. Often, too, he performed on stage as a "single." In New York he sometimes appeared with such famed folk-singing stars as Josh White and Leadbelly (Huddie Ledbetter).

Rustin never finished college. While at City College he decided that the best way to end racism in America was to change the entire political system. As a result he joined the Young Communist League, a division of Communist Party USA. Although he never became a Communist party member, he worked hard to recruit other students at City College for the league.

Until 1941 Communists had argued that America must stay out of the war between Nazi Germany and Great Britain, the only surviving democratic government in Europe. Then, when Germany launched a surprise attack on the Soviet Union, Communist Party USA changed its position overnight, demanding that America immediately enter the war against Hitler.

Rustin, a pacifist like his mother, re-

Bayard Rustin as a young reformer. *The A. Philip Randolph Institute.*

signed in disgust from the Young Communist League. Later in life he admitted that the Communists had fooled him. He had failed to understand that they cared little for the welfare of poor and suffering people around the world, as they claimed, but only for the interests of Russia.

Next, as America stood on the brink of war, Rustin became an organizer for CORE, the Congress of Racial Equality. He helped A. Philip Randolph of the Brotherhood of Sleeping Car Porters, a union composed almost entirely of blacks, to organize young people for a march on Washington. The march was planned to put pressure on President Franklin Delano Roosevelt to end discrimination against blacks in defense industries—factories producing arms and ammunition.

Just six days before the march was to begin, Roosevelt agreed to Randolph's demands. He issued Executive Order 8802, outlawing discrimination against black workers in defense plants, while also setting up the Fair Employment Practices Commission (FEPC).

To Randolph, Roosevelt's action signaled a clear-cut victory for blacks. Since the purpose of the proposed march had been achieved, he called it off. Holding such a demonstration, he said, could only anger whites and make blacks appear unpatriotic at a time of impending war.

Rustin, still young and fiery, was crushed. It seemed to him that all of his work had been for nothing. He argued that the march should have gone ahead, anyway, to illustrate how effectively blacks could work together toward a common goal.

It was only after many years that he and Randolph became friends again. In time, however, Bayard Rustin became one of Randolph's most faithful followers. He personally cared for the aging civil rights leader in his final years of declining health.

Following Japan's attack on Pearl Harbor, December 7, 1941, the United States entered World War II. As a pacifist and a practicing Quaker, Rustin was assigned to hospital duty instead of regular military service. Soon, however, he learned that a close friend, also opposed to war but not a Quaker, had been denied the right to noncombat service.

Was it fair, asked Rustin, that he should be spared the dangers of combat while his friend, with identical beliefs, should run a greater risk of death? As a matter of conscience Rustin notified the government that he would not report for hospital duty—or for any duty at all connected with the war. Instead he accepted a sentence of twenty-eight months in prison for evading the draft.

Years later, when Rustin was a nationally known personality, one United

States senator accused him of being "nothing but a Communist and a draft dodger." In reply Rustin stated that he had never actually joined the Communist party, only the Young Communist League, and that with his term in prison he had fully paid the penalty for refusing to serve in the armed forces.

In time he admitted that by not fighting in the war he probably had made a mistake in judgment. There was good reason for him, as a black, to have taken up arms in America's struggle against the evil racism of Hitler and the Nazis.

At the end of the war in 1945 Rustin once again turned his attention to the battle against segregation. He and others, both black and white, decided to test a Supreme Court decision declaring illegal the separate seating of blacks and whites on buses and trains. Especially in the South at that time, blacks still had to sit in special "colored" sections. On many occasions blacks who insisted on sitting with whites were arrested and sent to jail.

In 1949 Bayard Rustin was arrested for refusing to move to the "colored" section of a bus and was sentenced to serve thirty days in the state prison camp at Roxboro, North Carolina. He was released eight days early for "good behavior."

Later his article describing the experience, entitled "Twenty-two Days on a Chain Gang," was reprinted in the *New York Post.* In the article he recalls how prisoners were beaten for breaking the rules, were systematically starved, were taunted by laughing guards who put pistols or rifles to the prisoners' heads, fingers on the triggers.

Even old men too sick or too weak to work were forced to shovel dirt or break rocks with sledgehammers under threat of beatings. Many of the men were kept in chains. All of the prisoners were black. All were poor.

According to Rustin, vicious punishment did no good in reforming criminals. In a short time, he said, prisoners began to think of themselves not as persons but as "things, to be used." Such men, Rustin suggested, would return to society "not only uncured but with heightened resentment and a desire for revenge."

There was, he thought, a better way: the way of love. "What can be loved can be cured." Only when we have rejected punishment and turned to the healing power of forgiveness and nonviolence, claimed Rustin, would we be able to change the lives of criminals and make them into productive citizens.

When Rustin first arrived at the prison all of his money, stamps, food, and writing paper were stolen by fellow prisoners. Determined to prove that his way of dealing with crime really worked, he announced that the box where he stored his valuables from then on would be kept unlocked. It would become a "community kit." He hoped that anyone who took something from it would let him know.

Before long the stealing stopped. Other prisoners began to unlock their own strongboxes and contribute to the community kit. When Rustin organized a party for the inmates before his departure, he chose "the three men known to be the biggest thieves in the camp." Instead of stealing the food and eating it all themselves, as most prisoners feared, the three not only did not steal but made sure that everyone had enough to eat and that it was shared equally.

How much better might such people behave, asked Rustin, if in the future they were treated with trust and respect, given education, medical care, clean quarters, recreation? Isn't it just a matter of human nature, Rustin advanced, for people to behave as others behave to them? Love and nonviolence, he concluded, were far superior to punishment.

Rustin's article about his experience at Roxboro spurred a wave of public outrage at the conditions he had described. After an official state investigation, chain gangs were abolished in North Carolina.

Encouraged by that victory, Rustin joined confidently with the Reverend Dr. Martin Luther King, Jr., and other leaders in a national campaign to end segregation in public transportation. He also protested against segregated facilities such as lunch counters. Day after day he organized, he wrote, he spoke. But progress was slow.

Then, in 1964, when riots broke out among blacks in Harlem, Rustin went into the streets, trying to get blacks to stop the destruction. Instead of stopping, some threw bottles at him, calling him a traitor to his race. Still he continued to insist that violence was wrong and that it would win no friends for blacks.

Nor did he believe, as did some more fiery blacks, that the answer to the problems of the black community could be found in *separating* from white society. Eating "soul food" (traditional slave food such as chitterlings) and putting black studies into the schools (courses about black culture) would not help, he said. According to Rustin, it might make people *feel* good "to think black, dress black, eat black, and buy black," but it would make very little difference in their lives.

The real problems, Rustin argued, could only be solved by better jobs at higher wages, better housing, better health care, better education. Gaining those ends would mean working together with whites, especially through

Bayard Rustin with Martin Luther King. *The A. Philip Randolph Institute.*

labor unions. It would mean getting the vote for blacks—and then *using* those votes to influence Congress.

"Wearing my hair Afro style," he said, "calling myself an Afro-American, and eating all the chitterlings I can find are not going to affect Congress."

In 1963, to dramatize the goals he had in mind, Rustin joined with other leaders—both black and white—to plan the famous March on Washington for Jobs and Freedom.

On August 28, 1963, more than a quarter of a million Americans of all races and religions gathered together at the base of the Lincoln Memorial. There they heard Dr. Martin Luther King cry out, "I have a dream today!" expressing his vision of what America someday might be.

Electrified by King's message, many did not know that it was Bayard Rustin who carefully had prepared each part of the proceedings for that historic day. He had organized the movement of people arriving on buses and trains. He had arranged for first-aid stations and portable sanitation stations. He had rented public address systems, secured police permits, set up places for keeping lost children—all of the endless details that made the march so memorable. According to A. Philip Randolph, Rustin could only be described as "Mr. March."

In the years that followed Rustin kept working on the big issues—jobs and votes—that could mean real change in the lives of blacks. It made no sense, he said, to desegregate a lunch counter if blacks were too poor to eat at it. Such an economic task, said Rustin, must first be addressed at the ballot box, through political action. And since blacks were a minority in America they would need friends—white friends.

As a result, Rustin, aided by trade union and civil rights leaders, helped establish the A. Philip Randolph Institute. The institute worked to organize black voters. It worked to open up the American economy to blacks. It also fought against black leaders who themselves were racist—hating white society, hating Jews, trying to use their fellow blacks to gain money and influence for themselves.

As Bayard Rustin's fame grew, so did his responsibilities. He became chairman of Social Democrats, USA—the political party that once had been led by Socialists Eugene V. Debs and Norman Thomas.

He worked closely, too, with Freedom House, a group that reports on human rights matters around the world. He cooperated with the United States Holocaust Memorial Council to keep alive the memory of the six million Jews slaughtered by Nazi Germany.

Increasingly Bayard Rustin became involved in world affairs. He championed the rights of the poor in India. He tried to defend the victims of tyranny in Haiti and South Africa. He supported the struggles of Poland's trade union, Solidarity, against oppression by the Soviet Union. He insisted on the right of people *everywhere* to justice and human rights. That right must not be denied, he said, no matter who their tormentors were.

Rustin's position sometimes angered blacks who preferred to focus attention on the long history of white prejudice against them. Other Americans excused tyranny and oppression in such Communist countries as China, Cuba, the Soviet Union, and Vietnam, since those abuses took place to achieve a "higher goal" sometime in the future.

Rustin rejected the excuses. All human life is sacred, he responded, and deserves to be protected. All threats to democracy must be challenged, he said, including those coming from Communists, whose words made them sound like friends of freedom while their deeds proved just the opposite.

On August 24, 1987, Bayard Rustin died. To the very end, he had tried to persuade Americans of talent and influence, regardless of their race, that in their lives there was a special obligation to work for social justice.

"People," he once declared, "must be involved in the struggle for freedom. For if not us, who? And if not now, when?"

Cesar Chavez

1927–   Organizer of migrant farm workers against exploitation by their employers

A tragic reality of life in America today is the plight of the homeless—people without jobs or hope, often forced to sleep in the waiting rooms of railroad stations and bus terminals or shiver in the winter cold of public parks.

Yet one special group of Americans do have jobs. They work long hours, often at backbreaking labor, but sometimes do not know where they will be living the next year, the next month, or even the next day. They are the migrant farm workers, thousands of poor people who travel the country harvesting crops on other people's farms, housed in cheap barracks or shanties set up by the farm owners.

Migrant farm workers, like the poor in our nation's cities, once lived with little hope and little pride in them-selves. Their situation is still serious, but in many ways it is better and may improve still more. The reason for that dramatic change can be traced in large part to one man, the champion of America's migrant workers, Cesar Chavez.

Chavez knows what the life of thousands of poor migrant farm workers is like, because he has lived it. He knows what it is like to wake up at 5:30 A.M. to pick beans or strawberries until nightfall and then not be paid enough money for gasoline to drive to the next job. He knows what it is like to have to sleep under a bridge at night to protect himself from the rain. He remembers looking for wild mustard greens to save himself from starving.

And he remembers other things from his own life: a restaurant waitress pointing to a sign saying No Mexicans Served Here when he wanted to buy a hamburger; the policeman who pushed him out of the Anglo side—the white side—of a movie theater; towns that were so bad that people who lived in them said, *"Sal si puedes"*—"Escape if you can."

Chavez remembers these things. He cannot forget them. And now he is spending his life trying to put an end to them in his country, the United States of America.

Robert F. Kennedy, the brother of the late President John F. Kennedy, once called Cesar Chavez "one of the heroic figures of our time." When Cesar was born on a small farm near Yuma, Arizona, in 1927, his parents and their friends could scarcely have guessed that one day he would become a great American leader.

Cesar's grandfather had been a poor farm worker in Mexico. In 1889 he brought his family to America, finally settling on a 160-acre section of land in what is now Arizona. There he produced corn for tortillas, lettuce, beans, and a little cotton. He built a large house of many rooms, with adobe walls nearly two feet thick. It was in that house that Cesar spent the first ten years of his life.

With the coming of the Great Depression the Chavez family's fortune changed. Cesar's father barely managed to make a living from his farm. In 1937 the family had to sell out for whatever price the bank would give them. Packing their belongings into an old car, they headed for California. There they joined the many thousands of other workers who migrated from farm to farm as the seasons changed.

Cesar lived with his family in the miserable tar-paper shacks that farm owners set up for their workers. He went to more than thirty elementary schools in California and Arizona. By the time he dropped out of school, he was in the seventh grade, but he could hardly read or write. Through all of his childhood, Cesar had worked in the fields alongside his parents and his brothers and his sisters. Ten or twelve hours a day, six or even seven days a week, Cesar Chavez had worked in the fields.

During World War II he served in the United States Navy. It was a change. But after the war he went back to the life of the migrant farm worker—picking fruit, vegetables, cotton—whatever work he could get. He married and began to raise a family. The children had to be fed. They needed clothing. Cesar was poorly educated. He could not get a better job. It seemed as if he was caught in a trap and could not break free.

Then one day in 1952 the life of Cesar

Chavez suddenly changed. An organizer named Fred Ross asked Cesar to help him convince other Mexican-American farm workers to begin helping themselves.

Cesar's father often had tried to get the workers to join together in a union. There had even been strikes. But always the strikes had failed. The owners had only to bring in braceros—farm workers who would come from Mexico, work for low pay, and then return home. The braceros were poor, even poorer than Cesar's own people, who were called Chicanos—Mexicans who were American citizens living permanently in the United States.

What could be done? There always were plenty of fieldworkers ready to pick crops for pennies a day. Everything seemed hopeless. On the side of the owners, there was money and power. On the side of the workers, there was nothing.

Cesar agreed to help Fred Ross and the national leader Ross worked for, the famous community organizer Saul Alinsky. For the next ten years, Chavez worked with Saul Alinsky's Community Service Organization. He did many things. He showed Mexican-Americans how to register to vote so they could participate in elections. He helped farm workers who were having trouble with the police or who needed to receive welfare payments. He showed workers how to band together to petition farm owners for toilets, clean housing, safe drinking water—things the owners almost never provided unless they were forced to.

Meanwhile Cesar was improving his English. He was becoming an effective public speaker. Cesar's campesinos—poor farm workers—trusted him. He was one of them. He was poor. He was brown skinned. He spoke Spanish. Shy and soft-spoken, Cesar never ordered the workers to do things; he only suggested, nothing more. He urged people to talk about their problems. First he worked with them on the little problems—those that could be solved. Then he showed them that by working together they could have a whole new way of life—and that they deserved it.

Chavez, his jet black hair falling over his bronze face, became a familiar figure in the labor camps of California. He was well known for his sense of humor, but even more for his great willpower. It is said of him that he "burned with a quiet fire that never would go out."

In 1962 Cesar Chavez resigned from the Community Service Organization. He thought that the group no longer was serious about bringing poor people together. Too many people in the organization wore coats and ties; too few were real workers. Convinced that the leaders of the group were incapable of founding a farm workers' union, he quit.

With his wife and eight children, he returned to Delano, California, his wife's hometown. Once again he worked in the fields. Often his wife and children worked alongside him. On Sundays he dug ditches for extra money.

But now there was a difference. Chavez used every spare moment to talk to field workers. He asked them to join the new union he was starting—the National Farm Workers Association (NFWA).

He had twelve hundred dollars in savings. Soon that was used up. Sometimes he had to beg food for his family. Yet even that helped him to organize the union. Those who gave him food often decided to join. "If people give you food, they'll give you their hearts," said Chavez.

The union quickly grew. Word spread that Cesar's NFWA really could help workers with their problems. Cesar and his wife started a credit union— a bank that loaned money to workers to buy tires, gasoline, and parts for their battered old cars. Chavez next started a gas station and a grocery store, charging low prices for the things that workers needed. The union offered burial arrangements so workers would not have to go into debt for a funeral if members of their families died. Cesar

had the NFWA hire lawyers to help workers who were cheated by farm owners. Sometimes the union was even able to win small pay raises for its members.

In September 1965 Filipino farm workers near Delano went on strike. The NFWA voted to help them. Cesar's union began a strike against the owners of the large grape farms in the Delano area.

To Chavez and his followers, the strike—*la huelga* in Spanish—was more than just an argument between workers and their bosses. It was a struggle against everything they thought was bad about life in America. It was a way to show anger over all the years they had been crushed by poverty. It was not just a strike. It was a cause—*La Causa*, as it came to be known.

"*Huelga! Huelga!* Strike! Strike!" shouted the farm workers. "*Viva la huelga! Viva la causa! Viva Chavez!*"

The sign of the workers was a black eagle on a red background. It was printed on flags, buttons, pamphlets, even on kites sent flying in the sky. The black eagle was everywhere.

Help for Chavez and his striking migrant workers came almost by magic from around the United States. Doctors, lawyers, clergymen dropped what they were doing and flocked to Delano. College students who had worked to win civil rights for blacks joined in the struggle. The thrilling civil rights song, "We Shall Overcome," was translated into Spanish as *"Nosotros Venceremos."* It was sung throughout the state of California.

The United Auto Workers union promised five thousand dollars a month in aid. Important politicians including Eugene McCarthy, Hubert Humphrey, and Robert F. Kennedy gave their support to the Chicano migrants.

But it was Cesar Chavez himself who kept the spirits of the workers high as the strike dragged on month after month. He spoke at churches, at colleges, at union meetings. He wrote to newspapers and magazines for help. Finally he organized a march from Delano to the state capital at Sacramento—a distance of three hundred miles.

As the marchers made their way north, the road was lined with hundreds of Chicanos who had food and drink ready for them. Bands played. Crowds cheered. Many campesinos joined the march as it neared Sacramento. The major television networks were there with their cameras. Cesar Chavez became known across the country.

Some of the growers gave in. They agreed to let Chavez and his union bargain for the migrant workers. That meant higher pay and better working conditions.

But still the strike continued, especially against the growers of grapes. Many of Chavez's followers lost their patience. They urged Cesar to use violence. Cesar refused. He reminded the workers what had been done without violence by others in history—Mahatma Gandhi, Martin Luther King, Jesus.

The workers, said Chavez, were not all good, and the growers were not all evil. No strike, he said, was worth the life of a worker or his child or a grower or his child. The strike would continue to be nonviolent.

Americans began to notice what was going on in the orchards of California. In most of the nation's big cities, pickets marched in front of supermarkets. The pickets carried signs saying Don't Eat Grapes!

More and more Americans agreed. They refused to buy grapes, to show that they, too, believed in *la huelga.*

As people bought fewer grapes, the growers lost money. In the following months, many of them agreed to sign contracts with Chavez's union. The struggle then turned to growers of tomatoes, of lettuce. In April 1971 Chavez signed a contract for the United Farm Workers with the nation's largest independent producer of lettuce.

Next, after a long period of competition between the United Farm Workers

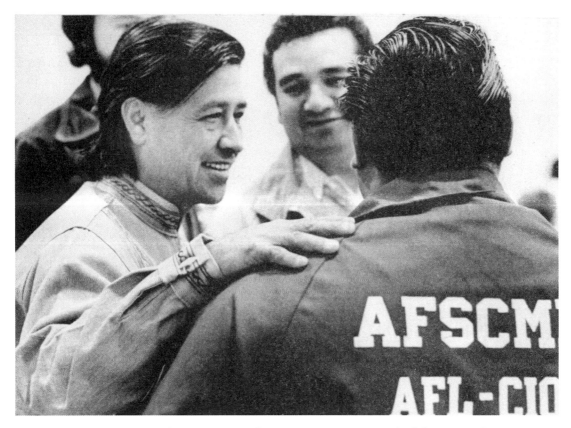

Cesar Chavez rejoices with supporters after agreement was reached between farm workers and the Teamsters Union in San Bernardino, California, 1973. *UPI/Bettmann Newsphotos.*

and the Teamsters Union, the two unions came to an agreement. They worked out a plan for deciding how to organize workers in the field of agriculture, not just migrant laborers but all farm workers. With some exceptions, that truce has lasted.

In recent years, however, Chavez has suffered serious setbacks. From 1978 to 1989, as unskilled laborers poured across the border from Mexico, the UFW lost some one hundred contracts that it had worked out with grape grow-ers, the largest employers of farm labor in California.

At the same time, a frightening development surfaced in the San Joaquin Valley, the very center of the state's agricultural industry. Farm workers and their children began to suffer much higher than normal rates of cancer. Environmentalists suspected that the cause of the drastic rise in cancer-related deaths might well be the contamination of water supplies by the pesticides used in growing grapes.

Chavez and the UFW protested to the grape growers. But the owners answered that there was no proof that pesticides were responsible.

In the summer of 1988 Cesar Chavez acted once again to bring his case to the American public. He began a water-only fast. The fast lasted for thirty-six days, greatly endangering the health of Chavez, by then sixty-one years old. On the day he finally ended the fast he had to be carried to a union rally. There some seven thousand union members and other supporters stood in silence as he sat through the celebration of a mass.

Just as Robert F. Kennedy had been present for that ceremony twenty years earlier in 1968, the Reverend Jesse Jackson, a former presidential candidate, this time pledged his support. He promised to help convince Americans to boycott growers until the growers agreed to give workers, through their unions, an equal share in decisions as to how pesticides are used.

Once, while testifying before a Senate committee, Chavez was asked how long the struggle for the farm workers would continue. "A lifetime," he answered. It would continue until all farm workers who wanted the protection of a union could have it.

Despite all of his fame Cesar Chavez had not changed. He continued to live in an old house with badly peeling paint. He still wore faded blue jeans and an old cotton work shirt. And he still supported his wife and children on not much more than the ten dollars a week in strike money paid to all field workers in the union.

Over the years Chavez and his union experienced many ups and downs—contracts signed and contracts lost. Yet, in spite of his problems, his many defeats, Cesar Chavez succeeded in raising the consciousness of much of the nation. He showed persistence, determination, in working for the cause of farm workers' rights.

True, the growers had money on their side. But the poor, on their side, had time. And Cesar Chavez was a patient man. He could say with certainty that surely, in time, "*Nosotros venceremos*—we shall overcome!"

Eleanor Roosevelt

1884–1962   Writer, lecturer, and vigorous supporter of social betterment causes; author of the United Nations' Universal Declaration of Human Rights

Eleanor Roosevelt was the wife of President Franklin Delano Roosevelt. But Eleanor was much more than just a president's wife, an echo of her husband's career.

Sad and lonely as a child, Eleanor was called "Granny" by her mother because of her seriousness. People teased her about her looks and called her the "ugly duckling." Her husband was unfaithful to her and continued to see another woman until the day he died. Nor did Eleanor's children find much happiness in their own marriages.

Yet despite all of the disappointments, the bitterness, the misery she experienced, Eleanor Roosevelt refused to give up. Instead she turned her unhappiness and pain to strength.

She devoted her life to helping others. Today she is remembered as one of America's greatest women.

Eleanor was born in a fine townhouse in Manhattan. Her family also owned an elegant mansion along the Hudson River, where they spent weekends and summers. As a child Eleanor went to fashionable parties. A servant took care of her and taught her to speak French. Her mother, the beautiful Anna Hall Roosevelt, wore magnificent jewels and fine clothing. Her father, Elliott Roosevelt, had his own hunting lodge and liked to sail and to play tennis and polo. Elliott, who loved Eleanor dearly, was the younger brother of Theodore Roosevelt, who in 1901 became President of the United States. The Roosevelt

245

family, one of America's oldest, wealthiest families, was respected and admired.

To the outside world it might have seemed that Eleanor had everything that any child could want—everything that could make her happy. But she was not happy. Instead her childhood was very sad.

Almost from the day of her birth, October 11, 1884, people noticed that she was an unattractive child. As she grew older she could not help but notice her mother's extraordinary beauty, as well as the beauty of her aunts and cousins. Eleanor was plain looking, ordinary, even, as some called her, homely. For a time she had to wear a bulky brace on her back to straighten her crooked spine.

When Eleanor was born her parents had wanted a boy. They were scarcely able to hide their disappointment. Later, with the arrival of two boys, Elliott and Hall, Eleanor watched her mother hold the boys on her lap and lovingly stroke their hair, while for Eleanor there seemed only coolness, distance.

Feeling unwanted, Eleanor became shy and withdrawn. She also developed many fears. She was afraid of the dark, afraid of animals, afraid of other children, afraid of being scolded, afraid of strangers, afraid that people would not like her. She was a frightened, lonely little girl.

The one joy in the early years of her life was her father, who always seemed to care for her, love her. He used to dance with her, to pick her up and throw her into the air while she laughed and laughed. He called her "little golden hair" or "darling little Nell."

Then, when she was six, her father left. An alcoholic, he went to live in a sanitarium in Virginia in an attempt to deal with his drinking problem. Eleanor missed him greatly.

Next her mother became ill with painful headaches. Sometimes for hours at a time Eleanor would sit holding her mother's head in her lap and stroking her forehead. Nothing else seemed to relieve the pain. At those times Eleanor often remembered how her mother had teased her about her looks and called her Granny. But even at the age of seven Eleanor was glad to be helping someone, glad to be needed—and noticed.

The next year, when Eleanor was eight, her mother, the beautiful Anna, died. Afterward her brother Elliott suddenly caught diphtheria and he, too, died. Eleanor and her baby brother, Hall, were taken to live with their grandmother in Manhattan.

A few months later another tragedy

struck. Elliott Roosevelt, Eleanor's father, also died. Within eighteen months Eleanor had lost her mother, a brother, and her dear father.

For the rest of her life Eleanor carried with her the letters that her father had written to her from the sanitarium. In them he had told her to be brave, to become well educated, and to grow up into a woman he could be proud of, a woman who helped people who were suffering.

Only ten years old when her father died, Eleanor decided even then to live the kind of life he had described—a life that would have made him proud of her.

Few things in life came easily for Eleanor, but the first few years after her father's death proved exceptionally hard. Grandmother Hall's dark and gloomy townhouse had no place for children to play. The family ate meals in silence. Every morning Eleanor and Hall were expected to take cold baths for their health. Eleanor had to work at better posture by walking with her arms behind her back, clamped over a walking stick.

Instead of making new friends Eleanor often sat alone in her room and read. For many months after her father's death she pretended that he was still alive. She made him the hero of stories she wrote for school. Some-

times, alone and unhappy, she just cried.

Some of her few moments of happiness came from visiting her uncle, Theodore Roosevelt, in Oyster Bay, Long Island. A visit with Uncle Ted meant playing games and romping outdoors with the many Roosevelt children.

Once Uncle Ted threw her into the water to teach her how to swim, but when she started to sink he had to rescue her. Often he would read to the children old Norse tales and poetry. It was at Sagamore Hill, Uncle Ted's home, that Eleanor first learned how much fun it could be to read books aloud.

For most of the time Eleanor's life was grim. Although her parents had left plenty of money for her upbringing, she had only two dresses to wear to school. Once she spilled ink on one of them, and since the other was in the wash she had to wear the dress with large ink stains on it to school the next day. It was not that Grandmother Hall was stingy. Rather, she was old and often confused. Nor did she show much warmth or love for Eleanor and her brother. Usually she just neglected them.

Just before Eleanor turned fifteen, Grandmother Hall decided to send her to boarding school in England. The school she chose was Allenswood, a private academy for girls located on the outskirts of London.

It was at Allenswood that Eleanor, still thinking of herself as an "ugly duckling," first dared to believe that one day she might be able to become a swan.

At Allenswood she worked to toughen herself physically. Every day she did exercises in the morning and took a cold shower. Although she did not like competitive team sports, as a matter of self-discipline she tried out for field hockey. Not only did she make the team but, because she played so hard, also won the respect of her teammates.

They called her by her family nickname, "Totty," and showed their affection for her by putting books and flowers in her room, as was the custom at Allenswood. Never before had she experienced the pleasure of having schoolmates actually admire her rather than tease her.

At Allenswood, too, she began to look after her health. She finally broke the habit of chewing her fingernails. She learned to eat nutritious foods, to get plenty of sleep, and to take a brisk walk every morning, no matter how miserable the weather.

Under the guidance of the school's headmistress, Mademoiselle Souvestre (or "Sou"), she learned to ask searching questions and think for herself instead of just giving back on tests what teachers had said.

She also learned to speak French fluently, a skill she polished by traveling in France, living for a time with a French family. Mademoiselle Souvestre arranged for her to have a new red dress. Wearing it, after all of the old, worn dresses Grandmother Hall had given her, made her feel very proud.

Eleanor was growing up, and the joy of young womanhood had begun to transform her personality.

In 1902, nearly eighteen years old, she left Allenswood, not returning for her fourth year there. Grandmother Hall insisted that, instead, she must be introduced to society as a debutante—to go to dances and parties and begin to take her place in the social world with other wealthy young women.

Away from Allenswood, Eleanor's old uncertainty about her looks came back again. She saw herself as too tall, too thin, too plain. She worried about her buck teeth, which she thought made her look horselike. The old teasing began again, especially on the part of Uncle Ted's daughter, "Princess" Alice Roosevelt, who seemed to take pleasure in making Eleanor feel uncomfortable.

Eleanor, as always, did as she was told. She went to all of the parties and dances. But she also began working with poor children at the Rivington Street Settlement House on New York's Lower East Side. She taught the girls gymnastic exercises. She took children to museums and to musical performances. She tried to get the parents interested in politics in order to get better schools and cleaner, safer streets.

Meanwhile Eleanor's life reached a turning point. She fell in love! The young man was her fifth cousin, Franklin Delano Roosevelt.

Eleanor and Franklin had known each other since childhood. Franklin recalled how once he had carried her piggyback in the nursery. When she was fourteen he had danced with her at a party. Then, shortly after her return from Allenswood, they had met by chance on a train. They talked and almost at once realized how much they liked each other.

For a time they met secretly. Then they attended parties together. Franklin—tall, strong, handsome—saw her as a person he could trust. He knew that she would not try to dominate him.

But did he really love her? Would he always? She wrote to him, quoting a poem she knew: "'. . . Unless you can swear, *For life, for death!*' . . . Oh, never call it loving!'"

Franklin promised that his love was indeed "for life," and Eleanor agreed to marry him. It was the autumn of 1903. He was twenty-one. She was nineteen.

On March 17, 1905, Eleanor and Franklin were married. "Uncle Ted," by then President of the United States, was there to "give the bride away." It was sometimes said that the dynamic, energetic Theodore Roosevelt had to be "the bride at every wedding and the corpse at every funeral." And it was certainly true that day. Wherever the president went, the guests followed at his heels.

Before long Eleanor and Franklin found themselves standing all alone, deserted. Franklin seemed annoyed, but Eleanor didn't mind. She had found the ceremony deeply moving. And she stood next to her husband in a glow of idealism—very serious, very grave, very much in love.

In May 1906 the couple's first child was born. During the next nine years Eleanor gave birth to five more babies, one of whom died in infancy. Still timid, shy, afraid of making mistakes, she found herself so busy that there was little time to think of her own drawbacks.

Still, looking back later on the early years of her marriage, Eleanor knew that she should have been a stronger person, especially in the handling of Franklin's mother, or, as they

Eleanor and Franklin Roosevelt in the early 1920s. *Oscar Jordan/Office Presidential Library, National Archives.*

both called her, "Mammá." Too often Mammá made the decisions about such things as where they would live, how their home would be furnished, how the children would be disciplined. Eleanor and Franklin let her pay for things they could not afford—extra servants, vacations, doctor bills, clothing. She offered, and they accepted.

Before long, trouble developed in the relationship between Eleanor and Franklin. Serious, shy, easily embarrassed, Eleanor could not share Franklin's interests in golf and tennis. He enjoyed light talk and flirting with women. She could not be lighthearted. So she stayed on the sidelines. Instead of losing her temper she bottled up her anger and did not talk to him at all. As he used to say, she "clammed up." Her silence only made things worse, because it puzzled him. Faced with her coldness, her brooding silence, he only grew angrier and more distant.

Meanwhile Franklin's career in politics advanced rapidly. In 1910 he was elected to the New York State Senate. In 1913 President Wilson appointed him Assistant Secretary of the Navy—a powerful position in the national government, which required the Roosevelts to move to Washington, D.C.

In 1917 the United States entered World War I as an active combatant. Like many socially prominent women, Eleanor threw herself into the war effort. Sometimes she worked fifteen and sixteen hours a day. She made sandwiches for soldiers passing through the nation's capital. She knitted sweaters. She used Franklin's influence to get the Red Cross to build a recreation room for soldiers who had been shell-shocked in combat.

It was in the autumn of 1918 that, as she put it, "the bottom dropped out" of her world. She discovered that Franklin had been having a love affair with her social secretary, Lucy Mercer. Eleanor offered Franklin a divorce, but he urged that "for the good of the children" they should stay married. Actually Franklin realized that a divorce—in those days considered a serious moral offense—would ruin his political career.

Eleanor forgave Franklin. She agreed to go on living with him and helping him in his career. Yet from that time on she determined to live her life, too,

to have her freedom and independence. Things would never again be as they had been. She could forgive Franklin, but she could not forget.

In 1920 the Democratic Party chose Franklin as its candidate for Vice-President of the United States. Even though the Republicans won the election, Roosevelt became a well-known figure in national politics. All the time, Eleanor stood by his side, smiling, doing what was expected of her as a candidate's wife.

She did what was expected—and much more—in the summer of 1921 when disaster struck the Roosevelt family. While on vacation Franklin suddenly fell ill with infantile paralysis—polio—the horrible disease that each year used to kill or cripple thousands of children, and many adults as well. When Franklin became a victim of polio nobody knew what caused the disease or how to cure it.

Franklin lived, but the lower part of his body remained paralyzed. For the rest of his life he never again had the use of his legs. He had to be lifted and carried from place to place. He had to wear heavy steel braces from his waist to the heels of his shoes.

His mother, as well as many of his advisers, urged him to give up politics, to live the life of a country gentleman on the Roosevelt estate at Hyde Park,

New York. This time, Eleanor, calm and strong, stood up for her ideas. She argued that he should not be treated like a sick person, tucked away in the country, inactive, just waiting for death to come.

Franklin agreed. Slowly he recovered his health. His energy returned. In 1928 he was elected governor of New York. Then, just four years later, he was elected President of the United States.

Meanwhile, Eleanor had changed. To keep Franklin in the public eye while he was recovering she had gotten involved in politics herself. It was, she thought, her "duty." From childhood she had been taught "to do the thing that has to be done, the way it has to be done, when it has to be done."

With the help of Franklin's adviser Louis Howe, she made fund-raising speeches for the Democratic Party all around New York State. She helped in the work of the League of Women Voters, the Consumer's League, and the Foreign Policy Association. After becoming interested in the problems of working women she gave time to the Women's Trade Union League (WTUL).

It was through the WTUL that she met a group of remarkable women— women doing exciting work that made a difference in the world. They taught Eleanor about life in the slums. They awakened her hopes that something could be done to improve the condition of the poor. She dropped out of the "fashionable" society of her wealthy friends and joined the world of reform— social change.

For hours at a time Eleanor and her reformer friends talked with Franklin. They showed him the need for new laws: laws to get children out of the factories and into schools; laws to cut down the long hours that women worked; laws to get fair wages for all workers.

By the time that Franklin was sworn in as president the nation was facing its deepest depression. One out of every four Americans was out of work, out of hope. At mealtimes people stood in lines in front of soup kitchens for something to eat. Mrs. Roosevelt herself knew of once-prosperous families who found themselves reduced to eating stale bread from thrift shops or traveling to parts of town where they were not known to beg for money from house to house.

Eleanor worked in the charity kitchens, ladling out soup. She visited slums. She crisscrossed the country learning about the suffering of coal miners, shipyard workers, migrant farm workers, students, housewives—Americans caught up in the paralysis of the Great

Depression. Since Franklin himself remained crippled, she became his eyes and ears, informing him of what the American people were really thinking and feeling.

Eleanor also was the president's conscience, personally urging on him some of the most compassionate, forward-looking laws of his presidency, including, for example, the National Youth Administration (NYA), which provided money to allow impoverished young people to stay in school.

She lectured widely, wrote a regularly syndicated newspaper column, "My Day," and spoke frequently on the radio. She fought for equal pay for women in industry. Like no other First Lady up to that time she became a link between the president and the American public.

Above all she fought against racial and religious prejudice. When Eleanor learned that the DAR (Daughters of the American Revolution) would not allow the great black singer Marian Anderson to perform in their auditorium in Washington, D.C., she resigned from the organization. Then she arranged to have Miss Anderson sing in front of the Lincoln Memorial.

Similarly, when she entered a hall where, as often happened in those days, blacks and whites were seated in separate sections, she made it a point to sit with the blacks. Her example marked an important step in making the rights of blacks a matter of national priority.

On December 7, 1941, Japanese forces launched a surprise attack on the American naval base at Pearl Harbor, Hawaii, as well as on other American installations in the Pacific. The United States entered World War II, fighting not only against Japan but against the brutal dictators who then controlled Germany and Italy.

Eleanor helped the Red Cross raise money. She gave blood, sold war bonds. But she also did the unexpected. In 1943, for example, she visited barracks and hospitals on islands throughout the South Pacific. When she visited a hospital she stopped at every bed. To each soldier she said something special, something that a mother might say. Often, after she left, even battle-hardened men had tears in their eyes. Admiral Nimitz, who originally thought such visits would be a nuisance, became one of her strongest admirers. Nobody else, he said, had done so much to help raise the spirits of the men.

By spring 1945 the end of the war in Europe seemed near. Then, on April 12, a phone call brought Eleanor the news that Franklin Roosevelt, who had gone to Warm Springs, Georgia, for a rest, was dead.

As Eleanor later declared, "I think that sometimes I acted as his conscience. I urged him to take the harder path when he would have preferred the easier way. In that sense, I acted on occasion as a spur, even though the spurring was not always wanted or welcome.

"Of course," said Eleanor, "I loved him, and I miss him."

After Franklin's funeral, every day that Eleanor was home at Hyde Park, without fail, she placed flowers on his grave. Then she would stand very still beside him there.

With Franklin dead, Eleanor Roosevelt might have dropped out of the public eye, might have been remembered in the history books only as a footnote to the president's program of social reforms. Instead she found new strengths within herself, new ways to live a useful, interesting life—and to help others. Now, moreover, her successes were her own, not the result of being the president's wife.

In December 1945 President Harry S Truman invited her to be one of the American delegates going to London to begin the work of the United Nations. Eleanor hesitated, but the president insisted. He said that the nation needed her; it was her duty. After that Eleanor agreed.

In the beginning some of her fellow delegates from the United States considered her unqualified for the position, but after seeing her in action they changed their minds.

It was Eleanor Roosevelt who, almost single-handedly, pushed through the United Nations General Assembly a resolution giving refugees from World War II the right *not* to return to their native lands if they did not wish to. The Russians angrily objected, but Eleanor's reasoning convinced wavering delegates. In a passionate speech defending the rights of the refugees she declared, "We [must] consider first the rights of man and what makes men more free—not governments, but man!"

Next Mrs. Roosevelt helped draft the United Nations Declaration of Human Rights. The Soviets wanted the Declaration to list the duties people owed to their countries. Again Eleanor insisted that the United Nations should stand for individual freedom—the rights of people to free speech, freedom of religion, and such human needs as health care and education. In December 1948, with the Soviet Union and its allies refusing to vote, the Declaration of Human Rights won approval of the UN General Assembly by a vote of forty-eight to zero.

Even after retiring from her post at the UN Mrs. Roosevelt continued to travel. In places around the world she

A highlight of Eleanor Roosevelt's career at the United Nations was the adoption of the Universal Declaration of Human Rights in 1949. *Franklin D. Roosevelt Library, Hyde Park, New York.*

dined with presidents and kings. But she also visited tenement slums in Bombay, India, factories in Yugoslavia, farms in Lebanon and Israel.

Everywhere she met people who were eager to greet her. Although as a child she had been brought up to be formal and distant, she had grown to feel at ease with people. They wanted to touch her, to hug her, to kiss her.

Eleanor's doctor had been telling her to slow down, but that was hard for her. She continued to write her newspaper column, "My Day," and to appear on television. She still began working at seven-thirty in the morning and often continued until well past midnight. Not only did she write and speak, she taught retarded children and raised money for health care of the poor.

As author Clare Boothe Luce put it, "Mrs. Roosevelt has done more good deeds on a bigger scale for a longer time than any woman who ever appeared on our public scene. No woman has ever so comforted the distressed or so distressed the comfortable."

Gradually, however, she was forced to withdraw from some of her activities, to spend more time at home.

On November 7, 1962, at the age of seventy-eight, Eleanor died in her sleep. She was buried in the rose garden at Hyde Park, alongside her husband.

Adlai Stevenson, the American ambassador to the United Nations, remembered her as "the First Lady of the World," as the person—male or female—most effective in working for the cause of human rights. As Stevenson declared, "She would rather light a candle than curse the darkness."

And perhaps, in sum, that is what the struggle for human rights is all about.

Martin Luther King, Jr.

1929–1968   Martyred leader of the nonviolent wing of the American civil rights movement; recipient of the Nobel Peace Prize

Christmas was coming. Mrs. Rosa Parks had been shopping all day. She was tired. Her feet hurt. She climbed onto a big orange bus, paid her fare, and took a seat.

Then something happened that changed the course of American history. The bus stopped and four passengers, all white people, got on. There were no more seats. In Montgomery, Alabama, it was the law that blacks had to give up their seats to whites if the bus driver told them to. Rosa Parks was black.

The driver ordered three other blacks to give up their seats. Without a word, they stood. They were used to that kind of thing. It happened all the time in Montgomery. Besides, in 1955, it was the law.

But this time, when the driver told Rosa Parks to stand, she simply said, "No!" She would not give up her seat. She was tired. She had paid her fare—just like the white people. Why should she have to stand?

The driver called a policeman. He arrested Rosa Parks. At the city jail she was fingerprinted. Her picture was taken, showing her holding a prison number—as if she were a common criminal. Then, after paying a few dollars in bail, she was allowed to leave. Her trial would come later.

The word spread quickly through Montgomery. A black woman had been arrested for not giving up her seat on a bus. It had happened many times before. But this time in the Negro part of town people buzzed excitedly. They were angry. "What can we do? This can't go on any longer!"

It was nearly a hundred years since the Civil War, and black people still did not have the rights of other Americans. In America's South—and in other parts of the country, too—blacks ate in separate restaurants from whites, went to separate schools, drank from separate drinking fountains in public places, even swore oaths on separate Bibles in the courtroom. Few of them were allowed to vote in elections. Before voting, they had to pass difficult reading tests and pay a tax called a poll tax. They could not get good jobs. They could not get good housing. In small ways and in large ways, black people were made to feel all the time that they were not as good as whites.

For a long time the blacks had accepted mistreatment without fighting back. They did not think anything could be done. But in 1954 something important happened. In that year the Supreme Court of the United States said that blacks could not be given separate schooling from whites.

Why? Because in schools for blacks the children did not receive as good an education. In America education is critical in determining how successful a person will be in life. If schools for blacks were not good, black youngsters would have less chance for success than whites.

After the Supreme Court ruling, black people had new hope. Perhaps, at last, they would have the same chance as other Americans for a good life.

That is why, in 1955, the black people of Montgomery, Alabama, were so angry when Rosa Parks was arrested. Their hopes had been high, and now it looked as if nothing really had changed. They decided that this time they would stand up for their rights. But what should they do? And who would lead them?

The new minister of the Dexter Avenue Baptist Church in Montgomery was the twenty-seven-year-old Reverend Dr. Martin Luther King, Jr. Born in Atlanta, Georgia, he was one of only six Negroes at Crozer Theological Seminary, where he went to study religion. Yet he graduated with the highest grades in his class and was also student-body president. After that he studied for a doctorate in philosophy at Boston University.

The night Rosa Parks was arrested, Martin Luther King and other Montgomery ministers met to decide on a course of action. They agreed that for one day, December 5, blacks should not ride the buses. This would show how they felt. Nearly three-fourths of all the bus riders in Montgomery were black. If they did not use the buses, the company would lose business. This strategy, called a boycott, is a peaceful way to bring about change.

Leaflets were quickly printed. They said: "Don't ride the bus to work, to town, to school, or any place Monday, December 5. . . . Come to a Mass Meeting, Monday at 7:00 P.M., at the Holt Street Baptist Church for further instruction."

On the morning of December 5, Martin Luther King and his wife, Coretta, awoke early. They were eager to see how many people were on the buses. If half of the city's blacks stayed off the buses, King would have been pleased. At six o'clock the first bus passed near the Kings' house. It was empty! The second bus was almost empty, and so was the third.

To Martin Luther King it was a miracle. He jumped into his car and drove around Montgomery. The buses were almost all empty. Black people walked. They rode horses and even mules. They shared rides in cars with their friends. But they did not take buses.

The boycott did not last just one day. It continued for 382 days. King and the other ministers held meetings. They urged the city's blacks to be peaceful and calm. But they should not pay a penny in bus fare until the owners of the bus company agreed to give blacks the same right to seats as whites.

The owners of the company were furious. Every day the boycott continued

they lost money. Many of Montgomery's other whites were angry, too. They were not accustomed to blacks standing up for their rights. Sometimes whites threw rocks at the drivers who were sharing their cars with other Negroes. They shouted and called the blacks names.

Martin Luther King told his followers not to fight back. He believed in love, not violence. In college he had studied much about Jesus, who said, "Love your enemies, bless them that curse you." He also had learned about Mahatma Gandhi of India. Gandhi helped India win freedom from Great Britain by refusing to obey British laws. Even when he was imprisoned, Gandhi would not allow himself to hate the English or advise Indians to use violence against them. Gandhi first had learned about nonviolence from the works of an American, Henry David Thoreau.

King, like Gandhi and Thoreau, believed that an unjust law should not be obeyed. Not obeying—known as civil disobedience—might mean going to jail. But if that was the price for doing what a person thought was right, Martin Luther King believed that the price should be paid.

He also believed that even if people did evil to you, you should do good to them. You should not hate them. As the great black Booker T. Washington once had said, "Let no man pull you so low as to make you hate him." King agreed. He wrote that no matter how badly blacks were treated they should not hate their white brothers. To become a truly great people they must learn to "turn the other cheek"—not hit back if they were hit.

But they must never stop trying to win their rights. Most Americans, King thought, believed in fair play. They needed only to be shown that blacks were not being treated fairly. Then they would understand. They would help black people achieve equal rights.

The story of the Montgomery bus boycott spread quickly around the world. Money poured in from Latin America, Asia, and Europe, as well as from many parts of the United States, to help King in his fight. Almost overnight King became an internationally known figure.

Seeing his picture on television and in the newspapers made some whites even more bitter. One evening a bomb exploded on the front porch of King's home. Nobody was hurt. A crowd of more than a thousand Negroes gathered. Many shook their fists in anger. Others carried guns, knives, rocks, and broken bottles. In vain the police chief tried to quiet them. So did the mayor of Montgomery. But the shouting crowd refused to listen. Someone had tried to kill their leader. And they demanded revenge. Nothing, it seemed,

could block the onset of a bloody riot.

Finally Martin Luther King himself stepped out onto the smoking ruins of his front porch. He raised his arms and began to speak. At once the crowd grew silent.

"Don't get panicky," he said. "Don't get panicky at all. Don't get your weapons. Please be peaceful," he pleaded. "I want you to love your enemies. Be good to them. Love them and let them know you love them."

Then King, who, along with his wife and children, had just barely escaped death, concluded, "I want America to know that even if I am stopped this movement will not stop, our work will not stop, for what we are doing is right. What we are doing is just—and God is with us."

Slowly, peacefully, the angry blacks began to disperse to their homes. The police relaxed. There was no riot. King's words were repeated on television and in newspapers across the country. Americans saw that he meant what he said about nonviolence, even when his own life was in danger. "The strong man," he said, "is the man who can stand up for his rights and not hit back."

The bus boycott went on. It lasted until 1956, when the United States Supreme Court ruled that segregation of blacks and whites on vehicles engaged in interstate commerce is illegal.

At last the fight was over. Dr. King

Dr. Martin Luther King, Jr., in his cell in the Jefferson County Courthouse, Birmingham, Alabama, in 1967. *UPI/Bettmann Newsphotos.*

and his followers had won a tremendous victory. Now blacks could sit where they chose on buses and trains. Never again would they be required to give up their seats to whites.

When King next spoke to his people he urged them not to boast about their victory. "I would be terribly disappointed," he said, "if any of you go back to the buses bragging that 'We, the Negroes, won a victory over the white people.'" He wanted them to join together with whites to make Montgomery a better place—and to remain nonviolent.

The bus boycott was only the first step in King's struggle to help blacks get their rights. The fight spread all over the South and then to the North. But always King taught black people to use gentleness and kindness—not force.

Sometimes, even for him, it was not easy. Whites cursed him and spat on him. They threw rocks and tomatoes at him. They kicked and hit him. They threatened his life. They threatened his wife and four children. They burned crosses on his front lawn. Often he was thrown into jail.

In spite of everything, King kept on fighting for the rights of blacks. He showed his followers how to stay still even when they were being beaten or when mobs called them names and threw things at them. He led peaceful marches against all-white schools, restaurants, and movie theaters. He tried to get the names of blacks on voter registration lists so they could vote in primary and general elections.

In Birmingham, Alabama, King was met by snarling, sharp-fanged German shepherd dogs, held on leashes by policemen. The police turned fire hoses on a crowd of Negro marchers, even the women and the little children. All across the country, people saw pictures on their television screens of the police dogs. They saw policemen clubbing people who would not fight back—blacks who wanted nothing more than the same rights that most Americans already had.

More and more King began to emerge as a new kind of American hero. Every time he was put in jail or beaten, he won followers to his ideas. Before long, white people joined in his marches. Together with blacks, they sang the most famous of all civil rights songs, "We Shall Overcome." The words of the song speak of a time when blacks and whites will live together in peace and happiness.

Martin Luther King believed that such a time really would come—someday.

In Washington, D.C., on August 28, 1963, he told more about his hopes for

Leaders of the March on Washington move along Constitution Avenue in Washington, 1963. *UPI/Bettmann Newsphotos.*

the future. That day he made one of the great speeches in all of American history.

More than a quarter million people—both black and white—were gathered in front of the Lincoln Memorial. They had come to ask Congress to pass the civil rights bill, then being considered by Congress. If adopted, it would give blacks many of the rights that King and his supporters had fought for so valiantly.

"I have a dream today," declared King. "I have a dream that one day this nation will rise up and live out the true meaning of . . . 'all men are created equal.'

"I have a dream that one day on the red hills of Georgia, the sons of former slaves and the sons of former slave owners will be able to sit down together at the table of brotherhood.

"I have a dream," said King again and again. Each time he told of his hope that the promises made for all Americans in the Declaration of Independence and the Constitution would someday come true.

"Let freedom ring," he cried out. Let it ring until the "day when all of God's children, black men and white men, Jews and Gentiles, Protestants and Catholics, will be able to join hands and sing in the words of that old Negro spiritual, 'Free at last! Free at last! Thank God almighty, we are free at last!' "

When King finished, men and women openly wept. His words were carried swiftly around the world by radio and television. Many newspapers printed his entire speech. Now, unquestionably, he had become the foremost leader of America's blacks.

In 1964 King was presented the Nobel Peace Prize, an international award given to those who make outstanding contributions to the cause of peace.

When King won the prize he was only thirty-five years old—the youngest person ever to receive it. In accepting the award, he suggested humbly that it really was not his. Rather it belonged to many people, black and white, still working with high courage toward an era of nonviolence and love in the United States.

Not all blacks agreed with King. Some argued that nonviolence was too slow. They pointed out that love, so far, was not winning equal rights for blacks. In Birmingham, Alabama, six children were killed when whites bombed a Negro church. In Mississippi, Medgar Evers, a black civil rights leader, was ambushed and killed in the driveway of his house. In Mississippi, three young people trying to help blacks register to vote were beaten and shot to death, their bodies found several weeks later buried near a dam. Who could love white people who did things like that?

New black leaders began to emerge. One of them, Malcolm X, called himself a Black Muslim, a believer in the Islamic religion. Malcolm said—at least early in his public career—that blacks never would be able to live with whites. Instead, he said, they should rule a separate country of their own, made up of one of the states of the United States. There they would live their lives completely apart from whites.

Among other black leaders who disagreed with King were Stokely Carmichael and H. Rap Brown. Carmichael demanded that blacks should no longer try to love whites who beat them and insulted them. Instead they should fight back. "What we need," he said, "is Black Power!" H. Rap Brown did not mind violence, either. "Violence," he once said, "is as American as cherry pie."

Many blacks believed that Malcolm

Dr. King is greeted by school children at Mount Calvary Baptist Church in Newark, New Jersey, March 27, 1968. He was touring Newark to seek support for his Poor People's Campaign in Washington. *UPI/Bettmann Newsphotos.*

X, Stokely Carmichael, and H. Rap Brown were right. They thought King was wrong. And, of course, it was easier for angry blacks to pick up guns and shoot white people than to try to love them. In city after city, riots erupted—Watts (Los Angeles) in 1965, in Cleveland, Chicago, Detroit, New York, and Newark in the following years. Buildings were burned and stores looted. Whites and blacks shot and stabbed each other.

By 1968 the battle for Negro rights had become a nightmare. To some it appeared that America was on the verge of widespread racial warfare.

King would not change his mind. He believed that violence was wrong. He also knew that in America it was whites who had both the weapons and the numerical advantage. A war between blacks and whites would end in death—the death of the Negro race in the United States. Meanwhile he remained convinced that most blacks still followed his ideas. What he needed was time to lead them away from violence and back to loving-kindness. He needed time to prove that nonviolence really could work.

But he did not have that time. On April 4, 1968, in Memphis, Tennessee, Martin Luther King was shot and killed from ambush by a white assassin.

The day after he died, angry blacks began riots across the United States. In Washington, D.C., smoke and flames rose high in the sky within sight of the White House. Soldiers with machine guns guarded the steps of the Capitol building. Violence, it seemed, was everywhere.

But violence was not the way of Martin Luther King. He did not want to be remembered that way. He wanted to be remembered with Jesus and Gandhi. They were men of peace who gave their own lives to make the lives of others better. King, too, gave his life to help build what he hoped would be a better world, a world of right and of justice.

Now Americans have had an opportu-nity to view their racial situation more clearly. In the years since Dr. King's death, most of his foes—both black and white—have faded into history. Meanwhile the name Martin Luther King has earned a hallowed place in the annals of human freedom. Streets and schools in the United States and abroad have been named after him. College scholarships have been established in his memory. A national holiday—Martin Luther King Day—has been set aside by Congress to honor his achievements, thus placing him in the front rank of American heroes, along with George Washington and Abraham Lincoln.

What has happened, then, is that time has proven King far more right than wrong. The American people, in honoring him, have affirmed what Lincoln called "the better angel" of our natures. It is not violence and hatred that America has celebrated, but rather the ideals of peace and love and the brotherhood of humankind.

And those, of course, are the ideals represented in the life—and the sacrifice—of Martin Luther King.

For Further Reading

Unlike poets and novelists, writers of biography cannot depend on their own experience. They must draw on the work of others who have gone before them—earlier historians and biographers, and in some instances the personal accounts of subjects who have written about themselves.

Even when the biographer has lived at the same time as his subject, perhaps even known the person he is trying to portray, the task of describing someone's life is infinitely complicated, delicate. Gamaliel Bradford, one of the truly great biographers, once expressed his frustration and, at the same time, his attraction to the "portrayal of souls":

> Souls tremble and shift and fade under the touch. They elude and evade and mock you, fool you with false lights and perplex you with impenetrable shadows, till you are almost ready to give up in despair any effort to interpret them. But you cannot give it up; for there is no artistic effort more fascinating and no study so completely inexhaustible. (*American Portraits*, 1922)

"Collective biography"—a collection of portraits including several personalities related by a common theme—is no simpler. But it carries with it enormous satisfactions. In preparing this book, for example, one challenge was to understand and then describe for young readers the diverse motivations of certain self-willed, politically active individuals. Each personality in the book is different—different in heritage, education, and strategies for achieving a wide variety of goals.

Yet all of the historical figures in the book are inextricably related. For in spite of the great differences that divide them, they are united in a common commitment to individual rights—free speech, free press, racial and religious justice, equality of economic opportunity, women's rights.

Because of their diversity, no single source of information possibly could prove adequate in exploring such extraordinary lives. For general background, however, two multivolume collections proved especially helpful: the *Dictionary of American Biography* (Charles Scribner's Sons) and *Notable American Women* (Belknap Press of Harvard University Press).

Clearly, if one hopes to capture the flavor—the texture—of a person's life it is essential to consult many sources. For the figures portrayed in this book the following sources have been particularly useful:

Part I: Human Rights in a New World Setting

ANNE HUTCHINSON

Battis, Emery John. *Saints and Secretaries: Anne Hutchinson and the Antinomian Controversy in the Massachusetts Bay Colony.* Chapel Hill: University of North Carolina Press, 1962.

Rugg, Winifred King. *Unafraid: A Life of Anne Hutchinson.* Boston: Houghton Mifflin, 1930.

ROGER WILLIAMS

Jacobs, William Jay. *Roger Williams.* New York: Franklin Watts, 1975.

Winslow, Ola Elizabeth. *Master Roger Williams.* New York: Macmillan, 1957.

JOHN PETER ZENGER

Rutherford, Livingston. *John Peter Zenger and Freedom of the Press.* Mount Vernon, N.Y.: A. Colish, 1984.

THOMAS PAINE

Conway, Moncure Daniel. *Thomas Paine.* New York: Chelsea House, 1982.

Fast, Howard. *Citizen Tom Paine*, 2nd ed. New York: Grove Press, 1983.

BENJAMIN FRANKLIN

Franklin, Benjamin. *The Autobiography of Benjamin Franklin.* New York: Modern Library, 1944.

Lopez, Claude-Anne, and Eugenia Herbert. *The Private Franklin.* New York: Norton, 1975.

Part II: A Search for Freedom and Racial Justice

SARAH and ANGELINA GRIMKÉ

Lerner, Gerda. *The Grimké Sisters from South Carolina: Pioneers for Woman's Rights and Abolition.* New York: Schocken, 1971.

DOROTHEA DIX

Lowe, Corinne. *The Gentle Warrior: A Story of Dorothea Lynde Dix.* New York: Harcourt, Brace, 1948.

Wilson, Dorothy Clarke. *Stranger and Traveler: The Story of Dorothea Dix, American Reformer.* Boston: Little, Brown, 1975.

FREDERICK DOUGLASS

Douglass, Frederick. *Narrative of the Life of Frederick Douglass, an American Slave.* New York: Penguin, 1982.

HARRIET BEECHER STOWE

Wilson, Forrest. *Crusader in Crinoline: The Life of Harriet Beecher Stowe.* Philadelphia: Lippincott, 1941.

WILLIAM LLOYD GARRISON

Merrill, Walter McIntosh. *Against Wind and Tide: A Biography of William Lloyd Garrison.* Cambridge, Mass.: Harvard University Press, 1963.

Thomas, John Lawrence. *The Liberator, William Lloyd Garrison: A Biography.* Boston: Little, Brown, 1963.

ELIZABETH CADY STANTON

Lutz, Alma. *Crusade for Freedom: Women in the Anti-Slavery Movement.* Boston: Beacon Press, 1948.

Stanton, Elizabeth Cady. *Eighty Years and More.* New York: Schocken, 1971.

THADDEUS STEVENS

Current, Richard Nelson. *Old Thad Stevens: A Story of Ambition.* Westport, Conn.: Greenwood Press, 1980.

Smith, Gene. *High Crimes and Misdemeanors: The Impeachment and Trial of Andrew Johnson.* New York: McGraw-Hill, 1976.

SOJOURNER TRUTH

Truth, Sojourner. *Narrative of Sojourner Truth, a Northern Slave.* Edited by Olive Gilbert. New York: Arno, 1968.

Part III: Human Rights in an Industrial Age

BOOKER T. WASHINGTON

Harlan, Louis R. *Booker T. Washington: The Wizard of Tuskegee, 1901–1915.* New York: Oxford University Press, 1983.

Washington, Booker T. *Up From Slavery.* New York: Penguin, 1986.

CHIEF JOSEPH

Josephy, Alvin M., Jr. *The Indian Heritage of America.* New York: Knopf, 1968.

Brandon, William. *The American Indian.* Adapted by Anne Terry White. New York: Random House, 1963.

CLARA BARTON

Barton, Clara. *The Story of My Childhood.* New York: Ager, 1980.

Stevenson, Augusta. *Clara Barton, Founder of the American Red Cross.* Indianapolis: Bobbs-Merrill, 1962.

SUSAN B. ANTHONY

Anthony, Katherine. *Susan B. Anthony: Her Personal History and Her Era.* Garden City, N.Y.: Doubleday, 1954.

Jacobs, William Jay. *Mother, Aunt Susan and Me: The First Fight for Women's Rights.* New York: Coward-McCann, 1979.

ANDREW CARNEGIE

Hofstadter, Richard. *Social Darwinism in American Thought, 1860–1915.* Boston: Beacon, 1955.

McCloskey, Robert Green. *American Conservatism in the Age of Enterprise.* Cambridge, Mass.: Harvard University Press, 1951.

SAMUEL GOMPERS

Gompers, Samuel. *Seventy Years of Life and Labor: An Autobiography.* New York: ILR Press, New York State School of Industrial and Labor Relations, Cornell University, 1984.

JANE ADDAMS

Addams, Jane. *Twenty Years at Hull House.* New York: Macmillan, 1910.

Kittredge, Mary. *Jane Addams.* New York: Chelsea House, 1988.

WILLIAM JENNINGS BRYAN

Clements, Kendrick A. *William Jennings Bryan, Missionary Isolationist.* Knoxville, University of Tennessee Press, 1983.

Cherny, Robert W. *A Righteous Cause: The Life of William Jennings Bryan.* Glenview, Ill.: Scott Foresman, 1984.

Part IV: New Frontiers in Human Rights: The Twentieth Century

EMMA GOLDMAN

Drinnon, Richard. *Rebel in Paradise: A Biography of Emma Goldman.* Chicago: University of Chicago Press, 1961.

Goldman, Emma. *Anarchism and Other Essays*. New York: Dover, 1969.

JACOB RIIS

Meyer, Edith Patterson. *"Not Charity but Justice": The Story of Jacob A. Riis*. New York: Vanguard, 1974.

Riis, Jacob. *How the Other Half Lives: Studies Among the Tenements of New York*. New York: Sagamore Press, 1957.

CLARENCE DARROW

Leuchtenburg, William E. *The Perils of Prosperity 1914–1932*. Chicago: University of Chicago Press, 1958.

Weinberg, Arthur and Lila. *Clarence Darrow: A Sentimental Rebel*. New York: Atheneum, 1987.

DOROTHY DAY

Coles, Robert. *Dorothy Day: A Radical Devotion*. Reading, Mass.: Addison-Wesley, 1987.

Miller, William D. *Dorothy Day: A Biography*. San Francisco: Harper & Row, 1982.

BAYARD RUSTIN

Rustin, Bayard. *Down the Line: The Collected Writings of Bayard Rustin*. Chicago: Quadrangle, 1971.

CESAR CHAVEZ

Newlon, Drake. *Famous Mexican-Americans*. New York: Dodd, Mead, 1972.

Terzian, James, and Kathryn Cramer. *Mighty Hard Road: The Story of Cesar Chavez*. Garden City, N.Y.: Doubleday, 1970.

ELEANOR ROOSEVELT

Jacobs, William Jay. *Eleanor Roosevelt: A Life of Happiness and Tears*. New York: Coward-McCann, 1983.

Roosevelt, Eleanor. *The Autobiography of Eleanor Roosevelt*. New York: Harper & Row, 1958.

MARTIN LUTHER KING, JR.

King, Martin Luther, Jr. *Stride Toward Freedom*. New York: Harper & Row, 1958.

O'Neill, William L. *Coming Apart: An Informal History of America in the 1960s*. Chicago: Quadrangle, 1971.

Index